A Jericho's Cobble *Miscellany*

Also by Tom Shachtman

Novels:

Echoes or The Insistence of Memory

The Memoir of the Minotaur

Beachmaster

Wavebender

Driftwhistler

Non-fiction:

The Founding Fortunes

How the French Saved America

Gentlemen Scientists and Revolutionaries

American Iconoclast: The Life and Times of Eric Hoffer

Airlift to America

Rumspringa, To Be or Not to Be Amish

Absolute Zero and the Conquest of Cold

Terrors and Marvels

Around the Block

Skyscraper Dreams

The Most Beautiful Villages of New England

The Inarticulate Society

Decade of Shocks, Dallas to Watergate

The Phony War, 1939-1940

Edith and Woodrow

The Day America Crashed

A Jericho's Cobble *Miscellany*

Tom Shachtman

Lake Dallas, Texas

Printed in the United States of America

FIRST EDITION

This is a work of fiction. Any of its characters' resemblance to individuals, living or dead, is unintentional and coincidental.

Permissions
Madville Publishing
PO Box 358
Lake Dallas, TX 75065

Cover Design: Kim Davis

ISBN: 978-1-963695-57-1 paperback
978-1-963695-58-8 ebook

Library of Congress Control Number: 2025947269

To Harriet

Table of Contents

Foreword
by J. Augustus Miller, March 2026

While clearing out my family's ancestral home in Jericho's Cobble, Massachusetts, preparing to sell it after the death of my long-widowed father, Richard Bond Miller, I discovered a treasure trove of materials about that small hamlet nestled in the rolling hills of the Southern Berkshires.

A true miscellany, the trove consists of diary entries, newspaper articles, oral history transcripts, roadside markers, business brochures, tombstone legends, a playlet, a sewn sampler, a nursery rhyme, snippets from Dad's "brief history" of the town—he was its designated historian—plus musings by living townspeople based on his conversations with them, and others by inanimate objects, which I assume Dad wrote although I had not known of his penchant for poetry.

In the Cobble my father is remembered for being the chair of the history department at Stillwater Mountain High, for habitually sporting bow ties—he had dozens—and for leading town parades in his great-great-grandfather's Civil War uniform.

"The past is never dead. It's not even past." This famous quote from William Faulkner, a favorite of my Dad's, spoke to the continuing presence and relevance of history in our lives. In this miscellany's pages the Cobble's history emerges, commencing with the area's geological origins and beginning in earnest with the 1638 settling of the area by the British Whitbreds. It features stories of the nineteenth-century Eastlund, Birdsong, and Niedermeyer families and the modern-era controversies relating to those families' legacies. The past provides counterpoint to the miscellany's contemporary focus on the joys, trials, and tribulations of Dad's fellow townsfolks, such as a weekender couple whose lives are upended by a life-threatening traffic accident; the recently-installed Congregational Church leader and his surgeon wife; and longer-resident "Cobblers," including a group of six female grads of the Stillwater class of '73, working mothers who lunch together quarterly, and their husbands—farmers, plumbers, hardware salesmen, and state inspectors—and their teenaged children.

In this crazy quilt of tales from "the country of the second chances," as one townswoman labels it, my favorite is of the unexpected alliance that develops between a twenty-something newcomer, museum director Mary-Beth Flaherty, and a matronly stalwart of the Jericho's Cobble Old Guard, Gertrude Beresford, who join forces to try to prevent the shuttering of the town's historic house, home to the nineteenth-century poetess Eleanor Birdsong, the Cobble's most famous resident.

(For clarity, I have supplied an appendix listing the Cobblers featured in the text.)

The nine months chronicled in the miscellany, between Labor Day 2003 and Memorial Day 2004, my father deemed critical to discerning how the Cobble's character was changing in the modern era. Those months were also difficult for him personally: after the spring 2003 death of my mother, Wilma Murfrees Miller, which ended a long illness, Dad needed to decide whether to retire from his positions in Jericho's Cobble, and if so, whether to remain there or to come live near me in Boston or my sister in Washington, D.C. He assembled the materials herein, I believe, to help him understand enough about his town and his neighbors to make his choices.

The miscellany apprised me of many things about Jericho's Cobble I'd never known although I'd lived there throughout my childhood and youth, which is why I maintain that it is about secrets hiding in plain sight. It is also an attempt, through the relating of many diverse individual tales, to tell a single meta-story of the beginnings, maturing, and aging of a small, interior New England town.

A glimpse into our shared past and shared values, it should be of interest equally to those born and raised in the United States of America and to newcomers willing to embrace America's promise, which—as these pages amply demonstrate—is intricately tied to its past.

—John Augustus Miller, Esq.,
Boston, MA, March 2026

A Jericho's Cobble *Miscellany*

Prologue: Labor Day Weekend, 2003

This Accident Victim Is Aware

(thoughts of Sam Newington)

This aging accident victim is aware,
although he knows he shouldn't be,
brimming with sweet sedation
and splayed on the carving board
of a steel-and-plastic operating table;

aware of mouthless-masked medics
rescuing what of him can be retrieved
from death's enveloping arms,
into which a speeding van hurled him,
right there in the crosswalk
of Jericho's Cobble's Main Street!

aware of *here* an eye-blink from *gone*;
unwilling to give up the ghost
yet curious about becoming one;
unable to cease playing with words,
conjuring a "box seat" in the cemetery
to view the Cobble's soothing vista,
with its backdrop, the eponymous knoll,
a stage across which the seasons strut;

insensate yet sensing everything,
the right now, the near past and the far,
the living, the dead, the beyond,
becoming permeable to them all
whilst searching them for answers,
urgent and essential, to questions
one never finds the time to ask.

Jousting with the Space Invaders

(Grace Newington, thoughts and dialogue)

Waiting in this limbo of a hospital "family lounge" as Labor Day Monday becomes work-a-day Tuesday, I am overwhelmed, both with the hope that my husband will recover from his terrible accident, and with the fear that even if he does he may never again be the man he was. Adding to my perplexity is the absurdity that next door in the operating room, surgeon Glenda Trainor is trying to save Sam's life while in this bland anteroom her husband Vernon, our Congregational Church's pastor, is praying for Sam's well-being! It's as though Sam's body and soul are the current rope of the Trainors' marriage-long tug-of-war.

In this waiting room Vern and I have long since exhausted our reservoirs of small talk and now pass the time reading materials placed here for that purpose, mine the new issue of *The Country Caller.* I skim the lead article, about the demand by critics to rename the Whitbred Elementary School because, they charge, the Whitbreds, the original European settlers, stole the land from the natives, to re-read my gardening column, e-mailed to the paper ten days ago. "Jousting With The Space Invaders " relates my late-summer gardening battles with such "alien-to-the-Americas" plants as Japanese Knotweed, Oriental Bittersweet, and Purple Loosestrife, whose exotic beauty disguises their aggressive displacement of native species. How petty that jousting now sounds to me, when measured against my husband's being slammed by a force so destructive that it nearly killed him.

Doc Glenda enters the lounge in her street clothes; I appreciate that she has changed out of her no-doubt bloodied operating gown so that I won't have to see my husband's gore. We two know each other a bit from singing together in Congo's choir.

GLENDA: Sam's in the ICU now, Grace. Stable. We put a cast on his arm, taped his damaged ribs, reflated his collapsed lungs. Later today I'll take out one of the tubes we inserted for the reflation, and tomorrow the other. He'll be on oxygen for a week or so after that.

GRACE: Is he still in grave danger?

GLENDA: Yes, but less so than when the ambulance brought him here. Grace, his insults are severe; healing is going to take time.

GRACE: There's a rehabilitation facility near our apartment in the city ...

GLENDA: No! He should not be moved that far! I'll call Moorehead Rehab to see if they have a bed available—more peaceful there than in the city.

GRACE: Can I see him now?

GLENDA: You could, yes, but I don't advise it as he's too sedated for interaction. Better off waiting twelve hours. Try this afternoon; he'll be more alert by then.

I believe Glenda is saying that Sam will make it but that the degree and pace of his recovery are still question marks. Only partially relieved, I am suddenly acutely ashamed of our recent marital difficulties—after thirty-two years, feeling pulled in separate directions, although still fond of each other. Now all I want is for him to return to good health. But I cannot help worrying about what will happen to us if he doesn't. Will he be able to walk, talk, and think well enough to resume work as a financial analyst? That's our main income.

Our two children need to hear the positive news. I phone

them. Each picks up on the first ring. My message: Your father is out of immediate danger, and by this afternoon should be able to speak to you, and we can then figure out the timing for visits, sans grandchildren—the little ones, we agree, mustn't see a banged-up Poppa Sam.

In the parking lot, our Volvo is almost the only car left. Through the darkness I drive slowly towards our house. Whenever Sam and I motor up from Manhattan, Sam likes to note and to salute as the first real sign of being "in the country" the Bald Knoll itself, visible a mile ahead. To see it makes him happy. Right now, since the sun is not yet up, I can't make it out.

Too keyed up to even cook for myself, I'll stop at Get'nGo and pick up something for breakfast.

The Bald Knoll

Five hundred million years ago,
as the Iapetus Ocean shrank
in its clash with the land,
shells and skeletons and sand
began to cluster, forming us;
four hundred million years ago,
the Taconic Orogeny in a torturous spasm
thrust us and all around us up and up and up;
ever since, our cradle has been diminishing,
chiseled by water, wind, and downflows,
condensing, amalgamating, shifting,
the sedimentary grinding the allocthonous,
what of us had been molten
congealing under the surface,
soon to extrude again
in a ground teeming with green,
but not us,
for as we weathered
we protruded unrestrained,
a bald spot in the foliage,
resistant to the progression
of beeches and birches,
pines and spruces,
chestnuts and hornbeams,
hemlocks and oaks,
and that of the beasts,
from mastodon to mammoth to moose,
spurring mankind,
upon its late emergence,
to render us reverence.

Sorority of the Brown Bags

(thoughts of Jeannie Johnson)

Whichever of us gals arrives earliest at Get'nGo starts in on the prep: there's eggs to bake, bacon to sizzle, tomatoes to slice, breads to arrange, butter to soften, coffee to brew—the whole nine yards. I crayon the lunch specials on the board; Bonnie seeds the register with singles, fives, tens, and coins (twenties go underneath); Hope lays out the muffins, donuts, scones, and coffee cups. An hour 'til our 5:30 a.m. opening is barely enough time but we work hard because, don't ya know, hard work is what we rube dames do, we who weren't born lucky or married lucky, we of the sorority of the brown bags.

We sneak glances at one another, checking on how we weathered the night as we been doing since we met as biker gals. Hope and Bonnie and Jeannie been toiling ass-to-ass six days a week like forever, and we still take vacations together! Without our guys.

Work is work—not uplifting, not demeaning, just what's there to be done. Sure we take pride in doing it well, but mainly we're here to make money for the fourteen hours a day that we're *not* here. Everything on the shop walls shouts that: the sassy-motto plaques, the baby pictures, the Christmas cards on the pinboard.

Moment we open, there's a line at the counter—brothers, sons, cousins, neighbors, former boyfriends—come to collect their sausage melts and corn muffins, josh us a bit, leave us nice tips. These big lugs in company-logo shirts, driving pick-ups and tool vans, they got roads to clear, tanks to fill, machinery to mend, and lawns to tend, so they need food for warmth, and our knowing smiles at the world's making them too, like us, wake every day at a very doggoned early hour.

Here's Vinny Djere (bacon-egg'n'cheese), still baby-faced though he's been through hell in Iraq and is now back home and working with the grounds-and-maintenance crew at The

Chancellery. Here's Chad Stucnowicz (cheese and tomato on a roll), going in early to Valley Hardware so he'll be there when the contractors need him. Here's Andy Borska (buttered toasted sesame bagel), handsomest plumber in town.

One early gal customer (buttered blueberry muffin, nuked) I sorta recognize as a weekender—husband plays in the pick-up ballgame on Sundays—but I don't really know her. Appears like she can't stop thinking about something awful as just happened. Well, ambulance crew did say they'd had a bad one on Main Street, late; bet it was her husband.

I'm slipping an extra treat into her bag. Probably stopped here because Jim's isn't open yet.

Jim the Baker's our competition—one of us, really, a hard-working Vietnam vet—in his tiny café the other end of Main Street. This hour he's definitely at it, ovens going a mile a minute. He opens a bit later and mostly gets a different type customer: the Gobblers—the weekenders, the retirees, the people up from the city—we call 'em Gobblers because they're so different from us born-and-raised Cobblers. Our customers are usually grads of Stillwater Mountain High, like me (class of '73), who can't spend more'n a few minutes or a few dollars at Get'nGo 'cause, don't ya know, they're on the clock!

Our Cobbler-customers make it possible for Jim's Gobbler-clients to spend nice weekends in their country houses. Yeah, yeah, but I gotta admit that it's also the other way 'round: Wouldn't be lots of service-type jobs in these parts without enough weekenders to pay good dollar for those services. If this town's going to survive in the 21st century as a great place to live and work, Cobblers and Gobblers are gonna have to figure out how to make a go of it together.

Jim's made-from-scratch pastries and designer coffees are fancier and tastier than ours, so he can charge more for them. But he can't match our bold tattoos and our purple-and-green hair and our tight sweaters.

Jonathan Menaker Nash

(1923-2003)

I am the most recent of those beneath the sod in Jericho's Cobble's Cemetery,
    and had hoped in death to be reunited with my left foot.

Just kidding!

That left foot, ankle, and adjoining small section of lower left leg,
    damaged by a landmine as our division took Mount Belvedere,
    were cut off at Bagni di Lucca so as to save the rest of me.
Ever since, I've felt the foot's loss, even though my substitute one
    enabled me to walk and even to cross-country ski,
    my poles giving me adequate balance.

In death, though, I am now gratifying my other yearning,
    to lie forever in Jericho's Cobble—
        not in Fort Myers, where I spent my last days,
        or in Burlington, where I spent my earliest ones.

Vitti, the nurse in that Italian hospital,
    whom I persuaded to come to America with me,
    promising her a nicer life
    than seemed possible in ruined Italy,
        did not immediately take to the Cobble,
        where I'd bought a small-animals practice.

Enduring tough winters and the raising of two children
    she yearned for a much warmer place,
    a sunny beach to walk, a sea to swim in.

So we took annual winter vacations to Florida,
    and in the Cobble applied ourselves to enjoying the wondrous autumns,
        mellow summers, and glorious springs.

The Cobble had it all: enough work for us to make a decent living,
    good schools for our children, friends for me, some for Vitti,
    churches that didn't harangue us, a congenial pub at the inn,
    good fishing, good hunting, good skiing,
        fresh corn and tomatoes.

In return, we strove to be of service to its people and domestic animals.
Does God ask more of us than that?

I was good old trustworthy Doc Nash, best vet in the Valley—
    even treated a man wounded by arrows, once—
    sang lead basso for Congo's choir,
    drove my 1938 Alfa Romeo on sunny days and in parades,
    and was the perennial winner of the handicapped division
        of the cross-country ski races.

After fifty years of being "Doc Reliable,"
    since my hands would no longer obey,
    I sold my veterinary practice,
    and my wonderful car,
        and bought Vitti that place in the Florida sun,
        so she could walk barefoot on the beach.

I walked with her on those sands as long as I could.

Don't know if she'll join me here, but I do know that I've come home.

Alice on her Morning Jog

(Alice Hadley Morely, diary entry
for Thursday, Sep. 4, 2003)

Schools R opening again today after the summer—and w/o me! Yay!

I'm on my now reg'lar early A.M. jog—nature path (X-country ski trail)—2½ mi. of mild ups 'n downs—2 earn my reward 4 exercise: a Morning-Glory muffin + a latté @ Jim's, & a chat or 2 w/neighbors. All-ways a pleasure! Nice ppl. By then the P Office will B open so I can fetch my mail. After that, a more leisurely return; a 5-mile RT, perfect 4 a recently retired schoolmarm. (74 days, but who's counting?) The best thing @ being in the Cobble is 2 get outdoors all the time! So B-U-TEE-full! So alive!

From this trail U can C a lot @ the town. I jog (slowly) from west to east along the edges of 4 of the largest tracts, each I w/plenty o' history.[1] *U wouldn't know it from their serene appearance, but awful things happened @ ea., long ago, & the reverberations R still being felt today: the Renwick State Forest, where the Pequabogue tribe met their doom—& more recently, just 20 yrs ago, where I of the arsonists that burned down R old Town Hall was shot 2 death; the stately fiefdom of the rapacious Whitbreds, now the home of the snobbish Chancellery prep school; the Eastlund Cottage*

---

1 Compiler's Note: The four properties along the jogging trail (in ski season, the cross-country loop) were once owned, respectively, by the Renwicks, the Whitbreds, the Eastlunds, and the Dawsons, although each property has since changed owners more than once. RBM.

estate, w/its generations of sexual scandals; & last but not least, the site of the former Dawson House + tannery, now razed, once the setting for poor Celia Dawson's madness, a place whose future is still B-ing fought over. Thank goodness we have a calmer, gentler town now than in the past!

Some trees R already showing a bit of fall plumage (thanx 2 an unusually hot Aug.), vivid in the slanting early sunlight—which is great for me, b/c these morns R among the more difficult 4 me 2 bear, since 4 the last 37 yrs. such A.M.s were when I was busy readying my classroom at Whitb. Elem. 4 the new 3rd -graders. Those 8-yr.-olds, so adorable & needy, @ a juncture on which all future academic + emotional development depends, in the early daze of the school yr. were so new 2 me—& 2 themselves!—that I'd be so engrossed in prepping that I wouldn't realize I was humming a B'way show-tune!

"MISS-us MORE-lee," my kids called me. 500-600 over the yrs, in a town of 4,000! Some, now grown up & still nearby, still greet me as MISS-us MORE-lee even tho they're old enuf 2 call me Alice—such as @ my retirement party, where a few announced, 2 my astonishment, that they're grandparents!

No 1 tells U how tough retirement is when U R alone. Or how best 2 put yr energy into leisure, as our weekenders do. Arthur ran off long ago w/his sec'y; I didn't miss him then & certainly don't now! Nor, truth B told, do I miss Mother—she made us both miserable during the 4 yrs she lived w/me before she passed. What I do miss, & terribly, is the 3rd graders' love, & even more, the oppor2nity 2 give them my own. We are on earth 2 love others, not just 2 B loved.

Glancing around a bend in the trail as I lope, I C, not 50 ft. ahead, a huge, multi-antlered moose—he is EEE-NOR-MUSS!—his sopping, shaggy, dark-brown coat shimmering from a recent dip in the waters, moss draped from 1 antler.

I stop. Never before seen a moose. He turns his head—looks calmly & directly @ me. We gaze at 1 another in mutual appraisal. And suddenly I know this moose! He is the magnificent, legendary Pequabogue guardian @ the Bald Knoll; & somehow he is also the spirit of Skanaska, the tribe's murdered sachem!

I hold my breath, hoping my stillness will prolong the moment.

What does the moose want of me? Something; but I can't figure what...

After a brief lowering of his massive head in my direction—an indication that we share such questions?—the moose strides in an unhurried way off the path & into the adjoining brush. By the time I reach the spot on the trail where the moose was, I find no trace of him anywhere.

ONE:
ANCHORS

Missing the Weekly Game

(thoughts of Sam Newington)

The sea of meds, now in ebb tide,
reveals as it recedes what I lost
'twixt harvest moon and hunter's moon
while confined in rehab's cocoon:

the sumptuous part of September,
brought to mind this Lord's Day
by bells sounding the call
to summon the churches' faithful,
while at the municipal recreation field
behind the gas and lottery-tickets mart,
twenty guys with worn leather mitts,
mostly middle-aged weekenders—
although we do welcome anyone!—
gather for the weekly slow-pitch game.

We preach the gospel of camaraderie,
grant indulgences for love handles
and knees no longer eager for grounders;
as hosannas rise from watching wives,
free, for once, to raucously razz;
from acolytes on bicycles, in dismay
at fathers engaged in boyish play;
from family dogs, vying for stray balls
that bipeds can't as easily recall.

We have no umpire, no roster card,
no dugout, no announcer, no organ,
but plenty of gimmes and do-overs,
and the score is a matter of opinion.

You ballers and you cheerers-on,
you out there having good clean fun:
Do you sense joy as you create it?
Bliss, communal as well as personal?
Belly-born guffaws, that as they echo
attenuate all earthly differences?

Here losers buy rounds for winners,
knowing next week it'll be vice-versa.

Class of '73 Monthly Lunch

(thoughts of Liliane Griswold)

We six were not that close at Stillwater Mountain, but at our tenth reunion in 1983, us and a few other class of '73 gal alums discovered we had so much in common—never went to college, married to a Stillwater grad or one from a nearby school, working for a local business, with a child or two in school—that we decided to grab a lunch...and for the last twenty years we've been doing that regularly! Our number has dwindled: Jeannie Johnson is too busy serving her own lunches at Get'nGo, Frankie Klecko couldn't continue coming because she works at night and needs to sleep during the day, and Delia Middleton—well, Delia's gone, God rest her soul. So it's just Kelly Lydner, Stacy Borska, Louise Gutwind, Jane Milch, Beth Galter, and me, Liliane Griswold.

For most of the thirty years we met at The Buttery, but recently Kelly, who's on their board, asked that we not lunch there anymore because it's being bought and won't be a co-op.[2] Today's our first meal at the Grey Griffon, at a table in a back section. The food's a tad more expensive, but I like the atmosphere, near the old upright piano that nobody's touched in years, so secluded that we can laugh loudly if we want to or pass on a secret with nobody the wiser.

Over the years we six have become very important to each other. We weren't the prettiest or the smartest or the most ambitious of our female classmates; those types couldn't wait to flee the Pequabogue Valley, aiming for colleges and big cities and guys with money or great prospects. But we not-so-brainy, not-so-great-looking sisters had little trouble snagging reasonable

2 Compiler's Note: The Buttery was founded by Kelly Murtaugh-Lydner's great-grandfather, Diarmuid "Muddy" Murtaugh, and his farming neighbors, in 1883. See *infra*. RBM.

husbands—not world-beaters, but then very few guys are—and mostly staying married to them. If it's old-fashioned to love your husband and your children and the beautiful countryside and the Cobble's smooth-and-slow style of living, which doesn't try to change the world every second—then we are truly passé. But I call us realists. Sure, our day jobs aren't the greatest, but we do them well, and our home lives are comfortable, although we're not rolling in luxury. Fact is, we're fortunate and we know it.

A hundred years ago we would've been the wives of farmers or of shopkeepers selling to farm families, and wouldn't have been allowed near the governing boards of community organizations—those were for the wealthy men—and wouldn't have experienced much of the world outside the Valley. That was my grandmother's way of life. And my mother's, mostly (she's 83). Today we six participate regularly in the wider world through the Internet and make regular day trips into New York City... though we're always eager to get back home on the last train.

We also recognize the need to toil to make sure our hometown doesn't become too much of a backwater. Jericho's Cobble is so small that it has no police department, no paid fire department or ambulance service, no town garbage collection, etc. It gets by on volunteers. Which means we need to step up, and we do. Stacy Borska, who has her hands full running her husband's plumbing-and-heating office, serves on the board of Meals For All (MFA), a charity that's a godsend for the old and infirm; Louise Gutwind, secretary to the Dean of students at The Chancellery, tends the hotline phone some nights at Females In Need (FIND)—plenty such needy women hereabouts; Kelly Lydner helps run her century-old Murtaugh-Lydner farm, which is more than a full-time job, yet she finds the time to serve as an elected, unpaid member of the town's Board of Estimate and a legacy trustee of The Buttery Co-op; Jane Milch, our only single mom, the staff scheduler at Moorehead, sings in the Congo choir; Beth Galter, assistant operations manager for Valley Fuels, a division of Valley Hardware, is a trustee of Valodia, the cross-country ski association; and me, Liliane Griswold,

I'm assistant manager of the Jericho's Cobble/Whitbred branch of the Southern Berkshire Community Bank, and a long-time ambulance service volunteer, part of the "Thursday Girls" crew.

Women's rights and feminism have made great strides in the U. S. of A. but mostly for the benefit of the highly educated—doctors, lawyers, and managers. I like that Eddie and I have a woman lawyer, a woman doctor, and a woman accountant. But for us half-dozen small-town sisters at this table, equality for working women is wishful thinking.

Our kids are mostly out of the house but still need us, our parents are more dependent on us than they or we ever expected, and we are fonder of our mates now than when we first got hitched, which most of us did before we or the guys were really ready. Thank God my Eddie is a rock and still thinks the world of me, as I do of him. He's older than the other husbands, sixty-two, a septic fields inspector for the state, leaning toward taking early retirement. Nobody can blame him for wanting out of that job! As for me, it really burns that for fourteen years I've been stuck as assistant manager of the smallest branch of the tristate bank. Yeah, yeah, I get that it's more about the bank than about me—they're only hiring as branch managers MBAs from top business schools, so everybody local's been passed over in favor of these know-it-alls, not just me. But still...

On to the gossip, which we do lots of. Janey confides that Sam Newington—we Thursday Girls scraped him off the roadway over Labor Day weekend—is doing better at Moorehead rehab, and that his wife Grace shows up there daily. We applaud that she's so attentive. They're trying for a settlement from the SUV driver's insurance, Jane heard from Grace at choir practice, but even if they get that, it won't cover all the costs. Well, since they can afford two residences, they've likely got money stashed away for this kind of rainy day.

Today's more important gossip item comes via Louise. The Chancellery, after years of rumors about Chip Garuzelski, who used to run their girls' sports program, has hired a big New York law firm to look into allegations of him sexually abusing female students. None of us ever had any contact with Garuzelski—we're not prep-school types—but we're certain that the scandal goes deeper than this one guy. And therefore that it's not only The Chancellery's problem, it's the Cobble's—and ours.

Regarding the Founding Whitbreds

A) "Whitbred Naming Controversy at Selectmen's Meeting"

By Felicity Ringell, *The County Caller*, Issue of Aug. 28, 2003

Despite vocal protests from two dozen townspeople in attendance at the monthly meeting of the Selectmen, the officials bucked the decision on renaming the Whitbred Elementary School back to the Board of Education.

Region Fourteen's Board, which oversees six elementaries, two middle schools, and Stillwater Mountain High has been debating all summer a demand by some parents and pupils to rename Whitbred Elementary because, it is charged, the original European settlers, led by Joshua Whitbred, stole the land from the Pequabogue, and later, that Whitbred descendants pyramided their fortune by using slaves to work their farms.

The Board sought guidance on the issue from the Selectmen.

During the meeting, all in the audience were keen to be heard, those arguing for the change and, just as forcefully, those arguing against the change. The "traditionalists," as the latter group call themselves, pointed out that the town's original public elementary school was built with funds donated by the Whitbreds during the nineteenth century, that the Whitbred name was continued when a new facility was constructed on the site in the 1950s, and that no documentary evidence of the alleged far-past Whitbred crimes exists.

The Selectmen, although under pressure to let audience members speak, decided not to do so, instead voting unanimously to return the matter to the School Board, which has sole jurisdiction over the naming of its facilities.

b) Massachusetts State Marker #379, Renwick State Forest

"On October 25, 1736, near this spot on the bank of the river, within sight of the Bald Knoll, the last of this area's indigenous peoples, the Pequabogues, led by their sachem, Skanaska, were overcome by the Massachusetts Bay Colony Militia in a battle that ended Native resistance to English settlement in the Pequabogue Valley."

c) Thoughts of Skanaska[3]

A rattler's nest of lies, that marker above where I rest,
I, Skanaska, the red-tailed fox:
By our death-day my Pequabogue were no longer a tribe, only a band;
the Adjidamo, the so-called river, was never more than a brook;
and there was no great battle here, only an ambush and a massacre.

A quarter-moon afore, since the whites five days east-by-northeast
would not trade women with us as a token of enmity forsworn,
to teach them a lesson I had my men steal two girls.
We took them with us along the path next the Adjidamo,
waters that squirrel-like twist and hop, alternately quick and still
on their way to the true river, the Ousatunnick.[4]

My scouts, sent ahead, beheld at the sacred bald knoll
its guardian, the many-antlered moose,
a signal permitting us to make our winter weatogue nearby.
The white girls' presence, too, would protect us,
since even the stupidest of settlers would know
that if they attacked our weatogue,
their daughters would be the first to die.

My prideful thinking so was our death song.
The whites' militia, after harvesting their fields,
oiled their rifles and followed our route,
dreaming of reward and revenge.

At the elbow bend in the Adjidamo,
at first light and in the season's first snow,
they silently overcame my sentries,
loudly fired their rifles,
and set our wigwams aflame.

---

3 Compiler's Note: Skanaska, sachem of the Pequabogue, (16?? - 1736) RBM.

4 Compiler's Note: Settlers later anglicized the name of the river as the Housatonic. RBM.

Only a few of us escaped, I not among them,
nor my wives, sisters, daughters, aunts,
sons, brothers, nephews, and those settler girls.

The whites took up their dead daughters
but left us where we fell,
not even stopping to remove our valuable scalps,
    so afraid were they of a little blizzard.

Winter's scavengers then had their way with us, as they should,
for we were but food for our animal brethren.

After two winters had returned to the sky,
new interlopers arrived,
gathered what remained of us
and jumbled our bones in a common pit.

That too was as it should be,
for here together The People forever lie,
even closer in death than we were in life.

D) Playlet based on diary of Anelise Whitbred (1717-1763)

(Author unknown; used since 1955
for Stillwater Mountain pageant)

TIME: May 1740. PLACE: Near the top of the Bald Knoll, 1,000 feet above the Valley. CHARACTERS: ANELISE CHELMSFORD WHITBRED, age 23, visibly pregnant.

JOSHUA COMMODUS WHITBRED, age 40, some gray hair.

ANELISE

Must we trek so far? Climbing is very hard for me, my love, pregnant and still despairing of our dead daughter.

JOSHUA

She rests in heaven, my wife. And you will soon have another child.

ANELISE

Twins, I think.

JOSHUA

The more the merrier! There. We have arrived at the top of the knoll. Let us sit to look out .

ANELISE

(As they sit)

You can see far in all directions.

JOSHUA

Tell me what you see.

ANELISE

Gently rolling hills, snowcapped mountains… the sparkling stream—really, just a brook, albeit you have grandiosely named it the Pequabogue River.

JOSHUA

And the forest springing into lushness…

ANELISE

And the smoke as it curls toward heaven from the small houses of our bondsmen and their families…

JOSHUA

(With passion)

You are queen of this magnificent Eden,
a greater queen than ever was in the
Norfolk Broadlands or ever will be!
And we have a realm to create!

ANELISE

That too is difficult.

JOSHUA

"Virtute Non Astuto," **my love .**

ANELISE

"By courage and not by guile," your family motto. What if courage is not enough? Our little band has not accomplished much beyond burying the natives from the massacre,asking forgiveness of Our Lord—not theirs!—for what our countrymen did to them.

JOSHUA

We have cleared acres and acres. Planted seeds in soil that had been forest. Reaped grain. Built our dwellings—less crude than they would have been without the iron nails we brought. Girdled trees to increase our moiety. Bred more cows, pigs, chickens—

ANELISE

—and dogs and children!
Must we always "share and share alike" with our bondsmen and their families?

JOSHUA

Any other split would harm us even more than them, Anelise. Life here is a struggle; best do it with partners.

(Pause)

Last winter was a bit easier than the first, was it not? The next will be easier still.

ANELISE

One must hope. Tell me, my Joshua, do you yet have a name for our realm?

JOSHUA

My inspiration being from the Joshua of the Old Testament, who brought Moses' band to the Promised Land and then had to fight the Battle of Jericho—as we with our small band have to continually fight with every element in this New World!... I shall call our settlement... Jericho's Knoll.

(A pause)

ANELISE

(Laughs)

Unusual for one born to a noble house, even as a junior son, my husband, you have the gift of seeing life more as a matter of humor than of honor. But 'twould better be named... Jericho's Cobble.

e) "Sources of the Whitbred Fortune"

(*The Country Caller*, September 4, 2003, "Ask the Town Historian" column by Richard Bond Miller)

READER QUESTION: At the recent Selectmen's meeting, it was charged that the original Whitbreds stole the land from the natives, and later that their descendants made their fortune from slave labor. Are those accusations true?

TOWN HISTORIAN: The short answer: No.

The longer answer: As we know from eighteenth-century accounts, in 1738, two years after the massacre of the Pequabogue, when widower Joshua Whitbred and his young second wife Anelise arrived here with seven vassal families, the land had been abandoned by native tribes. So the Whitbreds did not "steal" it. Their vassals, in exchange for passage to the New World had agreed to seven-year indentures. The vassals never wore shackles and had their own homes; they were not slaves but they were not entirely free. We must acknowledge that their indentured labor built the settlement, but must also understand that Josh Whitbred's enlightened leadership, based on his unusual embrace of communal principles, provided the key to its prospering. In most other European-settled areas vassals were never allowed to own anything; Whitbred, believing that such a lord-and-lieges arrangement could lead to revolt, let his vassals keep most of what they earned and invested the rest on the community's behalf, to erect a lumber mill, a cider mill, and other money-making facilities whose bounty was then shared with the vassal families.

However, at the end of the indenture period, even though those families accumulated some currency, the six surviving vassal chose to sell back their acreage to the Whitbreds for additional cash with which to move west and start their own farms. The freedom to try to make their own way was more important to them than staying put and prospering.

By the time of Revolutionary War, the founding Whitbred couple had died, leaving their twin sons, Joshua Junior and Robert with the largest farm in the area. The brothers alternated army service on the front lines, one joining the troops while the other stayed home with their two families and vended the Whitbred grain, cattle, pigs, hay, and lumber to the Continental armies. As with all other vendors, the Whitbreds were paid in government-issued certificates—Continentals—whose value soon sank. Most of the other certificate-holders, needing cash to survive in the 1780s, sold theirs for cents on the dollar but the Whitbreds, having fields that provided current income, held on to their certificates. In 1789, soon after George Washington's inauguration as our first president, the Whitbreds were able to redeem the certificates at full face value; the sudden influx of money catapulted them to the top tier of wealth in southwest Massachusetts.

Now to the question of slavery. The third, fourth, and fifth Whitbred generations—the latter, J. C. "Bucko" Whitbred V—rejected the family founder's community-inclusive philosophy and instead used their capital to buy up nearby farms and local businesses. This multiplied the family's power, enabling them, for instance, to erect housing for workers on their estate and to feed them from their fields' grain, cows, chicken and pigs, which allowed the Whitbreds to pay lower wages than their competitor neighbors. Today we could condemn as overly exploitative the Whitbred practices that kept workers poor and immobile—but that was not actual slavery.

F) "A REMEMBRANCE OF BUCKO WHITBRED"
(Interview With His Last Stable-master)
***THE COUNTRY CALLER*, ISSUE #7, AUGUST 1904.**[5]

THE COUNTRY CALLER: Rufus, you worked for many years for Bucko Whitbred?

RUFUS BARTUMS: Yessir. Sure did. Retired now. My fambly 'fore me live 'n wukk for his'n, when Mr. Bucko he built the mansion—they's freeborn and toiling for wages, my Pa in the stables, my Ma in the kitchens. Two other colored famblys doing the same. I'm born there, growed there, wukked there my whole life long. When young, I's friendly with Junior, but real pals with Chum.[6] Rode us a lot together. Did us some hunting, fishing.

TCC: So, you knew Bucko Whitbred as a parent as well as an employer?

RB: Yessir. Mr. Bucko he a hard boss to please, but he love his chillun. You see it in that *Green Lads* painting over the fireplace[7], when the boys're young and he's thin. Turrible thing for

5 Compiler's note: This article contains language offensive to modern sensibilities but that was typical in 1904 of whites' attempts to reproduce Black speech patterns. It is included unedited, in the interests of historical fidelity. RBM.
6 Chum, nickname of Chelmsford, younger son of Bucko Whitbred.
7 *The Green Lads*, 1853, attributed to Ammi Phillips, itinerant portraitist (1788-1865).

him and Miz Selwyn when Junior volunteer and get himself killt at Shiloh in '62. They never the same after. Chum, he's over to that Harvard school, while I'm a-getting hitched to my Ada, Miz Selwyn's colored housemaid as did all the laundry. So, when President Abraham Lincoln he call up every man, Mr. Bucko he don't want Chum t'go so he pay for summun else. I don't let him pay for me—gwine t'do my duty's I seen it. Puts in my three years in the 54th Massachusetts like all the colored mens here'bouts. But Chum, he don't fight, he don't stay at Harvard, he just ups and leaves for Santa Fe.

TCC: After the war, you continued to work on the Whitbred estate?

RB: Yessir. Hoped Chum might send for Ada and me come on out West and wukk for him, but no. Ada and me, we have us a good life here, though; no hunger, no worry 'bout a job, plenty firewood t'keep us warm.

TCC: Do you remember any talk with Bucko Whitbred about the railroads?

RB: Mr. Bucko, he very angry with his "friends," them railroad people he dine with in New York City, when they won't run nary a spur through Jericho's Cobble. Truth be tole, rest of us, we don't mind much—we like it the way it was.

TCC: What about the marriages of the Whitbred daughters, Anna and Lisa?

RB: Right big affairs. But Miz Anna and Miz Lisa, afterwards they gone away West too, with their husbands, and never coming back. Miz Selwyn and Mr. Bucko got to fighting over it, just like ordinary peoples. Then in '90 Miz Selwyn ups and dies, sudden-like—one day she's with us, next she's gone. Mr. Bucko, he keep to the house a lot, hardly go to his office. Mr. 'Zekiel Dunsmore, his dep'ty, he can tell you more 'bout that. Then Mr. Bucko, in '94 he pass on. The children, they don't want the Manor, so they sells it to them ed-u-ca-tors starting up The Chancellery. Miz Anna and Miz Lisa, they ask us only send 'em a few things, which we done. I wukked for The Chancellery three years more. Then my Ada, she leave this world too, and I don't want to be inside that Whitbred gate no more. I go out into the town and my daughter takes me in. My pension from the war helps us all, y'see.

g) Ezekiel Dunsmore (1840-1911)

I stole from the poor and gave to the rich,
only went to church when I fancied to,
lived large, dined well, used prostitutes,
drank excessively, was mean to my wife,
nasty to my children, set a bad example,
and died wealthy and in my bed of old age.

As Bucko Whitbred's deputy I learned my lessons
in cutting legal corners, the art of bribing,
and calling loans at the drop of a hat.

When Bucko, crumpled by family matters, passed on,
leaving the bank to his heirs but me in charge,
I let it be known that my heart had not softened.

I was as tough on the Cobblers as Bucko had been;
his heirs never knew or cared about that,
they just wanted the dividends to keep flowing,
which I made sure of, less an extra tithe for me.

People imagine a Hell because they want punishment
for those, like me, who transgress regularly
and are vicious, mean, unrepentant
and never pay the price for any of it!
They want us to suffer as they have suffered.

Sorry, suckers. I rest here just as easily—and just as hard—
as do the benevolent, the beatific, the penitent,
and those finally free from penury.

TWO:
THE DAWSONS *and* THE BIRDSONGS

"Public Meeting Set on Sale of Dawson Tract"

By Felicity Ringell, *The Country Caller*, October 9, 2003

At another contentious monthly session, the Selectmen, yielding to entreaties from vocal conservationists, postponed until next year the previously-scheduled vote on the sale of the Dawson 140 acres.

They pledged in the interim to obtain expert opinions about the potential environmental impact of the proposed motorcycle racecourse, and to post the results of these inquiries prior to a February 12, 2004 open forum at which the public will be invited to weigh in on the potential sale.

Rapido LLC, an investors' group based in Boca Raton, Florida represented locally by attorney Ademante Castelmara, has offered $420,000[8] for the tract, which it plans to develop as a motorcycle-racing venue. During the meeting, Castelmara assured the Selectmen that the enterprise will provide two-dozen full-time jobs, boost trade for local hostelries and restaurants, and pay $100,000 annually in local taxes beyond the fees for water, sewer, and sanitation.

Those in attendance calling for re-evaluation of the sale were led by Aimee Bishop, chair of the Pequabogue Protectorate, and (full disclosure) entertainment editor of *The Country Caller*. Bishop, also host of WCBL's daily *FM in the AM*

8 Compiler's note: Multiple-acre lots in the Southern Berkshires are regularly priced at $8,000-$10,000 per acre; Rapido's offer is $3,000 per acre. RBM.

Show, charged in her prepared statement that the proposed race-course would "compromise the integrity of the Cobble," and bring "air pollution, noise pollution, degradation of the forest, water despoliation of the Pequabogue River, and overuse of local roads and sanitation facilities."

Eight Dawson displays[9]

Local History Nook, Nils Eastlund Library

a) Dawson's Inn, ca. 1923, sepia photograph

Explanatory card:

Erected in 1832 by tannery owner Oscar Dawson as a home for him family, after he died in 1863 it was used as a facility for the insane for twenty years before becoming an inn for fifty years (1884-1934). In 1964, after its long-shuttered premises were razed desirable native trees and groundcover were planted, so that the area could become a thriving, town-owned open meadow with nothing visible of the site's former uses.

During that 1964 demolition, a sampler made by Oscar Dawson's daughter Celia was recovered and donated to the town.

b) The Sampler

those tiny hands as idle waste
a voice that praiseth not ev ry place
awfvl the cavldrons that menace
narrow the path to God s embrace

123456789abcdefghikl
mnopqrstvwxyz

9 Compiler's note: The eight historic objects in the Library's display are accompanied by explanatory cards, whose commentary is reproduced here. RBM.

Celia Dawson age 9
in year of ovr Lord 1844
Jericho Cobble

EXPLANATORY CARD:

As was the norm for the 1840s, Celia's alphabet lacks the letters "j" and "u," which were not introduced into the written lexicon until later. The format of the sampler is also typical of that era and of a small town, for instance not using the intricate patterns of samplers sewn at the better girls' boarding schools. Samplers demonstrated skill in needlework, a central task of girls and women, and once stitched were usually framed and hung as reminders of moral imperatives and expected proper behavior.

Troubled but purportedly brilliant, Celia was the only surviving child of tannery founder/operator Oscar Dawson (1802-1863) and his wife Ementha Helgelund Dawson (1814-1853). Her elder brother had died in infancy.

There is no known source for her sampler's God-fearing verse. It may have been her own thoughts or those dictated by a parent. Oscar's extant correspondence suggests that he was neither as literate nor as religious as the sampler's lines convey. Ementha, however, had attended Canterbury Boarding School in Connecticut.

Only in the modern era, and because of what happened in Celia's life subsequent to the making of the sampler, have some critics judged its verse a frantic call for help—a cry that, because it was never adequately answered, led to tragedy.

c) Bricks from The Tannery

Explanatory card:

As with the origins of many American fortunes, the founder's background and reasons for coming to a suitable place to make his mark remain murky. One version has Oscar Dawson arriving in the Pequabogue Valley ca. 1820, penniless but for a horse, wagon, and a hacksaw that he later acknowledged as stolen. An alternate version suggests that even earlier, while traveling with his father, an itinerant ostler occasionally employed by the Grey Griffon Inn, the boy was present at the 1816 religious "revival" held in Jericho's Cobble[10]; and so, ca. 1820, when in trouble with the law in Albany, he slipped over into Massachusetts and into the Pequabogue Valley.

Here Dawson functioned as a knacker, performing the much-needed service of collecting and disposing of farmers' dead or decrepit horses and cattle, an odious task. Soon Dawson was servicing most of the area's farms, and to do so he bought a second wagon and then a third, and hired several employees.

In 1829 Dawson erected his tannery, the only one within a fifty-mile radius. It was a logical step for a knacker—the word "knacker" derives from the earlier word "nacker," a harness-maker. He situated the tannery well east of the center of town, on acres that spread from the elbow bend of the Pequabogue, whose waters he needed for his operations, to the ridge and its turnpike,

10 Compiler's Note: The revival was held during the infamous "Year Without A Summer" of 1816, an important turning point for the entire Southern Berkshires. See infra. RBM.

over which he would send his finished goods to larger-city markets. The prevailing west-to-east winds, he knew, would carry away from the Cobble the noxious odors from decaying carcasses and from the chemicals used in the tanning and rendering.

D) Container of Dawson's Bar Soap (2' x 2' x 6')

Explanatory card:

Dawson Tannery products—leather, fats, tallow, glue, soap, and bone meal—were sold throughout New England, enabling Dawson, within a few years of starting his tannery, to become the Cobble area's largest employer.[11] To obtain hired hands for his unpleasant tasks Dawson paid higher wages than nearby estate owner and social rival Bucko Whitbred. The Dawson enterprises' wastes and odor became as widely known as their products, causing the town of Jericho's Cobble to become negatively identified in the public mind with both, which troubled Whitbred and many other Cobblers.

The knackery and tannery operations rapidly made Dawson wealthy, enabling him in 1832 to marry Ementha Helgelund, daughter of a Hartford exporter-importer. He erected a large home for her and the expected children, well upwind of the tannery. Dawson Manor was the largest building in the Cobble area for only a few years, until 1838 and Bucko Whitbred's creation of Whitbred Manor.

11 Compiler's Note: During the 1840s and 1850s, the Dawson and Whitbred enterprises' jobs allowed Jericho's Cobble to reach a peak of population, never since equaled. RBM.

E) CELIA'S DIFFICULTIES.

DISPLAY: PHOTOGRAPHS OF CONGREGATIONAL CHURCH ONE-ROOM SCHOOL; MISS ARCHDALE'S SCHOOL; AND MERIDEN CALVINIST ACADEMY

EXPLANATORY CARD:

Soon after Celia completed her sampler, her difficulties with schooling and demeanor became noticeable, causing her, in 1844, at the age of nine to be expelled from the Congregational Church's school. In 1846, at eleven, she was sent home from Miss Archdale's boarding school in Tonkatawpa, New York for "recalcitrant behavior," and in 1849, at fourteen, was similarly expelled from the Calvinist Academy of Meriden, New Jersey.

In 1850, claiming that the "horrible" odors from her father's tannery were making her "crazy," Celia compromised the sluice gates, allowing into the tannery not only a torrent of water but also a bunch of logs that had been floating downstream toward a lumbermill. The water and logs wrought havoc. Celia insisted that her actions against the tannery were in obedience to God's instructions to deter those responsible for killing His beautiful horses.

The Merriam County authorities, and not for the first time, strove to convince the Dawsons to entrust Celia to the care of a physician-mentalist, and to a facility appropriate to handling children of her sort. The authorities proposed the well-regarded Institution For The Wayward, run by Dr. Augusto Pinthaler in Nagan's Landing, Massachusetts, near the New Hampshire border, a location several days' ride from Jericho's

Cobble. While Oscar Dawson was amenable to this solution, Ementha was not, adamant that Celia must remain at home and would be adequately treated there.

F) THE COURT CASE
LEGAL PAPERS FROM THE LUCAS BIRDSONG ARCHIVES.

EXPLANATORY CARD:

In 1851, Massachusetts laws did not permit the state or any county to remove an underage child from a family without a court order. So Merriam County sued Oscar Dawson, as head of the household, with the objective of removing his daughter from the family home and placing her in an appropriate asylum. The Dawsons rejected the legal advice of those who wanted them to accede to the state's demands, and instead relied on the tannery's regular lawyer, Lucas Birdsong.

Previously, the legal practice of Lucas, elder brother of the by-then well-known poetess Eleanor Birdsong, had been limited to wills, deeds, real estate transactions, and minor infractions of business laws. Eleanor Birdsong encouraged her brother to accept the Celia Dawson case and thereafter worked closely with him on it. On at least one occasion, Eleanor's writing friends from Boston attended the Merriam trial in support of her.

Lawyer Birdsong argued that the county's real target was not poor Celia but the Dawson Tannery, whose noxious odors and sprawl were, according to critics, preventing other would-be businesses from locating in Jericho's Cobble. To convey that point, Birdsong called to the stand the Cobble's leading citizen, banker, and landholder, Bucko Whitbred. For the county, Dr. Pinthaler testified that Celia would only be manageable in a specially designed facility and warned that allowing her to remain at home posed a danger to herself and to the community.

Somewhat to the astonishment of the Dawsons and the Birdsongs, the magistrate, a great believer in the sanctity of the family hearth, sided with them. Celia Dawson would not be forced into an institution.

"Now you are free," Eleanor Birdsong was quoted as saying to Celia.

The county did not appeal the court decision.

In the wake of this case, the State of Massachusetts drew up new statutes to allow for the state to mandate institutionalization of juveniles on the recommendation of at least two physicians, and, if need be, over the objections of the parents.

The tannery was rebuilt along more efficient and less odoriferous lines. Birdsong's law practice blossomed, and he opened a satellite office in Merriam and thought about establishing one in Great Barrington.

Eighteen months after the verdict, while Oscar Dawson was out of town on business, at four in the morning Celia took a kitchen knife and killed her mother and then herself.

G) THE AFTERMATH.

DISPLAY: *Springfield Republican*, FEB. 7, 1853

EXPLANATORY CARD:

News of the bloody tragedy in Jericho's Cobble held the front pages of newspapers from Springfield and Hartford to Albany and Poughkeepsie.

Oscar Dawson, devastated, buried his wife and daughter in a mausoleum in the Jericho's Cobble cemetery that already housed his deceased infant son, and then shuttered the tannery and the Dawson House and decamped to Manhattan.

The closing of the tannery eliminated the jobs of forty men, many of whom then had to leave the area to obtain work; the Dawson closures were followed by those of other local industrial operations, commencing a seven-year period of economic doldrums for the Pequabogue Valley that only eased after hostilities began in the Civil War, which once again increased demand for the area's dairy, beef, corn, and hay.

After the Dawson murder-suicide, Lucas Birdsong never again set foot in a courtroom; he closed down his sate

lite law offices and thereafter confined his legal practice to non-confrontational matters. And for some years after the tragedy, Eleanor Birdsong did not send out her poems to magazine publishers.

h) Institute for the Wayward, Jericho's Cobble Branch

Display: Photo, Local board members (1866), in front of Institute, including Eleanor Birdsong, Selwyn Whitbred, and Miriam Beresford.

Explanatory card:

Oscar Dawson died in 1863, trampled to death

as he ventured out during the July draft riots in Manhattan that followed Lincoln's mobilization edict. As per Dawson's wishes, his body was returned to the Cobble for burial in the family mausoleum alongside those of his wife, daughter, and short-lived son. Dawson's last will—filed with Lucas Birdsong, and highly influenced by poetess Eleanor, according to markings on an early draft—bequeathed the Dawson House and acreage, along with an endowment to maintain the property, to Dr. Augusto Pinthaler's Institute for the Wayward.

Dr. Pinthaler had no interest in personally moving to Jericho's Cobble. Rather, as recounted in his textbook, *Mental Disorders Among Females*, his disciples established in the Dawson House a satellite Institute for The Wayward. Members of the Birdsong and Whitbred families (as identified in the exhibited photo) were among the trustees for the Cobble-based branch. It never lacked for clients, most from within fifty miles of the facility. Its doors eventually closed because not enough adequately-trained personnel were willing to live in a small town.

The Dawson property was considered for purchase by the French Protestant group of teachers who were then also mulling the acquisition of the Whitbred estate. The teachers ultimately rejected the Dawson House because of its tainted history. It was bought by former Institute cook Justin Youngblood, who soon re-opened it as Dawson's House Inn.

Oscar Dawson (1802-1863)

I was too much in Death's debt,
it having enabled me to amass a tidy fortune
from the spines, hooves, guts, and pelts
of the thousands of horses and cattle
I butchered, dismembered, and made into useful products.

Knackery—lucrative because despised—earned me no friends,
won me no civic honors, but bought me a better wife than hoped for,
gentle to my necessary harshness, her sweet pleas swaying me
when I should have remained adamantine.

Ashes to ashes and dust to dust:
I came from naught, made something of myself,
and gained the boasting belief that I had all the answers,
even though, as time and the world teach,
'twould have been smarter by far for me to have yielded:
to God, who demanded obeisance;
to Bucko, who sought an alliance;
to the State of Massachusetts, which wanted my daughter;
to dolor, instead of to curiosity
about the rioters at my Manhattan door.

Death teased me and tormented me,
refusing to scythe me quickly,
shearing off, bit by bit by bit
my pride, my children, my wife,
then my happiness, my dignity, and my faith,
and, only after I ceased to care about it,
my life.

Birdsong House Docent Script

(Docent or staff member, acting as Eleanor Birdsong in the summer of 1861)

Hello! Please come in! I am Eleanor Rummet Birdsong, a poet and assistant to my brother, Lucas, in his law practice. He and his family and I live in this house.

This war now begun with the Southern States is terrible, is it not? But the future of our beloved country is at stake, and so is its soul. Are we to continue to countenance slavery anywhere within our borders? We abolitionists hope at least to free the slaves down South, as has long since been done here in Massachusetts.

Let me tell you a bit about our home. Lucas built it in 1823, in the Federal style—nearly forty years later it's a bit old-fashioned, but we manage! This parlor is part of his law office. From time to time I assisted Lucas in his law practice, and particularly on the Celia Dawson custody case; Lucas and I bear some responsibility for its awful eventual outcome, a terrible calamity that, seven years on, still bothers me.

Lucas and Rachel have lots of room here now that their children, Maria and Simon, have flown the coop. (We do like bird metaphors here!) I helped raise my niece and nephew because my poor sister-in-law was often ill. But let me tell you about our ancestors.

My grandfather was born Friedrich Vogelsang. He was—I make no excuses for this—one of those awful Hessian mercenaries hired by George III to fight us in the

Revolution. Captured during the battle of Saratoga and then marched south toward a camp, he escaped! And came into the Pequabogue Valley and met and charmed my dear grandmother Gilda, who spoke a bit of the German, and her parents, the Nyswanders. After marrying Gilda and being given some acres to farm by his in-laws, Friedrich Vogelsang changed his name to Cedric Birdsong and became the valley's cheesemaker.

Then in 1798, Cedric and Gilda's son, my father Julius, decided that he preferred carpentry and apple-farming to dairy-farming and cheesemaking, and so moved to this site on the outskirts of town, planted an orchard and built a home. In 1822 that home burned to the ground, which is why Lucas, upon graduating from Tapping Reeve's law school in Litchfield—yes, that famous school—built this one.

For me, 1826 was the most dreadful year. My fiancée, Pieter Hogeboom from Poughkeepsie, an army engineer, was killed during a pacification mission in the Michigan territory. I was very distraught. I have only a small memento of dear Pieter, a physiognotrace silhouette - it's up in my quarters on my desk; you shall see it there.

After his death—well, I just did not seek to marry anyone else! Later in the year, Lucas urged me to visit our older married sister, Philomena, in Boston. I did, and she, knowing my predilection for poesy, secured an introduction to Josepha Hale, celebrated author of the children's poem, "Mary Had A Little Lamb." Josepha was about to begin editing the *Ladies Magazine*, and she invited me to contribute!

That was so wonderful. I came home and wrote scads of poems. Three years later, she published the one that became my most widely known, "The Purple Martin."

I'd rather swoop and soar than hop along,
Whistling, warbling, piping my song:
"Hello, sunshine, hello rain,
Hello forests, hello plains.
I am here, I am fine,
Midst poplar, birch, oak, and pine."

Short and sweet, but oh, my!—how much reading about birds and birdwatching it took for me to think up what to write! We already had purple martins in our apple orchard—very helpful in eating mosquitoes, black flies, and other pests. I begged my carpenter father to make nests for them, high upon poles—like bird-apartments!—and he did, and we placed the "apartments" around our property.

In the winters I'd go to New York and Boston and even to Philadelphia to visit Josepha and her friends, who became my friends: Anna Cora Mowatt, Ann S. Stephens, and Emma C. Embury—writers all. That cad Nathaniel Hawthorne—a wonderful writer but a nasty man—dismissed us all in a letter to his publisher as "that damned mob of scribbling women." But we wrote on! And in the summers, they visited me in Jericho's Cobble. We were all early abolitionists, and lovers of transcendentalism, and advocates for women's rights. Did I mention that I was a delegate to the second women's abolition convention in Philadelphia in '38? Very exciting. Dangerous for us, too, with our opponents throwing stones. Abby Kelley Foster spoke—she was magnificent.

My later writing has been much more for adults, dealing with longing, loneliness, isolation, and the ache that comes when beloved children grow beyond adorable preciousness. But I've never again had the level of success that I did with "the purple martin."

Shortly I'm to go to a friend's, along with other neighboring women, and together we'll make bandages for our gallant young soldiers protecting this country from disunion.

But I have a bit of time, now, to show you the rest of our home. Come, let us take ourselves upstairs to see my bedroom and writing desk…

Up at Three A.M.

(thoughts of Mary-Beth Flaherty,
Executive Director, The Birdsong House)

Needing to pee out the remains of last night's beer gets me out of the sack at three in the morning in my cozy caretaker's quarters of the Birdsong House. Last night's dancing at the Volta Club over in Springfield was pretty good—not as chill as a real clogging session (non-existent, hereabouts) but sweet, made more so by the beer and by the attentions of Benny, the hockey coach at Sprouls Academy, by far the best male dancer on the floor. Near midnight he asked me to stay over. I pleaded the need to return here for a morning meeting. Only a bit of a fib: I do have a meeting this morning, of great importance to the Birdsong House's future, but my main reason for begging off was that while Benny is a hunk, I'm not that eager for another affair with a jock that I wouldn't write home about.

After my bathroom session I can't get back to sleep, wondering whether I'd been dumb to push away Benny, and whether my real reason for coming back here was my worry that I haven't marshaled all the resources necessary to deal with the looming crisis for the Birdsong House, the Joshua's Cobble Civic Association's threat to close it permanently next July 1. The loss of the Birdsong House Museum would be a disservice to this town—and would also throw me out of a job and remove the roof over my head.

Actually, I've done a lot for this historic house in the two-and-a-half years since I landed here with my newly-minted MFA in Arts Administration from Kinsella College in Nashville, to become its first-ever paid executive director. Most people in the New England historic-houses community are aware of my having boosted the Birdsong's on-line presence, put in a garden specifically designed to attract birds—cornflowers and sunflowers, elderberry and cotoneaster—and beginning an annual birdhouse festival. Our profile is up. Admissions too, though not enough to offset the upkeep of the house and my salary. Doubtless the fuddy-duddies of the JCCA would be happier if I just moved on—which I am not ready to do. Because while this little village is absolutely too laid-back for a gal who lives to clog dance, I have come to respect and adore the sensitivities and wit of Eleanor Birdsong, for instance in her late-career poem (1862) that I rediscovered: *A Gloss On Hamlet*:

> To love or not to love, that is the question.
> Whether 'tis nobler in the main
> to suffer, yearn, and sob oneself to sleep,
> or to pursue what one must not obtain,
> court disdain, endure scorn so very deep?
>
> Life ought not to be a playground slide
> that one mounts alone;
> why not a teeter-totter, fit for two sides,
> that both of us may own?

It's deep yet playful. Deserves a bigger audience. And its maker deserves the continued preservation of her lifelong home.

Actually, I adore being Eleanor and conducting the house tours—I'm more of a performer than I've admitted to myself.

Once, early on a Saturday, I got into the Eleanor costume and was thinking of her as I came down those stairs in it, and I passed her coming up the stairs! I swear! And when my eyes met hers, she winked at me!

Then she vanished.

Visitors often ask me if the Birdsong House is haunted. I tell them I hope so.

Gertie's Primrose Path

(thoughts of Gertrude Merkin Beresford,
trustee, JCCA)

This morning, while I'm at the Birdsong House for a meeting, the Borskas will come to the cottage to dig that drainage ditch I should've had them do a year ago. Primroses adore moist soil, so I ignored any possibility of a flood from an underground stream until one drowned the roots of the six dozen I'd so carefully placed in walkable rows and showed off as "Gertie's primrose path." Most of the garden clubbers, when I escorted them along it, didn't get that joke—a primrose path as a reflection of a life more troubled than it should be for a Beresford, a DAR[12] stalwart, for Pete's sake! My lineage is through Sergeant George Oliphant Merkin's posthumous daughter Celandine, and my family money is from the 19th century Merkins' mining of the limestone cliffs. Pride in one's past doesn't necessarily mean avoidance of its seamier aspects. I digress; my bad.

Gracie Newington got my "primrose path" joke, but then she's a Holyoke girl if I'm not mistaken, wife of that Sam guy who does something on Wall Street and was so badly injured in the Main Street crosswalk. Gracie will have a Chardonnay with her sandwich if I do and likes to hear gardening stories and about the old days and old Cobbler families, and doesn't sneak glances at her watch while listening. She's now mostly tied up with caring for her banged-up husband, so we haven't lunched recently. One good thing from Sam's terrible injuring, though: she speaks of him with more affection. Don't think they're out of the marital woods yet, but I'm hoping. My last husband's straying and squandering forced me to sell Cliffsedge, the Beresford

---

12 Compiler's Note: DAR, Daughters of the American Revolution; membership restricted to those able to document their descent from Americans in the Revolutionary Era. RBM

ancestral home on Chariot Hill, to bail him out one last time. During my divorces I was grateful to have had some family money to see me through. There are things one can bear and things one absolutely cannot.

Today I haven't the fortitude to watch my garden being overturned, so I'm happy to go to the Birdsong House for a really crucial meeting with that executive director girl; her name will come to me in a minute. My parents knew the last of the Birdsongs, Maisie; and my great-grandmother Mimi was friends with the famous poetess. We've pictures of that.

For five years at the House, I was the Eleanor. Everybody said I did it well! I dearly loved doing it, yet I was among the first on the JCCA board to agree that the Birdsong House must have a professional leader. Mary-Beth Flaherty, that's her name! And she is a treasure. Cute and smart and polite—nothing like my daughter, who at thirty-five hasn't found her way, or my thirty-nine-year-old "free spirit" son who has no vocation but always manages to get some woman to care for him, roping in a new one soon after exhausting the old one.

Well, our Mary-Beth, a Southern belle from modest circumstances, has been doing a very innovative job with the Birdsong House, more so than what the JCCA could expect for the two-bits we pay her. The main complainer is that Collier gnome, the treasurer, a retired banker with an accountant's mentality—those green-eyeshade-types are everywhere, and I dread mine bristling at the bill from Borska and telling me for the umpteenth time to cut back my spending or I'll burn through the rest of my money.

I digress. Beg pardon.

Anyway, old Geoffrey Collier—got a decade on me!—wants to shut down the Birdsong House and has convinced most of the JCCA board to go along. His idea of saving a few thousand bucks a year by closing the Birdsong House is malarkey! The one place is town that honors a woman! What's a civic association for, if not to support a town treasure even if it doesn't run a profit? Geoffrey Collier, like most of the nouveau riche, has deep pockets but a shallow conscience.

Borska Family Heritage

(thoughts of Andy Borska)

Even with the van's windows open, the coffee stays hot in the cup for quite a while because at Jeannie J's request I cranked up the thermostat of the Get'nGo coffeemaker to the max. We of the fraternity who kneel on cold floors to work, we plumbers and carpenters and electricians and tile guys, we need that warmth in our cuppas as the early mornings turn cool. Today we'll be outdoors all day, digging the drainage ditch for Gertie Beresford.

Borska Family Plumbing and Heating was started by my grandfather, Karol, upon his arrival from Gdansk after World War I, and was continued by my father, Pyotr, on his return from Korean War service. After my stint in Vietnam, I was so blasted out I didn't care about anything but the next beer, but apprenticing with Dad and learning to love the work helped me. Eventually I took over from him. We now own three vans full of equipment, a backhoe and other heavy-duty machinery, and have enough steady business to keep me and my four other guys busy, plus Stacy in the office.

Gramp and Dad toiled all their days to build a rep for good service, great work habits, and a business solid enough to pass on to son and grandson, as crafts and guilds have been doing for thousands of years. They also instilled in me their love for the music of Frédéric Chopin. The Chopin CDs in my truck's deck are just as necessary to me as my morning joe.

But I'm no longer as ready to get out in the morning to face another plugged toilet. Part reason is not being able to pass on the business to my son. Hugo, twenty-one, has shown zero interest in getting dirty every day, in permanently callousing his hands and overtaxing his knees to unplug drains and prevent seepage, even at $79 per billed hour and with weekends and evenings free. Fortunately, my pal Zach Galter, the pharmacist at Prince's, took him on as the clerk in that department. Hugo's bored with it, though.

Well, growing up means becoming dissatisfied some, doesn't it? For me and for Stacy too. I married a girl I'd known all my life, and she's grown into her mother, who only ever tolerated me. Stacy is a good person who's let herself go a bit. I admit, though, that the problem gnawing at me is more about me than it is about her.

I thought midlife crises were for white-collar types. Yet I'm increasingly bugged by my "roads not taken," in terms of other women. Twenty-five years ago I felt keenly the need of a regular sexual partner, helpmeet, office minder, and prospective mother for our kids. Now—well, my eye does rove! I'll bet Stacy's class-of-'73 lunch pals have a field day talking that up. Some guys do keep a side honey; I haven't done, but I'm big and strapping, and more than a couple younger gals have flirted. There's one who has her eye on me now, in that wholesale appliance outlet in Merriam ...

Hardly a home in the Valley I don't know inside out, the newly-built and the centuries-old, for if I'm not in there unclogging pipes, then I'm there installing the latest award-winning toilet from the annual Las Vegas flush-off, or the handrail in the shower for my old history prof, or—this morning—enfilading a drainage trench for a grande dame, Gertie Beresford, who last year didn't want to hire me for a prevention ditch. The repairman's adage, "You can pay me now or you can pay me more later" has its truth proven once again.

Not everybody's as polite as Gertie and her old-money Cobblers. So I do understand Hugo's unwillingness to follow me into plumbing—it's not just hating the manual labor, it's not wanting to be looked down upon by the very clients so willing to give us the combos of their door locks while they're in New York or Boston, and who desperately need us to do what we're doing so they can be comfy when they arrive for their long weekends. Most of these weekenders barely acknowledge that I exist, even though on Saturday nights I attend the same classical concerts as them and on Sunday mornings I pray alongside them.

Today, to dig Gertie's drainage trench, in addition to the backhoe I need Chopin's Mazurka in A minor, Op. 17, No. 4 . It's an early composition, not his best, but still a cut above. Only Chopin can make music in a minor key feel so uplifting.

Maisie Birdsong Gaitskill

(1901-1943)

There are secrets that you never divulge,
that you take with you to the grave
because no one else needs to know them.
I have a few.

When my first love was leaving for the Great War,
I gave him my very best send-off, and six weeks later,
when he was killed, I knew I was pregnant;
that secret, for a while, I told no one,
not my mother, nor my pastor, nor my new suitor,
    Fred Gaitskill, automotive repair genius.
We married quickly, and Fred became father to Wally in every way.

We lived in the Birdsong house,
long since paid off and adequate to our needs,
    but every day there I was aware
    of my great-great-aunt Eleanor,
whose ghost chuckled at my not having a poetic line in my head.

Eventually I tired of the grease that never left Fred's hands
    and the cars that never left his mind,
    as well as of my second-rate existence
as the best voice in a back-country choir.

So when Wally was eleven and better able to fend for himself,
and I was twenty-nine and still a beauty,
I fled to New York and a new life as a Broadway chorine.

Although only occasionally employed on stage, I survived,
because I did not seek marriage,
which made it easier to find a man who'd support me.

As a mistress I lived well enough,
helping squares enjoy spending their money,
never asking whence it came
or whether their wives knew of me—
    secrets I did not need to know.

When Wally got a bit older he visited me.
He never asked why I had left,
only if I was happier now, which I said I was.
That he was the spit and image of his true father, I never told him.
How would that secret have helped him?

Fred remarried and established his own home.
Wally worked in Fred's business until sent off to war,
a prime mechanic of trucks and tanks,
soon killed in action in Italy.

I returned to the Cobble for my son's interment.
After the rite I put the Gold Star given me by the honor guard
in the front window of the shuttered Birdsong house,
like every other mother of a slain hero did,
    and shed honest tears,
more for what I had not given Wally than for my own loss;
and then once more left the Birdsong house,
    vowing never to return.

On our way back to the city, my current swain and I,
drunk and rounding a curve on the old turnpike,
swerved to miss an oncoming truck, skidded,
and died on impact with a century-old tree.

Since I was a Birdsong, and therefore, by the Cobblers' lights,
one of them,
they provided me with this cozy *pied-à-terre*.

Bloom Where You Are Planted

(thoughts of Aimee Bishop)

Ade Castelmara and I knew a day of direct clash would come, even though we never spoke of it during our dozen years as a couple, a period that ended a decade ago. Now it's here in the fight over the future of the Dawson House tract.

When I was thirty-three—a quarter-century ago!—I came to the Cobble to fulfill the promise of my favorite flower-child mantra, "Bloom where you are planted." The most diverse biosphere in North America seemed like a really neat place to start over. My inheritance from Aunt Berenice Childers, plus the proceeds from selling my half of the common property (our house) from my divorce from Ferdie Bishop enabled me to buy outright this 1921 gem at the end of Wisteria Lane, mostly surrounded by the forest, with just enough sunlight for an extensive vegetable garden. I really needed to get away from California: The era of wall-to-wall rock festivals, pot-haze summers, and cheap housing were long gone, and our former governor, Ronald Reagan, was aiming to take over the U. S. of A. and erase the Sixties. I was glad to push the reset button. The Cobble was a Brigadoon-in-the-Berkshires, a beauteous, mostly benevolent place, away from the roiling mainstream yet near enough to the big city to sample its offerings now and then. Perfect for me, because here I was able to find things to do that I liked—entertainment reviews and garden stuff for the paper and interviewing for WCBL—and that brought in enough money. Now and then I also snagged garden- and décor-related gigs—everybody knew I had style!

Ade and I found each other. He was a bit older, just as divorced, just as comely, and just as adventurous and ready to party. We had a great time! People liked us as a couple and invited us everywhere. Ade always claimed not to want children, and I wasn't going to bear one without him, so I didn't have any during the remainder of my fertile years; then, when I was

45 and staring at menopause and he was 48 and dreading the far side of 50, he dropped me and married his already-pregnant 27-year-old girlfriend, a secretary in the county clerk's office. She had no ambition but to take care of him and the children. They've since had two more! If he's been faithful to her, I'll eat my gardening hat.

After we went our separate ways I directed my energies into starting the Pequabogue Protectorate, the Valley's first locally based environmental advocacy group, for which I still serve as the chair. My work with the Protectorate has firmed my belief that I can make a positive difference here.

The Cobble is my forever home. I'm never leaving.

The battle is shaping up as between me and Ade. I'm not looking for revenge on him for finking out of me after I'd put a dozen years into our relationship, but this area's beauty, character, and serenity do need defending as well as appreciating, so for me to fight for them against assault-by-motorcycles is a no-brainer. What Ade touts as "progress" for this area, to me looks like "unnecessary wreckage" of the irreplaceable.

Also, in addition to protecting this tract of land, I feel obliged to guard the spirit of that poor deranged girl, Celia Dawson, who was unable to get help when she needed it most—we can all relate to that!—and the spirits of all the tormented girls who later lived at the Institute for the Wayward. I can't bear the thought of motorcycles ruining a locale so sanctified by blood and mental anguish.

Ade in his macho-lawyer way always underestimated me, and he's surely done so this time. Surrendering the Dawson acres to dirt bikes is not the kind of new enterprise that the Cobble can absorb and keep on being the Cobble. To mobilize public opinion against it I'll take to the airwaves, the newspaper waves, and even to the Internet waves.

I've spent my whole life becoming ready for this fight.

THREE:
ON A FINE SUNDAY MORNING

Jim the Baker's Early Start

(thoughts of Jim Skupski)

At 4 a.m., the flashing, silent alarm rouses me from my dreams of sweetness and balancing tartness, the piquant, the aromatic, the creamy. Making sure not to jostle Dinah, I creep downstairs in darkness, and in the living room change into the duds I laid out last evening, topped by my beret, for the brief walk to my Les Délices café through the deserted streets of Jericho's Cobble on a dark Sunday morning. Dawn's not for a couple hours.

"Jim the Baker" Skupski, Vietnam veteran,[13] is among those who love going about their business in the wee hours, when we have the world to ourselves.

Entering the café I doff my beret to the lush tropical mural of coffee-growing country, so unexpected by first-time customers in this white-clapboard town. Through the swinging doors into my tiny kitchen to start in on my ablutions—light my ovens, check that the overnight doughs are properly plumped, the nuts crisp, the jellies unfrozen, the raisins chewy. Be another hour before the bagels are delivered, and a half-hour beyond that 'til the first customer peers in to see if I'm open. I work quietly, so as not to wake old Hallie Prince in the upstairs apartment.

There's room for only one amidst the refrigerators, ovens, double-sinks, and cupboards wide and deep enough to hold five-gallon cans. It ain't perfect—but then, little in this world is, least of all me. Yet after the Bucharest terror of my youth, and Agent Orange in 'Nam, and the frantic Manhattan cab-driving, and the false starts, the business partnership gone sour, the heart attack, and the over-ripe daughters, this gentle village and this cozy café and this one-person kitchen is heaven to a man who lives to bake, which is what I was put on God's earth to do.

---

13 Compiler's note: Skupski's unit, the Third Brigade of the fabled 82nd Airborne, sent to Vietnam in 1968 in response to the Tet Offensive; returned to Fort Bragg in 1969, RBM.

This is the best time of my day. For while I enjoy chatting with customers—their how's-it-goings and little jokes and the conversations that now and then turn philosophical, the more so during the late mornings when patrons don't have to leave to go to their jobs—I crave more what comes *before* I open my doors, the measuring and blending and kneading and rolling and separating and dotting with butter and sprinkling with sugar. The sweet scent rises to my head like brandy. My breathing is too labored—that's my heart again. So I sit for a spell. And start fretting about whether Ina Mornay will renew my lease in a couple months, and for how much.

Can't solve my lease problem by worrying it, so I go back to work. Anyway, my hands know what to do. And I have wonderfully loyal customers awaiting the results. In these parts, coming to Jim's for a fancy coffee and a treat has become a ritual.

Dinah wants me to retire and sell before I croak in this kitchen—which I wouldn't mind dying in; but who'd buy the business from me? Too much work versus too little reward for most people. Yet the Cobble does need a place like this, where rich and poor, old-timers and newcomers, go-getters and retirees can gather. And what would I do at home? Can't read the papers or watch the TV news all day—what's going on in the world outside this lovely town would upset me even more if I learned about it in greater detail.

It's not yet dawn when I deliver to my primed ovens the greased sheets and tins bearing the four varieties of muffins, the bear claws, the elephant ears, the oatmeal-raisin cookies, all seeking the benediction of heat to become luscious.

Each one will be a delight to its future eater, as it already is to me.

Critical Responses?

(Patrick Tolland, publisher,
The Country Caller)

Standing in line waiting to order at Jim's on a Sunday—an important workday for us at the paper, since we close the weekly issue on Tuesday—I mull over how to respond to the unsigned letter-to-the-editor that came in yesterday's mail. We don't get many, and I feared this one would rail at rumored resurgent drug-dealing. No, thankfully; but it does allege something just as stomach-turning, sexual predation by the former women's athletic director of The Chancellery, Casmir "Chip" Garuzelski, crimes that, according to the letter-writer, the prep school has failed to address.

I remember Garuzelski's name. Eight years ago, just after Duke[14] had lured me back to the Cobble so he could retire, I was amazed to learn that decades after the inception of Title IX, a prestigious co-ed private school would still have a man as head of girls' sports. If the allegations are true about his fondling and raping of teenaged girls, and about a school administration that looked the other way, this is a huge problem for The Chancellery.

The writer of this unsigned letter, surely knowing our policy of only printing signed letters with verifiable addresses, only sent it to push us to an investigation of The Chancellery on this matter. If we were a major-city daily I'd be glad to—ask April[15] to assign someone to chase the story for a while and see what turns up. But being perpetually in the red, we must take care with every dollar and every reporter-hour spent, and the Chancellery is a very tough nut to crack. The town's largest employer, it is also

14 Compiler's Note: Malcolm "Duke" Duhamel, retired editor-publisher of *The Country Caller*; previously, features editor, *Army Times*, *Minneapolis Star*, and *Chicago Tribune*. RBM

15 April = TCC editor-in-chief April Lasko.

standoffish, able to brush away most attacks with its half-billion-dollar endowment—so large they can hardly spend it fast enough, recently putting in such innovative but unnecessary facilities as a geothermal heating plant. For what? To help the school compete properly with Choate and Exeter for the trade of wealthy families fast-tracking sons and daughters to the Ivies?

Many secrets are buried in this town, not all of them in the cemetery.

My train of thought is interrupted by Doug Flipkens, our new cub reporter, who has joined the line at Jim's, both of us getting espresso-based drinks to go. I need to talk to Doug about his draft review of the Pequa Players' production of Tennessee Williams' classic memory play *The Glass Menagerie.* The show is running at the VFW Hall for the next couple of weekends. It boasts a local elementary-school teacher as the ingénue, our assistant postmaster as the author's stand-in character and lead, and is directed by our most prominent amateur thespian, a retired librarian from Philadelphia, whose wife is playing the second leading role, the ingénue's mother, one of the most famous characters in American theater. Aimee[16] declined to do the review because she's become long-term pals with the director and star. Doug panned the production, soup to nuts.

"We cannot run this review as currently written," I tell the young man, just a year out of Boston University's journalism program, as we walk to the office with our coffees.

"Why not? They stank."

"Because this isn't Boston, Doug. This is the boonies. This is our neighbors trying to entertain us; and out here in the cultural desert we need all the locally based entertainment we can get."

"You just don't want the director and actors giving you the side eye at Jim's while you're getting your latté."

"Absolutely! But even more, I don't want to hurt the troupe's ticket sales. This is a big deal to them, they've worked months

16 Compiler's Note: Aimee Bishop = entertainment editor of *The Country Caller.* RBM.

at it, and if they're not very good in it—well, we're all amateurs to some degree, all trying to re-invent ourselves as artists, leave behind the humdrum of everyday lives or former lives. And besides, Doug, other potential audience members will like the show—won't be as hypercritical as you or me."

"So you want me to lie and say it's good when it's not?"

"No, I want you to write a different kind of review. Talk about the play itself, summarize the plot and characters, say how emotional the play is, how poetic, how good a writer Williams is, how hard the troupe is trying with the play, and how admirable it is of them to even attempt the production of something so complex and so important to the American theater."

"I'm to 'let it be a challenge to me?'"

"It is certainly that."

"Okay, okay, boss. Will give it a try."

To the general point: What are TCC's obligations in such instances? We know from surveys that our readers do not cherish us so much as a reportorial scourge as they do a source of information. They want to know what happened at that school board meeting they were too tired to attend, and at the high school ballgames, the bridge tournaments, and who's in the police blotter and in the obits. More difficult for us to figure is what our readers *need* to know as opposed to what they *want* to know, both aspects entwined with what local government, private enterprise, and volunteer entities prefer for us to tell them—or not to tell them.

Big city folks believe that communities like ours are even-tempered and easy-going. They're not wrong, but problems do regularly crop up that cry out for attention. To the rest of the world these problems might not seem like much, but to us here, they are. Some the paper can deal with right away; others I put into a tickler file and revisit them every so often. In my tickler file just now: the attempt to rename Whitbred Elementary; whether the Birdsong House will remain as a museum; the halting progress on building the new firehouse (way over budget); the future of the Dawson tract; and as of today, this Garuzelski matter.

The Mulroney news is another. A few days ago, Lene sent out a press release about it, and April assigned Felicity to do a short article. But the first few drafts were not quite right. Now, on my desk, there's the latest:

"New Leader for Small Luxuries," by Felicity Ringell

Small Luxuries, the Cobble-based chain of eighteen gift-shops offering "notions and potions " in small towns across interior New England, has announced leadership changes. Founder Darlene Mulroney, known as Lene, is stepping aside as CEO and will be succeeded by her daughter Margaret. Mrs. Mulroney will remain chairman of the board. Simultaneously, her son Charles Mulroney, Jr., known as Chuck, is leaving Small Luxuries to become a vice-president of Kinshauzer Corporation's Peyton's Corners shopping mall, off Route 91 between Hartford and Springfield.

According to published articles in retail consumer-goods trade papers, both the Small Luxuries firm and Mulroneys Marmalades, begun by Charles Mulroney, Sr. now gross in the millions of dollars annually. At present, several other sons of the senior Mulroneys continue on staff at Mulroney's Marmalades.

The firms were begun fifteen years ago as outgrowths of some specialties that the Mulroneys had developed during their quarter-century ownership of the Cobble's supermarket, now known as Grosvenor's, for the name of its current owner.

MEMO FROM PATRICK TOLLAND TO APRIL LASKO RE: FELICITY @ MULRONEYS, ETC.

(EYES ONLY, NOT TO BE CIRCULATED)

Finally! Felicity's draft doesn't say too little or too much. OK to go in this week's issue. I've sent her a congrat; you and I remember how much we appreciated such "good work, kid" memos from Duke, back in the day. In its current form the article should not provoke the Mulroneys to cancel their regular ads in the paper but should adequately hint to our readers what we must not state overtly, that behind these changes at Small Luxuries lies a real family mess as well as a new installment of an American success story.

Mulroney family history is important here. Fifteen years ago, after they sold the supermarket, Lene used her part of the proceeds to launch a trio of stand-alone gift shops in the Valley, using the Small Luxuries name of that nook of the supermarket that had been a profit center; and Charlie used his half to open Mulroney's Marmalades, its initial sweet being the locally-produced winner of state-wide taste-offs. Since then, Small Luxuries has added stores beyond the Valley but Mulroney's Marmalades has expanded more, with extensions into chutneys and, recently, three designer ketchups—did you see them at Grosvenor's?

And Lene and Charlie are fine Cobblers, charitable and civic-minded.

Which is why it bothers me that Lene seems to have favored Margie over Chuck. (I don't know this for sure—it could have been just Chuck wanting out of the firm.) But couldn't brother and sister have been co-presidents? Isn't the point of a family firm to provide niches for family members? That's what Charlie's done at Marmalades with their other children, whose presence in the MM firm is the main reason, he is fond of repeating, that he turns down offers to sell out for big bucks: so that the children (and grandchildren) can continue to have meaningful work and share in the profits. Why couldn't Lene have done the same with Chuck at Small Luxuries? I remember vividly her excitement, a half-dozen years ago, letting me know that she had lured him back to the Cobble after his divorce to work with her. But shortly after that, Margie announced that she too had a marital problem and badly needed to come home and restart her life.

I'd bet that in this current set of changes non-business matters were more important than business ones. Chuck is definitely not on the same political plane with his parents and siblings. But then, we must also acknowledge that Charlie and Lene Mulroney came by their beliefs as a result of themselves fulfilling the promise of the American dream, rising from modest means through hard work to create enterprises that are earning them small fortunes and that they are passing on to their children. That Chuck fundamentally disagrees with his family's political stance is, I believe, due to his quite different life experiences, including failures and blockages (he never did become a pro hockey player; his marriage went sour; he lived mostly in big cities). Is that reason enough for forcing him out? Has part of realizing the American Dream become the freedom to reject the beliefs and ideas of those who think differently from us?

Mulling all this, I've also decided what we ought to do in response to the unsigned letter about Garuzelski. I'll inform The Chancellery that we've received this anonymous allegation and won't print it because of our policy against doing so, but that we need them to tell us whether and how they're responding to its allegations—and that we won't wait too long for their response.

A Choirmaster's Wonderings

(thoughts of Victor Leighton)

The Sunday morning service went well, although we as a choir are still down a voice or three. I'm thankful that alto Grace Newington could participate alongside mezzo Glenda Trainor, soprano Jane Milch, and the rest of the ladies, given that Sam's still recovering at Moorehead Rehab. Grace, a good sight-reader, made no mistakes despite lack of practice. I'm also happy that today, in her chatter with other choristers, there was no repetition of what we all had noted this summer, disgruntlement in the marriage; rather, she marveled at how valiantly her husband struggles to regain health.

While powering down the Hammond B-3, I wonder: Do we have the vocal strength to do a *Messiah*? I've been singing the basso lines of the weekly hymns for us since the passing of Doc Nash, and frankly, the baritones of Herm Murfrees and Duke Duhamel are not as robust as they once were. Beyond that, men aren't volunteering for choirs nearly as much these days. But I'm convinced that we could manage a *Messiah* if the audience does a lot more sing-alongs than usual for the piece.

Giving the audience/congregation more opportunities to join in would be much appreciated by the Cobble community, I think.

Actually, Handel wrote it more for regular voices than for operatic soloists. To do the early performances he transposed to suit the available voices, so I'd certainly be justified in tailoring it to our needs. The original instrumentation was also sparse—a few strings, trumpets, and oboes; those I can do perfectly well with the organ.

Such an endeavor will require permission and financial backing, of course, from the Reverend Vernon Trainor. We've never done anything this big on his watch. I don't know that he'll go for it even if I stress the idea of the sing-alongs as community participation. Church attendance is not yet up to what it was during Peter Hickle's[17] last year, when we had a post 9/11 bulge.

To conduct such a masterwork before I shuffle off this mortal coil would be my gift to the Lord for having at last relieved me of the fleshly desires that for so long bedeviled me, that once brought me so low I was sure I would die. Fortunately, at that moment I landed this church job, and in the decades since I have hewed to the narrow path, though lately wondering how long one must atone for any sin short of murder.

Had I come of age in the Seventies rather than in the Fifties I would have lived a much freer life. But of the many things we can't change, high on the list are the year of our birth and the social morés that go along with being in that birth cohort.

As music director at Congo, I've enhanced the lives of many congregants—some have told me so directly and I've heard it secondhand from others. That, nobody can take from me. Whether it'll save my immortal soul I won't know 'til I'm at the pearly gates.

What I do know now, and what I glory in, is the music—the whole hymnal by heart, plus much classical music scored for organ, and the thousand pop tunes and Broadway show tunes that I used to tinkle on piano at parties, which I haven't done since Muriel took sick and needed me home to care for her, nightly except Thursdays, when our neighbor takes over for a few hours so I can lead the choir practice. As Muriel's condition deteriorates further, she'll require additional looking-after, but Medicare doesn't pay enough for that so we'll just have to cope. Fortunately we bought our small house long ago, when prices were low, and we've paid it off. Good houses and good wives and good bosses are not easy to come by. Tolerant ones. I remain grateful that twenty years ago Peter Hickle hired me as organist/music director without asking why my previous contract with The Chancellery had not been renewed after two decades.

---

17 Compiler's Note: The Reverend Peter Hickle (1930-2002) was only the eighth minister to lead the First Congregational Church of Jericho's Cobble since its gathering in 1768. RBM.

Looking back on Peter's decision, my guess is that he, too, must have had experience in the sinning line, probably during army service in Korea, and it made him willing to allow me to open a new chapter of my life. God has more aces up His sleeve than the Devil.

People come to church as much to be together and sing together as to be preached at; once I understood that, I sounded the hymns with fervor and in the musical interludes sought to entertain as much as to soothe. No one does it better, not even at Notre Dame de Paris. Is it arrogant of me to think so? Even a sinner can have legitimate pride.

And can become more devout.

I never imagined that a man like me would do so, just as a result of spending a lot of hours each week in a church, but today, more than ever and more deeply, I know the Lord to be my shepherd. I also feel that there is a growing divide in the Cobble, not between the Cobblers and the Gobblers, but between those like me who have faith in God and those who do not. I want to bridge that divide by employing everybody's affection for the *Messiah*, which non-believers like as much as believers do, to bring us together.

When Congo's council chose Vern Trainor to replace Peter, I worried. Although Vern is a man of rock-solid faith and fairly experienced in the pulpit, so far, he has been a less-insightful preacher than Peter and has not stood up to the Congo elders as Peter did. I continue to hope that on both of those counts Vern will improve with time. Peter Hickle always counseled that the Lord's way is not to be too quick to judge. I think that is also the Cobble's way—or, I should say more accurately, the way of the Cobble at its best.

Vern and I have understood that we march to different drummers, and so far we've been able to do so without a flare-up. He recognizes that music is not just a language for me, it is a way of life, one that comes easy to me; my relations with bosses, not so much.

The View from Moorehead Rehab's Third Floor

(A Newingtons' dialogue)

SAM:

In my third-floor window, level with
the tips of the courtyard's deciduous:
the trees, providing me entertainment,
the breeze tickled into dropping their leaves.

GRACE:

Your attention is sapped by self-pity,
and by the quite rational worry
that the snail's pace of your recovery
delays your return to the city
and to the office that depends on you.

SAM:

Providing, of course, that it still does!
Stock symbols are adrift in my head,
more flotsam than jetsam:
disjointed letters, mismatched numbers.

GRACE:

Chaos, taunting you to set things in order,
which is more my specialty than yours.

SAM:

Rehabilitate means "restore to normal,"
a definition to like, a target to aim at,
although for people nearing sixty,
as we are, the goal's not so simple.

GRACE:
Are you tired of hearing, as I am,
that you're lucky to be alive?
And therefore that you shouldn't worry?

SAM:
Impatient patient. Inquisitor visitor.

GRACE:
Imagine coming home before the trees go bare...

SAM:
The better to continue our conversation there.

What She Saw In Me

(thoughts of Herman Murfrees)

Often on Sundays, after singing in the choir I stop at The Buttery to get an ice-cream to take to Pamela at Moorehead. Today so did one of our altos, Grace Newington, getting a treat for her Sam, who's recuperating just down the hall here.

Seeing Pamela hold the chocolate cone in two hands to eat, I am reminded of the sweetness of the moment, going on twenty-eight years ago now, when our lives melded.

It was just after a tiresome Selectmen's meeting at the town hall—the old town hall, before it got burned to the ground—with an audience of two-dozen Cobblers shouting their disagreements over a matter so unimportant I can no longer recall it, a brouhaha that Pamela gaveled to sullen silence. After everyone else left, we two stayed to button up the place and I came up behind and put a hand on her shoulder and she put her hand over mine and turned to me and we were too close not to embrace.

Turned out, we'd both been imagining it for years.

Cloris was by then long gone from the cancer, but Paul, Pamela's husband, although retired from the State Department, wasn't quite dead, and her mother Letitia Renwick, the original Grande Dame, was still hanging on; and so for a while we kept our affair secret.

What Pamela saw in this overalled farmer I don't know. I wasn't a polished or a learned man; I didn't have money like her and hers; I never went to the good schools. We even worshipped at different churches, and at fifty-seven I was pretty set in my ways. I guess she liked that I say what I mean and mean what I say and never set out to do anything without knowing why. She'd run into too many people who did otherwise.

Her charm was more obvious: beyond the pearls and fine diction a well-educated woman of impeccable taste, firm decisions, and a willingness to forgive some who behave badly, including one whose name I won't say, who with his gang set the fire that destroyed our gem of a town hall!

People are full of mysteries.

Once we started being together I found her more adventurous than I'd figured, always up for doing what was new to her: driving a tractor, hunting ducks, a midnight skinny-dip. She got me into reading books I'd never thought to try: Dickens, Trollope, George Eliot. Learned a lot about human nature. We pushed each other more than a bit. Everybody said I became less of a grouch.

After Paul passed, Pamela and I spent more time together and in public; and the grand thing of it was that our children, by then all grown, had no objections and even liked what we brought into the family circles. But I sure wasn't going to suggest that we get married—a farmer's not inclined to change how things are done just for the sake of change.

Even though our intimacy is just memories now, and she's not always "present" when I'm here, I come to Moorehead to see her, regular as clockwork, rain or shine. And no matter whether or not I bring her an ice cream from The Buttery, every time she sees me she breaks into that great smile.

We talk about the old days, and whether the Cobble as we knew and loved it can survive much longer in this new century.

Raising the Flag?

(thoughts of Ernie Melchior)

It's not easy, being Black in Jericho's Cobble.

Acceptance by the Congo church, where we worshipped this morning, has happened quicker for us Melchiors than it has in the town as a whole, since the church was eager to demonstrate its inclusivity. They also need a bass for their choir, and I'm thinking about that; only thing is, I can't promise to always be back from my work trips on Thursday evenings to take part in practice. And some Sunday mornings, frankly, I'd rather be playing slow-pitch baseball.

Actually, I've a more problematic invitation to ponder; it came up at the bi-monthly Guardians lunch at the Griff. In the three years since Katy and I and our kids moved here and I joined the Guardians chapter at the urging of my bosses at Harwin House of Knoxville, I've nudged the Outpost to do more community support. #267 now awards a second annual scholarship to college, and does added nature-trail cleanups and food giveaways. As a result, the Guardians now want to promote me from second vice-president of 267—there are currently three of us in that position and it's a mostly ceremonial thing, with no responsibilities—to first v.p.

Most of this Outpost's members are small businessmen like general contractor Jemmy Tillotson and hardware store owner Danny Romano, a client of mine for HH, but I've discovered that a surprising number of "guardians" are not. These include a semi-retired lawyer from a white-shoe firm who just can't stand being alone, the female librarian who likes being at the center of male attention, and the gay male writer, half of a long-term partnership that just wants to be accepted like other couples.

In semi-rural New England towns like this one there's always background-level discrimination against Blacks. How could there not be, when 95-plus percent of the population is as white as they come? And when on top of that there's also long-standing rural insularity and regular drawing of lines between those born here and newcomers/ weekenders, no matter their color? Yet most Cobblers are aware that they have had Blacks in their cemetery since the eighteenth century, as well as some from the post-Civil War era.[18]

When we arrived here, Katy and I knew that it would take a while to be accepted as no more than and no less than the college-educated, middle-class family-of-four next door. But while our children are already part of the mix at Whitbred Elementary, invited to white age-mate friends' homes for cookies and sleepovers, we grown-ups are not yet among the professional-class Cobblers who regularly meet at their homes for dinner parties, private wine-tastings, and small-group play-readings. I'm seldom asked how my job as regional manager for a national wholesaler is going, and Katy's not often queried about her sculptures, which use hardware parts and are sold in reputable galleries. Broader acceptance will come in time, we hope, because we do like living here: a nice place, with very little of the constant confrontation and competition of the big cities. It's a real blessing to have people around you that are friendly, and not to have to be wary all the time.

When I was a running back with the Vols, a boy from a dirt-poor patch in Tennessee south of Cookeville, I couldn't even have imagined ever earning a solid income from anything but football, much less living in a beautiful, peaceful place like this. Then I met Katy. Smart as can be, she steered me into taking business and management courses so I'd have something to fall back on if I didn't make it to the NFL. Sure enough, the Steelers cut me, second week of camp. After two years in the Army, I put in seven years at HH of Knoxville, on the road across the South selling to retailers, before they promoted me to New York State manager and sent me to Albany. We were happy to go. But our

18 Compiler's note: See, e.g., the headstones of Nathan and Mathilda Archer, infra. RBM.

years there weren't so great—once you get well north of Harlem, being a Black man is no picnic.

After the birth of our second child, and my elevation to regional manager for HH, we decided to move to the Cobble. Its location is perfect for me to service HH's Western New England territory—equidistant from Hartford, Springfield, Albany, Vermont, and western New Hampshire. Our choice was between a townhouse in Poughkeepsie—a 30 percent Black, medium-sized city with so-so schools—or being in an almost entirely white small inland town where the schools are better and where our money bought us a whole acre with a sizable house and a barn for Katy's sculpture studio. From here we can easily get onto nature trails. We're even becoming better skiers. Fact is, skin color aside, we Melchiors are not that different from the other parents of grammar-school-age kids, and we love what those born here and those who relocate here do: the natural environment, the relaxed pace, the quiet, the strong faith in God, the benevolence of neighbors.

And now here come the Guardians, who I pegged as the least forward-thinking group, the most behind-the-façade biased, asking me to step up to the vice-presidency, which has actual responsibilities and comes with the understanding that in two years I'll be more-or-less automatically elevated to the presidency of this local chapter. Outpost elections are show-of-hands, so fewer members who might oppose a nominee in a secret ballot will likely do so in front of everyone else. The problem for me—for Katy and the kids and me—is, do I take this step-up or not? Being president would mean a bit of applause, an article in *The Country Caller*, and being asked for quotes now and then on local issues, chairing meetings, attending national conventions. Harwin House would love that. But it would also raise my flag high enough, hereabouts, so that Cobblers who don't want Blacks leading them in any way might come out of the woodwork and take potshots, whereas if I remain just a Guardians member, those types won't have reason to do so. Do Katy and I and the kids need more attention being paid to us than we may be able to handle? That's the crux of it. The actual election for first v.p. will be at next month's luncheon. There's time enough between now and then for Katy and me to hash it over thoroughly before making a decision. I'm inclined to go for it, but I won't do it without my family's blessing.

An Upright's Lament

I haven't been seriously caressed in a long time. A 1903 Hamilton, an upright crafted by the famed workshop of Hamilton Baldwin of Cincinnati, with a lovely American walnut case, keys made of real ivory and ebony, luscious felts, and "strings" of good American steel, I reside in the seldom-used back dining room of the Grey Griffon Inn with its fading wallpaper. In my heyday, when many people still knew how to play a piano, I was the focus of attention in the pub, where late of an evening, after enough alcohol had been downed, there would always be someone opening me up and striking my keys, to general enjoyment. Every now and then a classically trained pianist would seriously explore my tonalities and resonances—tonic for me; for weeks afterwards I'd shiver with excitement. Once someone did Rachmaninoff's Fourth! What a work-out! On the weekends, I would be used on regular concerts for the town, especially in summer when I'd be rolled onto the porch. Weekday afternoons, amateur choral groups would practice with me, and on weekday evenings traveling salesmen over-nighting at the Inn on their New England-territory routes would unleash unexpectedly fine singing talents on *Ol' Man River* or *September Song* and accompany themselves with my tones. These days I'm neglected by tinklers, pounders, and serious players alike: a constant trial. Occasionally a child will open my keyboard case and bang away for a few minutes, until the noise disturbs a grown-up and the child is lured away—to my utter dismay, since we were just getting acquainted. I've not had a rigorous tuning since the Inn changed hands, and no keys replaced since 1984, when surgery removed that clunking E flat below middle C, so often sounded in accompaniment to pop songs. I fear the coming winter's continuously roaring fires in the Inn's many fireplaces: their dry heat will wick away the last bit of moisture from my woods, leaving me fit only for the garbage heap and the lumber pile.

FOUR:
ARSON AT TOWN HALL

Town Hall Arson Articles

from *The Country Caller*, 1981-1991

1. "Historic Town Hall Burns To The Ground"

Issue of November 12, 1981, by Patrick Tolland

Early on Tuesday morning, November 10, the Jericho's Cobble municipal building burned to the ground. No one was in the town offices at the time.

Firefighting crews from the Cobble, aided by those from Great Barrington and Merriam, prevented the blaze from spreading to nearby structures but could not stop it from destroying the historic town hall, portions of which dated back to the 1820s. It is now just charred beams and twisted iron above its stone foundation.

According to First Selectman Pamela Markle, the fire consumed all of the paper-based files in the offices of the selectmen, the assessor, the town clerk, tax collector, children's services, services for the aging, sanitation, and other agencies. "It's a catastrophe for us, that's for sure, but thankfully no one was injured and not everything was lost," Mrs. Markle observed. She explained that some records had been stored in the only part of the building that appears to have survived the fire intact, the walk-in steel vault, originally commissioned for the Whitbred Bank in 1921 and donated to the town during the bank's 1971 renovation.

By press time for *The Country Caller*, that vault, whose records date back to the town's incorporation in 1768, had not yet cooled sufficiently to be opened.

Fire Chief Lorenzo Mattis declared the cause of the fire to be arson, based on the noxious fumes coming from the site and from the melted plastic gas-cans in the wreckage. He also opined that this arson was similar to the August fire at the town's equipment shed on Shandy Lane.

Markle characterized the burning of the town hall as the "the biggest event in the Cobble's history since the flood of 1955" that destroyed or seriously damaged twenty riverside homes, and she promised that "the perpetrators of this crime will be found and prosecuted, and a new town hall will be built on this very spot."

Until the new municipal offices are ready, town employees will work from alternate sites such as the rec rooms of the Congregational and Methodist churches.

Markle pledged to make available to this newspaper a complete list of the relocated offices and their new phone numbers in time to appear in next week's issue.

No witnesses to the onset of the blaze have come forward. However, State Police Lieutenant Jonah Wycliffe said that whoever set it had probably stayed long enough to watch the flames while consuming a pint of liquor—the discarded bottle was nearby. His men would be following up the bottle and other leads. He declined to add details about possible perpetrators other than to assert, "This was not an act of random violence."

2. "Arrests Made In Town Hall Arson"

Issue of December 3, 1981, by Patrick Tolland

Lieutenant Jonah Wycliffe of Barracks F announced on December 1 that three long-time residents of Jericho's Cobble had been arrested for the November 10 arson of the municipal building. They are Lamarr "Lem" Klecko, 35; his brother Holcomb "Hoke" Klecko, 32; and Arthur "Artie" Stilton, 31.

Lem Klecko has had many prior run-ins with the law, including convictions for drug dealing. He served time at Cedar Junction, a state facility, for distribution of controlled substances (cocaine and methamphetamine) prior to being paroled last February. His brother Hoke Klecko was also on parole after serving part of a sentence for the theft of automotive tools from the Jericho's Cobble Town Shed on Shandy Lane. He is a suspect in the still-unsolved August arson of the town shed, although he denies involvement. Artie Stilton has no prior convictions.

Lt. Wycliffe cited several unidentified acquaintances of the accused trio, who told the authorities that the Kleckos and Stilton boasted of drinking to excess in Red Horse Tavern in northwestern Connecticut and, while on their drive home, stopping to set fire to the fortunately-empty municipal building and watching it for a while.

A preliminary hearing for the trio is scheduled for December 4 in Pequabogue County Court in Merriam. It is expected to result in bail being set and in the suspects being released on bond pending a trial, which is scheduled for March-April of 1982.

3. "Troubled Pasts Of Alleged Arsonists"

Issue of Thursday, December 17, 1981, by April Lasko

According to Klecko family acquaintances, neighbors, Jericho's Cobble elected officials, and law enforcement officers, Lamarr "Lem" Klecko and Holcomb "Hoke" Klecko, accused with Arthur "Artie" Stilton of burning down town hall on November 10, have been in trouble with the law since childhood.

Lem and Hoke were frequently suspended from school for attacking or threatening classmates and for carrying concealed knives and firecrackers. Each attended Stillwater Mountain High School but did not graduate. Their father, a housepainter, was seldom home and died when eldest child Lem was 19 and Hoke was 15. Their mother, Crystal, a beautician, still works in area salons. Lem and Hoke's sisters, Angela Marshall, 34, and Ginny Klecko, 30, currently reside in Great Barrington.

Senior Police Sergeant Claude Zoldano of Mackenzie Road, responsible during his quarter-century on the force for the Jericho's Cobble area, estimates that the Klecko brothers and their hangers-on accounted for "a third or more of all complaints filed in the district in the years when they were not incarcerated." He also contended that the Kleckos' strength in numbers—"four to five at a time"—kept them from being booked more on minor offenses, since the gang was often more than a single officer responding to a call could counter by himself. According to Zoldano, the Kleckos were so brazen that they sometimes sold drugs from the bar at the Grey Griffon Inn after terrifying the staff into not complaining to the authorities.

Grey Griffon owner Fritz Paley declined to comment on the Kleckos but categorically denies Zoldano's accusation of the inn being used as a site for drug sales.

Town officials confirmed that Hoke Klecko had been employed by the town until the theft from the town shed of a year ago, after which he was fired for the second time. First Selectman Markle stated that after his first firing she had re-hired him because he had promised her personally to remain sober. "He's a Jekyll-and-Hyde personality. Hoke is an extremely moral fellow except when he's drinking—then he's a terror." She added that during the interim when he was not employed by the town, she engaged his services for weekly yardwork at her home, in part to assist him in supporting his family, wife Francine Mryzsk Klecko and daughter Bella, currently a sophomore at Stillwater Mountain.

Darnton Harris of Harris Metzlinger in Merriam, a defense attorney who has previously represented both Kleckos, has declined to be their counsel in the forthcoming proceedings. No other counsel has yet been retained or appointed by the court.

4) "A Long-Lost Secret From The Fireproof Vault"

Issue of March 25, 1982,
by Richard Bond Miller, town historian

A treasure and a puzzle confronted the members of Stillwater Mountain High's history club[19] as we inventoried the older items in the fireproof vault that survived last November's fire at the town hall.

19 Compiler's note: The Stillwater Mountain History Club, begun in the aftermath of the 1981 fire, is still thriving at the high school in 2003. RBM.

The treasure was also the puzzle: a list of over a hundred men from Jericho's Cobble who fought in the Civil War. Some were substitutes, and we had to figure out who they were. After the national draft was instituted in 1863, many wealthy families, and some not-so-wealthy ones who did not want to lose their breadwinners, paid substitutes to fight in their stead. An estimated 100,000 substitutes served on both sides. The average cost of one was $300. The vault's list noted a dozen substitutes. Our research task was not only to determine who those Jericho's Cobble substitutes were, but also, which of the area's men had paid for substitutes rather than serve.

Other documents in the vault provided clues—notarized copies of contracts between substitutes and purchasers. Several purchaser names were not previously known to us, and we will continue to search for more details about them. However, one name among the purchasers was quite well known to all Cobblers: Chelmsford Whitbred, a descendant of the original settler family.

Known as Chum, in 1863 this junior son of Bucko (Joshua Whitbred V), was 18 and a student at Harvard, his father's alma mater. A year earlier, his older brother, Joshua VI, known as Junior, had volunteered for the Union Army and had been killed at the Battle of Shiloh. Junior's body was then brought home for entombment; the Joshua Whitbred VI monument is one of our cemetery's largest.

As boys Junior and Chum, along with their father, had their portrait painted by itinerant artist Ammi Phillips, a painting now titled *The Green Lads*, which still hangs in the great hall of Whitbred House.

It is known that in 1863 Bucko and Chum had a severe disagreement over the young man's zeal to respond to President Abraham Lincoln's national draft. So it is likely that Bucko paid for a substitute despite Chum's wishes to serve. That substitute's name, we have discovered, was Lester Throckenberry. A seasonal farmhand, not born in this area, in November of 1863 he joined the II Corps of the Army of the Potomac in Whitbred's stead and was soon promoted to corporal. In February of 1864, at the Battle of Morton's Ford near Culpeper, Virginia, Throckenberry was killed in action. An unknown person then paid to have his body and rough casket returned to Jericho's Cobble for interment in our cemetery.

It is our history club's belief that that unknown benefactor was Chum Whitbred, who shortly thereafter left Harvard to resettle in New Mexico. He never returned to Jericho's Cobble, even after the deaths of his parents, refusing to claim the considerable estate. Indeed, it was the Whitbred family's lack of male heirs willing to take over the estate that spurred Bucko's daughters to sell it to the group that began The Chancellery.

5) "'Execution-Style' Death of Town Hall Arson Suspect"

Issue of April 13, 1982, by Patrick Tolland

Town hall arson suspect Arthur Stilton, 32, was found dead on the banks of the Pequabogue River on the morning of Sunday, April 9, with two bullet holes in the back of his head. The body was located by dogs while their owners had them out for an early walk.

The Merriam County coroner's office said preliminary indications were that the victim had been dead for six to eight hours, and had been killed elsewhere, probably further up toward the ridge line in Renwick State Forest, before being carried to the river's edge. Police officials have not yet located the actual site of the murder. In a preliminary autopsy, the bullet removed from the victim was determined to be too badly damaged to reveal the make or model of the pistol used. A second slug is believed to have gone through the neck area and out again but has not been found. The investigation into the death is continuing.

According to Pequabogue County Prosecutor Lars Wertham, the murder victim, Artie Stilton had recently agreed to plead guilty to a lesser offense and to testify against the Klecko brothers, his co-defendants on the arson charge. Stilton's death has postponed the arson trial, originally set to begin next Monday, April 17, before Judge Alonzo Thornton.

Wertham's office assured the public that the court delay will be minimal, and that murder charges for the Kleckos may well be added to the arson charges. There are no other suspects in the death of Stilton, a friend since childhood of Hoke Klecko. The brothers proclaim innocence of the murder.

6) "GUILTY PLEA IN ARSON OF TOWN HALL"

MAY 26, 1982 ISSUE, BY PAT TOLLAND

Judge Alonzo Thornton of the Merriam County Criminal Court accepted a guilty plea from Holcomb "Hoke" Klecko to two counts of arson, the first involving the Jericho's Cobble municipal building complex in November 1981, and the second, the town's equipment shed the previous August. By agreement with the prosecutor's office, these guilty pleas on the arsons will result in Hoke Klecko's avoiding trial on the more serious charges stemming from the murder of Arthur Stilton, who had been set to testify against Hoke and his brother Lamarr "Lem" Klecko before he was murdered.

Lem Klecko is being charged with Stilton's murder and will shortly go on trial for it. Hoke Klecko has refused to give evidence against his brother and has stated that if called to the witness stand, he will invoke his Fifth Amendment right against self-incrimination. According to court sources, Hoke was adamant that even though he may have benefitted from Stilton's death, he regretted the passing of his lifelong friend and had not asked for Artie to be silenced.

Each count of arson carries with it a separate sentence of three years.

7) "Editorial: A New Beginning?"

Issue of July 1, 1982, by Malcolm Duhamel, editor-publisher

Now that Lamarr and Holcomb Klecko have been convicted and incarcerated for long terms for their crimes it is time and occasion in Jericho's Cobble for a new beginning. In fact, we have already begun: according to law enforcement officials, in the six months that the Kleckos have been behind bars, our crime rate has dropped, an unambiguously good thing.

Yet our area will continue to be roiled by the same underlying conditions that fostered the Kleckos' anger and resentment, unless and until we forthrightly address its social and economic source, the growing divide in this town between the "have-a-lots," most of them weekenders, and the "have-a-littles," most of them lifelong residents.

Inequity does not always make people respond as the Kleckos did—most of us, regardless of our financial circumstances, do respect and uphold the laws. Yet it is also important for us to acknowledge that the wealth divide exists here, and glaringly so, and that it hurts some people more than others, and that it is not an easy problem to fix.

So as Independence Day in 1982 approaches, it is incumbent upon us all to work harder toward esteeming our neighbors for their characters and for what each contributes to this beautiful valley that we call home, rather than to judge them by their net worth. We are all Americans and all neighbors, and as such deserve each other's respect, and our collective as well as our individual assistance. The wealth divide exists in Jericho's Cobble; to strive to better reach across it is of the essence in our cherished New England village, and in America.

8) "LETTER-TO-THE-EDITOR"

ISSUE OF JULY 21, 1983, BY HOKE KLECKO

I hear there's grumbling in town over paying the $5,000 reward to the family of Arthur Stilton. It was offered for information leading to the arrest and conviction of those who torched the Jericho's Cobble municipal building in November 1981. Before Artie was killed, he was ready to ID me and my brother Lamarr as the ones as set that blaze. He would definitely have fingered us and earned that reward fair and square. His family should be paid.

(S) Holcomb Klecko, Norfolk Correctional Facility.

9) "A Prison Death For A Notorious Inmate"

Issue of July 18, 1985, pg. 1, by April Lasko

Lamarr "Lem" Klecko, 39, of Jericho's Cobble was found dead of stab wounds in his cell at Massachusetts' Cedar Junction Correctional Facility on July 16. Klecko was serving a 25-to-life sentence for the murder of Arthur Stilton in 1982. According to the state correctional authority, "There is no reason to believe that the killing of Klecko is related to the earlier crime." They believe it likely that Klecko ran afoul of inmate drug dealers. An investigation into his death is continuing.

Klecko's immediate survivors include two children who reside in Colorado with his ex-wife Darleen; his mother Liz Klecko; sisters Angela and Ginny of Great Barrington; and brother Holcomb "Hoke" Klecko, currently incarcerated at the Norfolk Correctional Facility for the arson that destroyed the old town hall.

Hoke Klecko's expected parole date from Norfolk, a medium-security prison, is several years off. According to the warden's office, although Hoke has been a model prisoner since arrival, it is uncertain whether the authorities will allow him to attend his brother's funeral, next week in Jericho's Cobble.

10) "Solemn Remembrance On Tenth Anniversary Of Arson"

Issue of November 14, 1991,
by Malcolm Duhamel, editor-publisher

Last Sunday, November 10, 1991, the tenth anniversary of the destruction by fire of the old Jericho's Cobble town hall, special prayers were offered in all of the town's churches. An exhibition of photographs recounting the devastation of the fire and the erection of the new town hall is available for viewing at the new one, along with a display of key historic documents salvaged from the fire. The exhibit will remain on display until January 1992.

First Selectman Pamela Markle characterized the burning of the old town hall as "the most traumatic event of my tenure," but opined that in retrospect it was "also a turning point in the history of Jericho's Cobble, after which many things started to get better."

During the last decade, according to local and state statistics, the crime rate in Jericho's Cobble and the Pequabogue Valley has declined markedly from what it was in the heyday of the Kleckos' crimes. At the same time, housing and land prices have increased by half. According to local realtors, nearly every sale of an existing home has been to purchasers from the New York City or Boston areas; there are now perhaps a hundred more "weekender" families in town than there were in 1981. They have increased the town's tax base, and with it, municipal spending. Efforts are under way to replace the town garage, upgrade the municipal ballfield, and refurbish Pequabogue Middle School.

One local home seller was retired Police Sergeant Claude Zoldano, formerly of Mackenzie Road, who while in uniform had clashed for years with the Klecko brothers. Reached for comment at his new home in Dunedin, on Florida's Gulf Coast, Zoldano insisted that Jericho's Cobble is "the better for the changes."

Interviews with various Cobblers as they visited the anniversary exhibits confirm that, in general, they share Zoldano's and Markle's sunny assessments.

Thinking of Apples

(thoughts of Hoke Klecko)

A.A. meetings begin at seven, weekdays and Saturdays, in the downstairs "community activities" space of the Congo Church and are over by eight.

Though we're Alcoholics Anonymous, we also welcome people trying to live beyond drugs; all of us addicts know that to get through the day and the night to come, we need help and solidarity with others who are also struggling against the demons.

Mostly we're hard-scrabblers—I'm not the only one as has spent more than a few days behind bars—although a couple are worth millions; they've screwed up just as bad as us scraping-by ones, they've had the same ugly binges, wipeouts, have hurt loved ones, been through the sort of crap we'll regret for the rest of our lives. Upstairs in the church, on Sundays, the rich attending services don't have to interact much with us peons, but on every other day, downstairs at A.A., they darn well do, and also need to fess up to the same things we do—having lots of money didn't protect them from drinking and snorting to excess.

Lately at meetings, even though I'm pledged to give my best attention to whichever recovering brother or sister is speaking, my mind's been wandering. After literally thousands of these meetings over twenty years, Hoke Klecko has heard all the temptation and panic stories he ever needs to hear. Been there, done that! I'm as sober as a man needs to be. Out of prison more years than I was in. Don't drink, except for a beer now and then at home after a hot day's yard work, which Frankie lets me have since I can stop after just one.

Nobody judges me now tougher than I judge myself.

Every time I drive past the town hall I renew my commitment to that judging task. I have some remorse for burning down the old one, but I don't hate myself for it—a dumbass, drunk thing to do, but nobody got hurt and the place was a firetrap that would've gone up in smoke soon anyway. Plus it was insured, and this town's flush enough to have easily found the dough to put up a better one. Even if it's not as pretty as the old one.

What I do not forgive myself for is my part in the murder of Artie. I didn't pull the trigger. Lem did. Then he tried to get me to confess to the murder! I was almost ready to cop to it because just then I truly believed that Lem had protected me all my life and so I owed him. How much of a lie his "protection" was I didn't realize until I'd been inside three years and finally figured out that while I'd always looked up to Lem, he'd always told me what I should think about myself—what I was good for and, more usually, what I was *good-for-nothing* for. Only then was I able to get clean and stay within the lines.

Worst part of my nine years inside was missing Frankie and not getting to see Bella grow up and be married. Frankie had ditched me, and for good reason. But she always knew I loved her. When I got out I begged her to take me back, and thank God, she did.

Since then I've worked hard to stay clean, keep away from trouble, earn an honest living, and care for my family. I take Frankie on vacation in the winter every year to some warm place, even if I have to deny myself many other things. And my grandson Morrie means the world to me. I'm trying to keep him and Bella on track; I talk to them better than any social worker or guidance counselor, and don't hesitate to chew them out when that's needed. It starts with my warning to stay away from booze and coke and meth. Lots of people think they can just take a swig or a hit and not go off the deep end. Most can't.

What I was thinking of today at A.A., while listening to yet one more guy fessing up after his umpteenth fall off the wagon, was bringing some of my Honeycrisps to Sam Newington. Everybody likes apples! Sam and Grace been nice to me since I started doing their yard: "Come in out of the sun, have a glass of water, use the bathroom, how's that grandson of yours doing?" Most of my other weekenders don't do these normal, polite sorts of things.

The Newingtons know about my garden—I go on about it a lot—but probably don't know I was in prison for torching town hall, and while in, that I dreamed about having a garden when I got out. Most of my weekenders don't give a hoot about my life so long's I show up, do the work neat, and don't charge too much—but from the Newingtons I get a bit more. And so I want to bring Sam a little present, my way of telling him—without having to say out loud where it comes from, inside of me—that since he's been knocked on his ass mentally as well as physically, he now has an opportunity—really the obligation—to restart his life so as to make it better.

FIVE:
LOCAL CHARACTER

Attending the Firehouse Ribbon-Cutting

(thoughts of Rose Serkin)

Late afternoons in high leaf-color season are glorious in Jericho's Cobble. This one provides the perfect backdrop for the ribbon-cutting ceremony of the new firehouse. In the outside world there are new questions about why the U.S. went into Iraq, and whether the European Community can hold together, but in this small town we measure our progress in the erecting of a new firehouse and the acquiring of associated equipment for it.

Though I've done my part to make the new facility a reality, I'm not on the dais for the ceremony, and am just as happy not to be there. A nurse, I'm not by nature a limelight-seeker, unlike my pal sitting with me, radio show host Aimee Bishop.

Initially, neither of us deemed a new firehouse necessary. But our town's volunteer firemen insisted on it, threatening to retire *en masse* should the town not agree. Such a retirement would force Jericho's Cobble to hire paid firemen, and in order to pay for them to hike the admirably low mill rate, freaking out Cobblers and Gobblers alike and deterring potential new weekenders. Aimee, engaged with environmental matters, couldn't take on this fight for the new firehouse but urged me to. As unofficial "mayor" of Cobble Gardens, the townhouse complex, and as a stalwart of the Visiting Nurses Association, I drummed up support, urging all to attend public meetings, sign petitions, and write letters-to-the-editor, which cumulatively made the difference in the town-wide vote to fund the firehouse.

During that campaign I learned more than I'd ever suspected about the intertwinings behind the scene. Take, for instance, the purchase of the new high-ladder truck, so huge that the new firehouse has to have big back doors as well as front ones so the truck can be pulled through rather than only backed in. This very expensive hunk of machinery will enable firefighters to reach the top floor of the tallest building in town, which is—ta-da!—The Chancellery's new six-story dorm. Which is why the prep school paid for the truck.

I worry, though, that this new firehouse and equipment is the proverbial finger in the dike holding back the flood, and that when our current firemen retire we will have to hire paid ones anyway, causing the mill rate to zoom. When that happens, will long-term resident Cobblers who discover that they can't afford the new taxes be forced to relocate elsewhere? Will the Cobble remain the Cobble we love? By means of this new firehouse, we're putting off having to answer those questions for a while longer.

No Chancellery reps on the dais today, and no Ina Mornay, the multi-millionaire weekender whose willingness to buy the old facility jump-started the funding of the new one. She professes not to know yet what she'll do with the old one but I've no doubt she'll fit it into her long-range plan to transform Jericho's Cobble into the next East Hampton, a retreat for the wealthy—which gives me the willies.

But then, this ceremony's being held on a Wednesday, which is a mistake because it limits the crowd to Cobblers, since by definition weekenders are not here mid-week, and the fact is the new fire station was largely funded by local taxes paid as much by weekenders as by full-timers. More care should have been taken to include the weekenders in this celebration—they must be involved in the future of this town if it is to survive.

At least Grace Newington is here, tending to husband Sam, who's still recuperating at their "country house." Doubtless she's here today because she needs a break from that. She and Aimee have been sort of rivals in writing the newspaper's gardening columns.

I recognize in the crowd three of our more interesting Cobblers. Seeing them in one place together makes me realize what they have in common: 1) They grew up poor—in tough homes roiled by drunkenness, near freezing from lack of adequate heating, etc. 2) None takes any guff from anyone. And 3), their outsized characters owe a lot to the small-town surroundings in which they've spent their whole lives. In big cities, eccentricities like theirs get shunted aside or smothered; our less competitive, more forgiving setting has allowed them to fully blossom.

Sadie Durmaz is a petite, silver-haired, childless widow of indeterminate age who lives in a trailer with her dog GoFetch but never comes to Main Street unless properly dressed, usually overdressed, with her hair firmly coiffed, her make-up perfect, and her acid tongue ready for action in English and, when she feels the need to curse, in her birth language, Romanian. I first met her a decade or so ago in the post office, where everybody goes to get their mail from their boxes. Coming in, I overheard an outburst in a foreign tongue that I did not recognize, being uttered by Sadie in response to being teased by Timmy, the long-serving postal clerk, who was pulling her weekly *TV Guide* out the rear of her post office box just as Sadie was trying to grab it from the front!

She fumed in outsized irritation. After Timmy let go of the magazine, and her vitriol was vented, Sadie turned in my direction and asked, "Was that terrible of me?" "No," I said, "just appropriate." She invited me to have coffee. At Jim's we got acquainted. Even in that first encounter she was very direct, knowing who I was and asking about my divorce from Dr. Sandor "Rusty" Serkin and how I was faring on my own with my daughter. I was frank and told her that Margot was doing fine but that being a single, working mother was rough. Fifteen years later, Sadie and I are friends, although I'm not yet at the level of being asked to join her weekly poker game—that's for those born here, and mostly for the subset born at home on their kitchen tables.

Beetle Oostendyck is one of the regulars in that game, the only male in it. He is the youngest son of a janitor who lived with his family in an unheated summer cottage; in winter the five kids, male and female, slept in one bed to keep each other warm. Beetle acquired his nickname in his teens after doing enough illegal things to be classified as a juvenile delinquent and be sent away to a training school. There he became a ruggedly handsome man and, I guess, determined that he was a homosexual. Certainly he has been a careful one, not displaying in public any affection for another man, even though he is quite gregarious; as a result, most Cobblers give the sexual aspect of him no weight in converse with him; and weekenders and visitors usually have no idea that he might be gay.

Using a gift from a "mentor" to buy a small building near the hospital, in it he ran a medical devices shop—canes, strollers, slings, crutches, bandages—working seventy hours each week and "living small," so he could put his money to work buying real estate and stocks, all of which prospered. Ten years after he'd bought the little building he sold it for three times what he'd paid for it. Today at seventy-plus he's a millionaire several times over, yet still mows his own lawn and walks five miles a day into town and back in all but the most extreme cold weather, wears clothes bought at secondhand shops, and can be spotted at every funeral, church supper, and public event chowing down on the free eats.

The third member of the trio is the least approachable: Starker, a burly, sunglasses-wearing, tobacco-stain-bearded volunteer fireman and transfer-station employee who is the power behind the throne at both institutions. At the ramshackle garbage dump, the middle-aged, basketball-size-paunched Starker can usually be found relaxing with other employees in rickety reclaimed beach chairs, regaling them with stories as his eagle eye makes sure we civilians put our garbage and recyclables in the correct bins. When there's a toss into the wrong one, Starker rises from his throne, accosts the perpetrator and supervises the correcting of the offense. Once my aim was so bad that I missed the receptacle. Horrified, he came out to instruct me. "Now girlie," he said, "you plant your feet this-a-way, and then you look in the direction you're gonna throw. Then you fire away." I did. It worked.

So the next time I came in I greeted the beach-chair trio with a cheery "Good morning, gentlemen," only to have Starker growl, "Ain't no gentlemen here." Hoots came from his chorus. I grinned and was not offended, knowing that Starker meant it as a joke and that he is among the most devout, community-minded, and indefatigable of the area's volunteers, unmistakable in his beard, bulk, and bright orange vest authoritatively directing vehicular traffic at every house fire, road accident, stream flooding, and celebratory parade.

I don't know Starker's birth name, or even Beetle's, just as most people in town don't know my maiden name, which I mothballed early in my marriage to Rusty Serkin. Direct from nursing college in Boston I came to work for his medical office—a tall, willowy brunette who wore long, dangling earrings, attended peace demonstrations, and listened to opera—and I fell in love with the generation-older redhead even though he was married and had two children. A few years into our own marriage I learned that Rusty was cheating on me. "What did you expect?" Aimee asked of me. The divorce settlement enabled me to buy the newly constructed townhouse. By then my ex-husband was becoming the "Ask Dr. Rusty" columnist, soon to be syndicated in two hundred newspapers.

At the firehouse, after the dignitaries pose for the ribbon-cutting photo they descend from the dais to have the obligatory bite to eat from the banquet table with us ordinary folks—and one of them, directly and unexpectedly, comes over to me: State Representative Jerri Schussler, a former schoolteacher, the obtainer of the state grant that helped underwrite the new firehouse. Praising me for my role in making this day possible, Jerri asks me to dinner soon—date TBD—at Chez Guillaume, the new bistro.

Sure, I say; and wonder what Jerri could have in mind.

An E-mailed Olive Branch

Dear Aimee:

Thanks for re-introducing yourself to me today at the firehouse ceremony. To underscore what I said to you there, I'd no intent of encroaching on your territory at *The Country Caller*, and during the coming months I won't be writing many gardening columns, since my main task will be helping Sam recover, even after he's returned to work in the city. We've resolved to come up here more regularly, so I'll be quite available to chat at length, and you and I can jointly figure out which of us will do what gardening subject for the next few seasons. I'd also like to offer to edit your *Pequabogue Protectorate* newsletter and will try to recruit more weekenders for that mailing list.

Regards,
Grace

An Offer She Won't Refuse

(thoughts of Sadie Durmaz)

I was the ugliest girl at Stillwater Mountain High, and the wildest, and from the grubbiest of foreign backgrounds, and I married the class hellion. Gus and I drank, we smoked, we cussed, we revved up our secondhand Harleys when near rich people's homes and otherwise had us a ball. Then in '42 he was drafted, and three years later the s.o.b. comes back from the Pacific hardly willing to work for a living.

I'm putting in my fifty hours a week for the phone company and in my off time I'm cleaning houses. Even so, we're living hand-to-mouth in a crummy place. No kids. Couldn't afford'em; and anyway, no kid would've wanted me for a mom in those days. Eventually I'm the Valley's afternoon and evening party-line operator, connecting people, talking back to idiots who're cranky about delays, knowing everybody's business—and their monkey business. "No, Doc Rusty's not home; he's over to Judge Alonzo's poker game. If you're ready to pop that baby out, I'll ring him there." That was a lie, too; I knew Rusty was elsewhere, poking his latest honey.

Once I got a letter in my P.O. Box even though the address was only "SAY-D" and the zip code. Liked that so much I put it on my license plate! Most people enjoy that vanity plate of mine but there's a few thinks it means I'm putting on airs. Screw them!

Gus died twenty years ago, more from spite than anything else. I used the insurance to buy the trailer. I retired from the phone company when they finally put in the direct-dial. Which they did late, of course; everything takes a long while to come to the Cobble—indoor toilets, electricity, telephones.

Since retiring I been doing mostly what I want. I got a lot of body problems, including from the cancer that I beat twice, so I don't smoke no more and hardly ever take a Scotch. Long ago traded in my motorcycle for a sedan. I live alone except for my dog GoFetch—I'm too ornery for any other human being to live with! Spend my days at Jim's, having a coffee and bagel and yakking with the other regulars—sometimes I say outrageous stuff just to see how they'll react—and then motoring to visit pals in neighboring towns, do a little clothes shopping. Mostly I buy four things and soon return three. Thursday afternoons are for nickel poker with our crew, and every Sunday I go to Congo because I know that God has been good to me, and I'm grateful. But I don't really like this new minister, so when he's preaching I turn off my hearing aids.

One of the regulars at Jim's, Freddie Ritter, comes over to chat. Raunchy Ritter, they call him behind his back, for having almost as foul a mouth as me. Has a couple cute kids that I like and that like me, and a beauty-queen nightmare of a wife who treats him like dirt and is just waiting for Jack and Jill to grow some more before she leaves him and holds him up for a pretty penny. He's got plenty of pennies. He comes on as a tough guy who knows everything—he doesn't—and will tease you about anything. So now, when he comes over and tells me he's making me an offer I won't refuse, I laugh at him. Then he says it's for grandparents' day at Whitbred Elementary, that his Jilly is inviting me to go with her, since her real grandparents are gone or live far away.

I don't know if he's pulling my leg, but he swears to Jesus he's not.

Imagine that! Me, a grandmother! I can't stop grinning like a fool. I'm going to have to get a new outfit...

Starker's Lunch Special

(Joseph "Starker" Stucnowicz)

When Jeannie and her gals see me coming in for lunch at Get'nGo , I don't have to say what I want because her crew gets cracking right away on 'Starker's Special'—not on the menu but they make it for me, three different meats and salad-y stuff on top, plus mayo, mustard, and hot peppers, overpacked the way I like it. That'll hold me a few hours. Other transfer-station guys now order it too.

Waiting on Chad, my son, for a sit-down. We do this every once in a while. This time's to plan our deer-hunting and turkey-hunting—Jug End or Beartown state forest—seeing as it's the season.

I nod or pass a word or three with most customers—I know about everybody comes by here at lunch, except for this guy in a business suit that's saying hello. Can't place him but I politely ask how he's doing, and he's smart enough not to give me a long answer. Then I remember: a weekender; spoke to him once about baseball. He's a regular at that Sunday slow-pitch. Aside from it being on at the same time as Holy Mass, I wouldn't be in it—my five years in triple-A is way above their pay grade, last couple pitching for the PawSox.[20] Quit when Frieda got pregnant and I needed to make money regular. Maybe never would've got to the big show. Thirty-three years ago! Taught me life's toughest lesson: If you got it you got it, and if you don't you don't.

Never said that to my son. Never will—might hurt him too much.

Chad comes in from Valley Hardware, down the road. Not quite as big as me, but big enough. A couple people pat him on the back in greeting—nobody does that with me more than once, though Chad don't seem to mind. Orders and sits down

---

20 PawSox = Pawtucket Red Sox, a farm team of Boston's Red Sox.

with one of those bottled waters. Fills me in about my beautiful-cranky grandson Petey and my princess Jessica who's now in second grade and likes to tug on my beard. Chad's a better father to them than I was to him—I was pretty tough. Quiet guy, maybe too quiet. Knows his hardware but not much else. Didn't want to be with me in the firehouse or the Turners Lodge. Only takes communion now and then.

Being my son in this town ain't easy, I admit. People coming in this sandwich joint pay their respects to me but sometimes talk right over Chad, though most everybody's known him since he's little. Can't figure what's to be done about that other than for him and Sheila to move away, start over in a place where people don't know about that big old dawg always out directing traffic and telling off people at the dump. I don't want Chad and Sheila to head out, though, because then I won't see Petey and Jessica.

Chad's being pleasant enough, eating his salad, but I think he's hiding something. Maybe he's getting fired. I heard Valley Hardware's cutting back to compete better with the big-box stores. Wouldn't be Chad's fault this time; and what Sheila makes at Grosvenor's won't be enough for the four of them.

I'm going to bag my deer and turkeys, get them prepped, butchered, and double freezer-wrapped, and give them to Chad for the family.

Beetle's Challenge

(thoughts of Beetle Oostendyck)

I like paying cash for everything, just as I like mowing my own lawn and having in my safe deposit box the actual stock certificates of the shares I own. I could pay with a credit card, trade stocks through a broker and never touch a certificate, and get my lawn done by one of the many landscaper guys I know, but I don't. I suppose that's the child-of-rural-poverty way, though I haven't been poor since I turned 30. I'm 72 now and have a bankroll that'll last me the rest of my life and beyond, so I don't see a reason to change my ways.

Friends who know I'm well-off think I'm silly as well as stubborn not to pay for hired help around the house, a winter home in a warmer place, trips to Europe and Asia in search of thrills, etc. They tease me about my tight-fistedness. I pooh-pooh it, but they're right-on in insisting that at my age I ask myself, How much can I spend, legit or even rashly? I bought the beautiful old Rolls I always wanted, to ride to church on Sundays. (Now worth more than I paid for it.) I can only stomach Las Vegas once in a while—it's tough for me to throw away money I earned the hard way. I even tried a couple rent-boys at my gay pals' urging, but that didn't appeal to me any more than high-falutin' French cooking does—I'm a meat-and-potatoes guy. Give me a great, broiled, medium-rare, juicy hamburger and crispy curly fries, preceded by a martini and washed down by a frosty beer, in the company of friends—what could be better?

So my old crowd in Manhattan—the bunch of us that've been meeting and eating and drinking and getting it on together on the third Wednesday of every month for more years than I want to count—challenged me: Have the top-priced ($199), top-quality restaurant burger in Manhattan and see if that'll convince you to spend more money on yourself.

So I did. And the burger was really, truly, spectacularly

great. Wagyu beef, truffle butter, quail egg, caviar, a fantastic bun, wonderful melted artisan cheese, and speared with a gold toothpick that you get to keep. Perfect! And I paid for it with cash, which pleased the restaurant people no end. Even left them a $50 tip.

And then I started figuring: If I wanted to, I could splurge on this fabulous hamburger weekly...a thousand or so bucks a month...and it wouldn't make a dent in my finances.

And in a roundabout fashion, that made me begin to think more about the need to give away most of my money now, rather than when I'm dead, so the recipients can enjoy it and I can get some big thank-yous, which I would like. Giving it out's no easy task, though; lots of needs to be balanced among my sisters and nieces and nephews, a couple special friends, and a few charities I respect. You've got to give enough to each to make a difference but not to derail them. I'm calling it the Joost Fund, after my real first name. It's one of the toughest things I've ever tried. But it's essential for me now, and the results will last a heck of a lot longer and be a tastier thrill for me than that $199 burger.

Never Bill

(thoughts of William Beecher)

Shall I legally change my name to Guillaume? Chez Guillaume, my bistro *hommage à la France*, is fully booked most nights, even though tourist season is over. Already a few customers, mostly weekenders that I barely know, address me as Guillaume. Which is a hoot—I've always been William, never Bill or Billy; no diminutives for me; no sir; never.

Despite being sixty-two and divorced for the third time—this one from Chelsea, mother of Missy—I'm still able to balance many things well: the new restaurant, and the new thirty-seven-year-old girlfriend, and spending time with my daughter and, most days, getting in a swim at Marc Posner's and a cappuccino at Jim's.

Over the years I've capitalized and blown so many opportunities—restaurateur, photographer, jazz sideman, art gallery owner, lover of dozens of women—that one could assert that my real skill is vending my charm. *D'accord*, but while I know I'm smart, sophisticated, and seductive, I also know I'm too avid for conquest and costly pleasures and far too easily lured and bored. There've been as many disasters as triumphs.

When Missy was three, Chelsea convinced me to sell the Brooklyn joint and our apartment and find us a country place so she could keep a horse to ride, and Missy could attend a good school, and I could be a gentleman of leisure. I knew just the area, which I'd come to love decades ago as a student at The Chancellery. But after we transferred to the Cobble, the misbehaving stock market in the wake of 9/11 trashed my stash, and my eye resumed roving. Chelsea should've accepted both as coming with the territory of me being me, but she didn't. So now I have another monthly alimony-and-child-support payment to meet. These nights, to save money I sleep on the sofa of the office above Chez Guillaume and am none the worse for it.

Not everybody likes my juggling act, but fortunately my new pal Marc Posner does. Early this morning we had one of our swims in the heated outdoor pool of his fabulous historic cottage, exercise and therapy for him as well as me, because in that pool we talk frankly about everything—hopes, fears, guilty pleasures, fantasies, nightmares. Marc is super-smart and super-savvy, a lawyer who's amassed millions servicing corporate honchos and can now travel and do whatever else he and Martha feel like; but he's never before had a "brother" with whom he can confide frivolous ideas, scandalous urges, philosophic flights—the sort of stuff that's central to being a charmer and juggler. Which I am and, as I discovered at a Chancellery reunion, so are some of my old prep-school prankster pals. We all have larceny in our souls.

But I now cherish another quality in myself that those old pals laugh at, a willingness to do as Marc does, work incredibly hard when that's required. With a restaurant it's *always* necessary. By our professions we are shaped. But what's work without fun? So even though I could make good additional money opening Chez Guillaume for lunch, I won't, needing to make time for that swim with Marc, that cappuccino at Jim's, that matinee with my new squeeze.

This morning I'm bothered by twinges in the gut and back that woke me during the night and that haven't gone away now that I'm up and about. Then too, the bathroom scale shows I'm down another pound—probably the result of doing too much making food for others while not properly feeding myself. To be shy five pounds in as many weeks is worrisome. But I've no time to see a doctor about it.

The Babysitter's Complaint

(diary entry of Laurie Milch)

Babysitting on a Thurs. nite for the Maldones. A home s'posedly once a farmhouse. Long driveway. Mom dropped me off, will pick me up later. I got my driver's license now, but she still won't let me drive at night!

Last-minute call, sit a 3rd and 2nd-grader, Jonathan (older one; chubby, shy) and Cecily (cute but snotty), newbies in town, only up after 9/11 when lotsa Noo Yawkers rushed to leave the city. No Towers gonna fall in this hick burg! 100 miles from anywhere! Real estate agents here sold it all—old, new, falling apart, you name it. I knew the Schlumbergers, Jewish family, traded in this house for top dollar and moved; and I know the next-door neighbors here, the Newingtons—she sings in the choir with Mom—but never before met Walter and Polly. He's usually in the city during the week, making money, while she's here minding the kids. Tonight he's taking her to a fine dinner—I approve of that!

Pair of them seems nice enough, even though the duds they're sporting are fancier than what anybody needs to go to that Chez Guillaume place on a weekday nite—after all, this is the sticks! And she really ought to have eye shadow on. Been crying too much, I bet—is what you get for having two kids so close together!

My sr. yr.'s just starting and already I want it over. I'd like school to be more of a challenge, but at Stillwater Mountain they mostly "teach to the norm" (Xcept for Mr. Miller's

"Our History" class), and frankly the norm is t-o-o-o … l-o-o-w. Can't think about that now, because every five minutes I'm fetching the snack, the toy, the pillow, chasing the dog from the pantry.

I'm never going to have kids! At least not anytime soon.

Mom didn't wait long enough to have my older sister Charlotte, and never got out of this town. Twenty years at Moorehead before they finally promoted Jane Milch to scheduler of the nurses, aides, techs, candy-stripers. Whoopee! I don't want that kind of yucky yob. Same with her pals—ordinary, blah jobs. I mean they're really nice, these Stillwater grads from, like, thirty years ago—class of '73! Great moms, too. But kinda dull …

Laurie Milch will not allow herself to be trapped in Jericho's Cobble! Everybody and her cousin doesn't want to be a virgin when they graduate high school, but I won't even go steady to avoid being pressured into having my cherry popped. Who cares if I can't brag about it to my posse? And that's not to say that I didn't fool around this summer with my boyfriend Stewie—I did, just not all the way.

Nine more months at Stillwater Mountain and I'm outta here. My BFFs are spending their babysitting money but I'm saving mine for my getaway. THE PEQUABOGUE VALLEY IS BORING, BORING, BORING. I've heard all the crap as to why boring is your problem, comes from within—yeah, right. But there's sumpin' called STIM-you-LAY-shun, *and here we ain't got none. No dance clubs. No rock bars. No wild parties. Hardly any Blacks or Asians. No cul-chah. Whatever is really happening in the world is DEFF-IN-IT-LY not happening here. Nothing ever did happen here, and nothing ever will! My Dad knew that; it's part of why he left the place—and us.*

Don't know why anybody sticks around here unless they've been knocked up or have to go into the family business or are too dumb to make it into even a junior college. I don't have the grades for regular college and couldn't afford it if I did. Even the community colleges in Pittsfield and in Holyoke are several large a year, plus a lousy long commute. And I can't stand the idea of going into debt for it.

Showing One's True Colors

(Sam Newington)

The leaves of most deciduous trees,
although in summer wholly green,
conceal red and yellow within,
due to chlorophyll overpainting
of their flavonoids and carotenoids—
until rationed sunlight and chill nights
dissipate the verdant cover story,
revealing the true colors beneath.

Newly discharged from rehab—
surely as much of a change in phase
as autumn brings to maples—
will I be stripped to my emotive bones?

And what will that reveal?

That what I had always cherished
as my calling and utility
to profession, family, and society
was arbitrary, just a drug of choice?

That my marital partnership,
challenged deeply by adversity,
has become so much firmer,
the basis for flights of fancy?

That opportunities are not confined
to those leading to fame and fortune,
and henceforth should be pursued
for their promise of re-evaluation,
with an emphasis on appreciation?

Having had impressed upon me
that my days are numbered—
indeed, indexed and cross-referenced!—
I want to savor them, one by one,
while testing the capabilities of,
the autumnal vividness of,
my basic, that is my true, colors.

SIX:
THE MURTAUGHS
and the NIEDERMEYERS

The Berkshire Buttery Co-op

(from its brochure)

In 1883, dairy farmer Diarmuid Murtaugh carried into the general store of Jericho's Cobble ten pounds of his wife Liona's hand-churned, clabbered butter, expecting to exchange it for credit but could not, since a half-dozen other farmers had already brought in theirs, taking up all the room in the coolers. In reaction, Murtaugh, known as "Muddy" for seldom removing his mucking boots, took the lead in founding The Berkshire Buttery Co-operative.

Muddy and Liona soon enlisted in the Co-op thirty small farms in the Pequabogue Valley, a number that grew to seventy-five. Three times a week the Buttery used wagons with ice-coolers to haul several thousand pounds of those farms' butter to the rail depot in Great Barrington for transport in refrigerated freight cars to New York City, where it fetched good prices. Shortly the Buttery added collective purchasing for the farms to the vending of their dairy and orchard products. An onsite retail counter and restaurant followed.

In the 1920s, when rural electrification and internal combustion engines provided farmers with alternate ways of storing, transporting, and selling their butter the Co-op lost steam, and was further diminished by the Great Depression, which forced sales of many Pequabogue Valley farms and their acres' conversion for housing and other non-agricultural uses.

Still a Co-op, today the Berkshire Buttery functions more as a restaurant, ice cream counter, and souvenirs and produce shop than as an organization for the wholesale buying of supplies for farmers and the selling of their farm products. In addition to its famous ice cream and unmatched apples, it now provides cider and donuts for the fall's visiting leaf-peepers, and eggnog and hot toddies for those attending the annual February cross-country ski competitions .

Contemplating the Last Harvest

(thoughts of Kelly Murtaugh Lydner)

Just after dawn, my Corey uses the new gadget for measuring the corn's moisture and texture. We've already harvested most of our ears and only have left about 2,000 bushels from 12 acres. The gadget, he says as he comes in from the field, shows today as optimal for bringing in the rest, since there's just enough moisture in the kernels and husks to keep the texture firm while we truck the corn to the distributor without first needing to refrigerate it a week, as we had to do with the last batch, for which we ended up with no profit.

Over breakfast, neither of us mentions the elephant in the room: That this may well be the very last harvest, not only of the 2003 growing season but of the entire 116-year-old Murtaugh-Lydner farm, started by my great-grandparents Diarmuid and Liona Murtaugh in 1887 after they'd toiled for a decade at Niedermeyer's. In 1898 they bought an adjoining ten-acre plot, then ten more, and later their son, my grandfather, acquired even more acreage, so that today we have eighty mostly-contiguous acres, thirty now in crop and the remainder in pasturage for our two-dozen Galway Belteds.

Farming is constant work. Leisure for us means not having a chore to do this very second! We don't get to loll in cafés but once in a while, or even go to a movie because we're so tired that we know we'll likely fall asleep in the theater. It's a stretch for me to make the regular lunch meetings of our class of '73 gaggle, but I do. And I find the time to work on The Buttery Co-op—also started by my great-grandparents—which is deeply in debt and as a result is now, to my dismay, about to go out of co-op hands.

Well, farming's changed, and so has the need for such co-ops.

Actually, since our daughters got married and moved away,

Corey and I have only been able to operate our farm with the toil of our employees/tenants, the Ecuadorean cousins Angel and Jorge Paredes, who live with their families in a little compound we've set up for them on the property. Angel, Jorge, Manuela, and Maria are essential to this operation. And no one could possibly work harder. Brought up as farmers in Ecuador—I don't ask what crops they raised—they know what hard work is and how to do it without complaining. God-fearing Christians, they are polite and always ready to roll.

Corey understands that now, but when they first came to work and made the usual beginner mistakes he raged on, as many people around here do, about foreigners coming to take our jobs. But the plain fact is that farm jobs are tough, dirty, exhausting, and low-paying, and few local people will work them. Moreover, and as I argued to Corey, we must accept the Paredeses as just the latest in a long line of immigrants who, like my great-grandparents and his, are working their way up from the bottom. Now he agrees that the Paredeses are terrific people; we're sponsoring them for American citizenship in cooperation with their church, Our Lady of Mercy in Merriam.

This is still the Murtaugh farm because I wouldn't allow it to pass out of my family's hands after a hundred years. As a child I learned to appreciate farm life: chores mixed with the fun of our own swimming hole, hay parties, chickens underfoot, the warmth of their just-laid eggs, an intimacy with the land and our animals and our parents and grandparents and great-grandparents, and our pride at doing the important task of feeding the world. At age four I learned to accept the trauma of death when Pokey, my favorite cow, had to be led away to slaughter. Death is a fact of life—one that we farmers know much, much better than do people who never grow their own animals for slaughter.

At Stillwater High I took ag courses and joined the Future Farmers of America so as to be more likely to meet a properly-trained husband. Corey Lydner of Merriam was two years ahead of me in the ag program, and we hit it off. Got married, and we've been working the farm ever since, by ourselves after my parents retired and moved to Florida. But Corey and I, too, have produced no sons, and our daughters had zero interest in working the farm or marrying would-be farmers. Corey's brothers have their own family acreage to deal with, twenty miles away, too far from ours to be operated in tandem.

Fact is, there are only eight farms left in the township of Jericho's Cobble where once there were two dozen, and a couple are horse farms. Is it inevitable that the remaining crop farms will soon no longer produce crops? The real Jericho's Cobble will vanish if that happens, I fear.

We have been over and over the numbers, and the numbers—the facts!—have brought us to a firm decision: we must sell the farm. Eighty acres at $10,000 per, the average price for farmland in the state, would be $800,000, and the cows could fetch a couple thousand dollars apiece, plus whatever we could get for the machinery. And the farmhouse. My estimate, a million bucks for the whole lot, a number Corey likes, a dollar amount that's always been beyond our reach but is not unreasonable as a sales price.

Can I bear to sell the house I've lived in all of my life, as did three generations of my family before me? I want any new resident family to continue to use it as their home, but I'm aware that a non-farmer buyer able to spend a million on this property may well want to tear the house down and build something grander. I'd also prefer that the acreage continued in agricultural use. The notion that my family's farm could be carved up into a half-dozen estates for McMansions, with broad, close-mown lawns and horse-jumping pastures, galls me as much as the idea of tearing down our home.

Abandoned Barn

Hmph!—another human stopping by to take my photo:
Red Barn in Late Stage of Decay. Leaning to one side. Roof
partially collapsed. Holes all over. One door torn off—okay,
granted, I'm not looking my best these days. It's age, sure,
but it's also abandonment. Haven't been workaday and
sassy for many a year, and less so after the last rough winter.
What gets me, right in the planks, is the heating up and the
freezing down and the higher heating and deeper freezing:
Peels my paint, splits my boards, holes my floors, lets in
the mice and carpenter ants that chew me up and the weeds
that widen my cracks, not to mention damages my roof, whose in-
ability to stand up for me any longer is a constant trial. Time
was, I could handle these assaults—with, of course, a bit of
patching up from my caretakers. Didn't require much, just a
slat or two, done in a timely and regular manner. Now my
roof no longer protects me from the sky, and my sides have
more holes than a woodpecker's favorite tree. But I'm
still here while most barns my age have collapsed. Well, my
memories sustain me: hay-parties, good cow-talk, machinery
whirrs, horse-sense, my favorite cat, picnics, trysts. What has
hurt me the most, caused the most damage, is losing purpose:
no more cows to shelter, hay to cure, tools to store, Thunder-
bird coupe to be hidden under moth-eaten horse blankets.
Owls have even gone away. Got other birds, though, with their
droppings, twig-and-straw nests, crumbling eggshells. They
know me: I am still shelter; I am respite from the wind; I am safety
from hawks and foxes; I am a beacon, cool on a hot day, and
on a frigid one a warm-enough haven. I'm here!

Liona Murtaugh

(1855 - 1919)

I never knowed my birth name or day.
When Immigration wanted a date
    we told'em St. Patrick's Day,
    because everyone said I've the map of Ireland in my face.

When I's eleven, at the St. Ciaran of Saighir Orphanage,
    near worked to the bone at the millinery,
    Diarmuid, second eldest of the groundsman's seven,
    began to chat me up quite regular,
    and when he's fourteen and I's thirteen we run away together.

In Boston there was already too many Irish!
In the Valley 'twasn't hard to find work so long's you'd do the dirtiest jobs.
Darry mucked out Heinz Niedermeyer's barns and slopped his swine,
    whilst I cleaned and cooked and tended to Lisette's little ones.

Heinz don't treat us no better than the nuns at the orphanage did;
    but Lisette and me, we become like sisters, best of friends.
Ten long years Darry and me saved every penny, and then bought us
    ten acres so scrabbly that no one else wanted them.

My firstborn girl and boy died.
    I had six in all, three thriving.
An orphan myself, I loved them all, and mightily;
as I did our other family, those in the co-op that Darry begun.

Nothing of value comes without pain, they say ,
    and whilst that should make the reward sweeter,
    'twas never my lot.

Darry and me, though, we had a good-enough run,
    from before our voices cracked and we was like slaves
        and poor as dirt,

to when our hairs was white and we was free and owned our farm
and fed ourselves and people elsewhere
and raised our children and grandchildren
to be upright, God-fearing Americans.

Most of us lying here don't have
no big accomplishments to our name, good or bad,
as would have got us notice in the newspaper,
but we've naught to atone for—that, the big shots can't say.

So here I be, next the love of my life, near my dear Lisette,
amongst kin and Buttery Coop brothers and sisters,
patiently awaiting Our Redeemer's return.

Some spirits in this cemetery, they migrate into animals.
I thought I'd want to be like our dairy cows,
having such a pleasant time grazing,
sheltered, groomed, cared for at night,
milked easily, then feeding more people.

But if ever I leave here I'd rather be a drab gray squirrel,
hopping gaily about the forest floor,
nibbling on fresh acorns,
scrambling up piney trees for a grand view of the horizon.

Playground Rhyme

(recited in Jericho's Cobble for many decades)

"Do it once, and
Do it twice, and
Do it til you're beat...
In the house, and
Out the house, and
All along the Main Street."

Lisette Gordon Niedermeyer
(1851-1893)

For a girl of fifteen, huddled in a hovel in East Canaan
with my widowed mother and sisters
near the limestone quarry that broke and swallowed
my father and many other strong men,
Heinz Niedermeyer seemed answer to a prayer.
Whence he came, he never said, nor explained the awful welts scarring
his back—
punished for desertion in the Civil War, I guessed—
nor his readiness to flash his pistol.

Once we settled into our Cobble farm, Heinz beat me regularly,
as he did our son and daughter when they come along,
his toughness needed, Heinz claimed, to expand our acreage
so he could become a big shot like Bucko Whitbred.
I knew that wouldn't never happen.
"Ease up on yourself and the world," I pleaded to him. 'Twas in vain.

Our hired hands, Muddy and Liona, done our dirtiest jobs for a pittance,
yet Heinz rewarded them with curses, slaps, and worse.
Ten years on, when the Murtaughs left to start their own farm
and Heinz called them ingrates,
for the first time I laughed at him.

When Muddy started the Buttery Co-op, and Heinz wouldn't join
and we soon lost out to our neighbor farmers' collective power,
again I laughed loudly at my husband.
Perhaps that was unfair, but stubbornness is not always
the measure of good character .

My loudest laugh came from dallying with Skeet McKenzie.
Yes, I was a sinner!

It began innocently enough, me going to his apothecary for headaches.
Skeet gave me a powder and let me lay on a horsehair settee in the back;
after a while, so relaxed was I that I took off my corset
and invited his ravishing.

For six months we met weekly. My headaches vanished!
For Skeet too it was exciting, yet also agonizing:
    believing himself happily married, he was appalled to learn
    that our animal nature has its own demands.

I'd no interest in Skeet's forsaking wife Dotty for me,
nor did I yearn to abandon my children for him.

Heinz learned of our affair—small villages keep no secrets—
flogged me near to death,
and dragged me to the Congregational Church,
to have the flock chastise me
    for my terrible transgressions.

My blood, freshly seeping into my blouse, gave our neighbors pause.
The congregants did not condemn me:

Back in our buggy, when I continued chortling
at the churchgoers' benevolence
Heinz strangled me, right there on Main Street
    and for good measure, shot me through.

Put on trial for my murder, Heinz was
convicted quick and executed quicker.

Then, since no one would claim his body,
Heinz was laid to rest in a prison field,
whilst I continued to lie here
in the cemetery of Jericho's Cobble,
    without him—alone, but not lonely.

And so the children sing:
    "Do it once, and
    Do it twice, and
    Do it 'til you're beat...
    In the house, and
    Out the house, and
    All along the Main Street."

Everybody's First Boss

(Interview of Henrietta Prince by Gertrude Merkin Beresford, for the JCCA Oral History Archives, 1998)

GERTRUDE BERESFORD: Hallie, you've sold the Prince's Pharmacy building and business and retired, yet you still live in the upstairs apartment.

HENRIETTA PRINCE: I have a lifetime lease, Gertie—part of my arrangement with Ina Mornay, who bought Prince's. The apartment is small, so during the days I spend a lot of time next door at Jim's café—it's my parlor, where I receive visitors.

GMB: Tell us how the pharmacy came to be Prince's.

HP: Thanks for asking! Nobody knows that story anymore, though everybody's heard of the scandalous affair between pharmacist Skeet Mackenzie and Lisette Niedermeyer—

GMB: Her husband murdered her over it! The nursery-school rhyme!

HP:—Yes—but here's my point: Skeet survived the Lisette affair, and afterwards went on living with his wife, Dotty, until the Spanish-American War—the one with Teddy Roosevelt going up San Juan Hill? Well, Skeet volunteered as a battlefield medic, caught yellow fever in Cuba and died there, leaving Dotty a widow. She then remarried...to the much younger apprentice in the pharmacy, Clete—Cletus Prince.

GMB: That would be your father, right?

HP: By his second wife, yes. After Dotty's death, Clete remarried and changed the name of the pharmacy to Prince's. I grew up there, and have been around it my whole life.

GMB: But you never became the pharmacist of record?

HP: Well, after my brother Hiram died in France during World War II, I suppose I might have done, but my father—by then, quite old—didn't want me going to pharmacy school.

GMB: Because you were a woman?

HP: Partly. But also partly because he and other people thought I was a bit feeble-minded.

GMB: I did hear that about you when I was young.

HP: Wasn't true, Gertie. Ever. I had what they called then "word-blindness." Today they know it as dyslexia, and they know how to deal with it. I did eventually get beyond it, teaching myself how to read better.

GMB: Now you read all the time! At Jim's you've always got your nose buried in a paper!

HP: Jim likes having the newspapers around for customers—it's what they do in Paris cafés, he tells me—I've never been abroad to check on that—but for him that's too much of an expense, so I buy them.

GMB: Now Hallie, I remember a portrait of you as a child by Oregon Wilberson.[21]

HP: It's upstairs; come and see it some time, Gertie. I'm eleven, it's summer, I'm wearing a shift and I'm playing with one of those big old running hoops—remember them?—and a stick to keep it rolling. I'm just about to take off with it down a country road.

GMB: "Portrait of Hallie as every-girl."

HP: My parents hoped I would do what every girl should, get married, and then my husband would become the pharmacist; but no young man wanted to marry me, and after a while I didn't mind being alone. Nor did I miss having my own children, since I babysat a lot, and in the store I supervised so many teenagers.

GMB: You were my first boss!

HP: I was everybody's first boss, Gertie. Let's see: For decades I ran the soda fountain, and then the whole store, with three-four apprentices a year, mostly in the summers—that's a hundred Cobblers or more. Even with hiring the pharmacists and then letting them do the prescriptions, there was plenty for me and my apprentices to do: The fountain, the shelving of everything other than medications—that's where we made good money; newspapers, soap, greeting cards, bath accessories.

GMB: I loved your Strawberry Dream ice cream floats. Everybody did.

---

21 Compiler's Note: The landscapes and portraits of Oregon Wilberson (1918-1993), a resident of Jericho's Cobble since the 1950s, hang in museums from Boston to San Francisco, Maine to Texas. RBM.

HP: You know, Gertie, when my obituary appears in *The Country Caller*, it won't list a husband or offspring or credit me with any accomplishments like growing a business or in charge of this or that charity or being an important artist like Oregon.

GMB: What do you think the obituary should highlight?

HP: That I never short-changed anyone. That I was a good neighbor and friend. That once every month, for forty-eight years, I had lunch with my sister-in-law, until she passed. That I made people happy by making the best "Strawberry Dream" floats this side of Chicago.

SEVEN:
HOMECOMINGS

Nathan Archer (1743?-1779)

My grave and gravestone are side-by-side to Mathilda's,
as though we were married,
and both stones bear the same legend, "Devoted Servant."
We were never married, and "devoted servant" is deliberate trickery too,
trying to make us out to be servants of the Christian God.
We were not "servants," we were slaves!
And not to Christ, either! Just to the Reverend Jedediah Sampson,
that started the Congregational church of Jericho's Cobble,
and to his demon of a wife, Mary Mercy.[22]

I am Yoruba. My name is Tafàtafà, my god the father Olorun Baba.
At nine, in Africa, I was torn from my mother's arms,
taken as payment for what my father owed.
Big men are the same everywhere: always selling, always bullying.
These brought me in chains to the coast, sold me to a Dutch trader.
I nearly died crossing that endless ocean,
and nearly died again in Barbados.

Beaten many times for insolence,
I ached so much I could hardly work,
causing me to be sold another time
and given an English name, a translation of my own.

Then being sixteen, large and strong,
on the voyage north to Providence I got better.
There the Sampsons bought me, him fresh out of Yale,
heading into the wilderness to lead a newly-gathered flock.
He baptized me—coldest waters I ever felt!—and other than
keeping me in light chains, treated me well.
He and his ill-named wife, Mercy,
were the only slave-owners for many miles around.
We did the Sampsons' work; they got rich.

---

22 Compiler's Note: There were very few slaves in the Pequabogue Valley in the 18th and early 19th centuries, and most were owned by the clergy. RBM.

When Mrs. Mercy saw some white girls glancing at me
    while I was working in the summer with my shirt off,
    she made her husband buy Mathilda.

The Sampsons cared not that Maddie was Igbo,
    enemies of Yoruba!
    Maddie's scars told me that.

Yoruba and Igbo had been fighting for a thousand years,
    back to the birth of the sacred city Ilé-Ifé.
In my home village, had this Yoruba boy taken up with an Igbo girl,
    he would have been stoned to death.

But Maddie's and my tongues shared many words,
    so we found ways to get along, and then
    to be as one and to rely on each other,
        a pair of blacks against a white world.

Before she came to the Cobble they had taken her two children.
So angry was she about losing them
    that she would not work even when whipped,
    which was why the Sampsons could buy her cheap.

We had no children together. I would have liked some.

Maddie and I went regularly to Sampson's church.
You must always pray to something, we told each other,
    and hoped one god was as good as the next.
What sort of god allows slavery?

We thought of running away—but where would we go?
We thought of killing the Sampsons;
    I even sharpened a big old scythe to cut them down
        like sugarcane in Barbados.
But Maddie argued that if we did it we would be hunted, not free.
So I did not kill them.

One day the church's bells started in to ringing,
and when I came in from the fields to find out why,
the Reverend descended from the belfry
to tell me that all men were now created free and equal,
and that someday soon this would mean Maddie and me.
He hoped that when that day came, we would all rejoice together.

I died before that day. Never did get to rejoice.

Dialogue in the Congo Vestry

(while changing out of robes after a Sunday service)

REVEREND VERNON TRAINOR: To have both Grace and Sam Newington here today, so soon after his release from Moorehead, means he must be recovering well.

DOCTOR GLENDA TRAINOR: Trying hard, according to the nurses there.

VERNON: I'll bet he's chafing to get back into the city and to his job. Grateful to be alive. No longer taking life for granted. Awaiting God's plans for him.

GLENDA: Is God's eye always on the sparrow?

VERNON: There's a loaded question! Nathan Archer, subject of my sermon today, had reason to not believe that God's eye was always on the sparrow. I certainly used to think that it was; but after a quarter-century in the pulpit I now feel that God is aware of the sparrow mainly when He deems such awareness needed—not at all times, nor in all circumstances; mostly, Mister Sparrow is on his own.

GLENDA: After *my* quarter-century in the *OR*, I now believe that God, after prepping *Ms.* Sparrow, launched her on the thermal currents, her procedural norms set by bodily construction, gravity, air pressure, hunger, the sense of predators nearby, and the urge to keep the species going.

VERNON: No current divine awareness by the sparrow?

GLENDA: Nor any need for the sparrow to praise Him every Sunday.

VERNON: So: you no longer believe in God?

GLENDA: Talk about your loaded questions! Believing in God is not an "either-or," Vern, at least not for this surgeon. I grant, as you do, the need for morality to assure the goodness of mankind, not as an ideal but as everyday guidance—inculcate that, and we needn't bother debating whether it comes from God! Anyway, we've no urgent need of Him in the Cobble – it's quite peaceful, protected, no outrageous sins. Elsewhere in this world there's more screwed-up stuff going on that cries out for His attention.

VERNON: Good thing you're not the one leading the congregation today.

GLENDA: Agreed! But if I were, I'd sure green-light Vic Leighton to do a sing-along *Messiah*. Won't hurt, could help. Even sparrows need to take risks.

VERNON: Another prayer offered to the Lord?

GLENDA: Amen.

Antique Autos Now On Parade!

(thoughts of Sam Newington)

Antique autos, now on parade!
Nostalgic passions, throbbing through
our village's fresh-cleared streets,
ignoring stop signs and speed limits:
Vettes and T-Birds, Beemers, Jags,
broughams, landaus, touring cars,
woken from Rip Van Winkle sleeps
in grubby garages and dusty barns,
little flags waving from every nook,
their drivers sporting broad grins,
their ladies riding shotgun,
carrying flasks to warm them
although quite sufficiently aflame
with pride, display, and adventure.

Some cars cost a fortune, I'm told—
those driven by the usual suspects
who have money and time to spare.
While formerly I appreciated those best,
this invalid now waves more gaily
at others, steered by neighbors
who are far from rolling in dough,
the drab, the habitually overlooked,
they who scrimp and scheme
to salvage old, rusted machines
that when repaired and burnished
are the more glorious to behold.

You ordinary-guy owner-drivers:
your grins tell me you've stirred
life from dormancy,
resurrected a mechanical Pegasus
to loft you through the difficult times,
exhilarate you when the world will not.

You've no need to trade up
to transport more exotic
or simply priced much higher:
you are content to be in command
of the secret object of long desire.

Notes @ ’03 Hometown Holiday Fest

BY PAT TOLLAND, PUBLISHER,
The Country Caller

Sunny, crisp, breezy. Late October. We’re past high color but plenty left on the trees. Perfect for annual eve-of-Halloween fest, one of the most Cobble-ish of events. Always a treat. “Early-birds” wear light sweaters. Some leaf-peepers & some Chancellery parents—easy to tell the latter: overdressed.

Scarecrow Contest. A hit since Aimee Bishop organized it in the Nineties. Charming. Outlet for creativity. Makes village look even more quaint & folksy. This yr.’s blue ribbons already pinned on winners. Adult division: Grace Newington and Aimee—Yay for TCC’s dueling gardening columnists!—with “The Mustard-Weed Menace.” (Will non-gardeners get the joke? Also, will Grace allow Sam—not that long out of rehab—to stay home by himself so she can come and accept the award?) Club or association: VFW, “Saddam-Crow Hussein.” The Iraq leader is in hiding somewhere, supposedly invisible to U.S. forces. Grade school kids: “Big Bad Bear,” but it looks quite adorable.

People in costumes. This is just the 2nd yr. for the Pre-Halloween Costume contest. There are the Melchiors—one of the few Black families in the area—dressed up as the superhero foursome in The Incredibles*, the animated hit movie. Definitely a contender! There’s the pony-tailed outdoorsman Cullen Wilberson, son of the most famous* painter ever in these parts, wearing his usual duck-hunting waders and camouflage—no need for an actual costume! Another top contender: the Parkfords, Lionel & Ronnie, in their riding-to-hounds outfits—they could pose for one of those Hunt Country-type magazine covers—or how about Starker, in his old "Pawsox" uniform 'neath his Day-Glo vest, as he directs traffic? Oh my!—here's Glenda Trainor, famed surgeon, w/ Tinkerbell wings! Did she win a bet or lose it? Hmmm: Haven't seen last yr.'s costume winner, Wm. Beecher, proprietor of Chez Guillaume, who had looked so dandy in his chef's uniform, toque, and drawn-on little moustache. NOTE: follow up?

There's so much going on with people in this town—each one a story in and of himself and herself—that we reporters are always playing catch-up ball. The natural setting for this festival is so lovely and serene that one might expect the inhabitants to be equally untroubled…though when you get to know us as individuals, we're each a bit…complicated.

Chant heard @ Main Street: "MISS-us MORE-LY," with clusters of teens glomming onto Alice Morely, once their 3rd grade teacher, retired since June. She hugs them all. Outside of class, it's OK.

Ina Mornay, walking while chomping one of Jim's terrific "bear claws" (impossible to eat daintily). Look out for the powdered sugar, Ina!

Booths.

- Buttery's, serving ice cream (a melting asset), & hot cider. Can't say which attracts more customers.

- DSL-line sign-up, with Rose Serkin handling the

petitions. Is she now getting active in politics? Hmmm.
NOTE: follow up.

- Eastlund Library, with reams of old books @ $1 each. They simply don't have room for these, though some are great reads.

The Moorehead van slowly unpacks 3 in wheelchairs, accompanied by as many aides and a few of the riders' younger family members, to take a leisurely look through the village & exhibits. Two geezers I recognize, but not the 3rd. No former First Selectman Pam Markle?
NOTE: follow up!

A bushel basket of honey-crisp apples, with a sign that says "Take One." Nobody can tell me who put them there. They're delicious!

"A Foxhunt at Signet Oaks"

by April Lasko, *The Country Caller*, issue of October 23, 2003

On Saturday, October 25, "unless the weather is very uncooperative," Mrs. Veronica Parkford states, she and Lionel will host a foxhunt on their Signet Oaks estate. The fifty hunters will be in full regalia, "red coats for the men, black for the women." This will be a private event, although the public may catch some glimpses of the hunt in progress from the various county roads.

Out-of-town guests will begin to arrive on Friday from "as far as the Vinyard, Greenwich, and the Hamptons," for a gala evening "in keeping with the Halloween season." Most will bring their own mounts; the Parkfords will provide horses for the others. Extra overnight stalls for visiting mounts will be offered by The Chancellery's stables, and bedrooms for their riders by the Parkfords' next-door neighbors, Marc and Martha Posner, as well as by local hostelries.

Mrs. Parkford said that other local participants, in addition to the Posners, include golfing entrepreneur Jess Krauthammer and his wife Karla, and woodsman/guide Cullen Wilberson.

Lionel Parkford, 64, is vice-chair of the board of Balthazar Transports, a world-wide shipping and trucking firm with annual sales of $10 billion. His father founded the firm in 1945, and Lionel served it in various management capacities between 1975 and 1998, when it went public, after which he stepped aside as CEO. Veronica, 49, is a former model and socialite, previously married to Italian shipping magnate Ugo Brolino, with whom she had two children, both now in college. The Parkfords married in 1993 and in 1997 bought and restored Signet Oaks. They also maintain residences in Manhattan and in the Bahamas.

The traditional quarry of Pequabogue Valley hunts is a red fox, common to the area. Since no hunting packs of dogs are kept in the Cobble any longer, the Parkfords have imported a pack of two-dozen foxhounds from Louderberry, CT. The hunt-hosts hasten to assure the public that while those hounds will pursue and corner the fox; at hunt's end the wild animal will be released unharmed.

Arrangements have been made for the hunt to take place partially on the neighboring grounds of The Chancellery and the Posner (formerly Eastlund Cottage) estates, grounds that according to Mrs. Parkford also have some old stone walls and split-rail wooden fences that can be expected to provide "fun and challenges for the riders."

According to town historian Richard Bond Miller, this hunt is a throwback to the 1870s through the 1920s, when hunts were regularly convened at the Whitbred and Eastlund estates.

Ina's Annoyance

(thoughts of Ina Mornay)

I am beyond furious! Ronnie Parkford did not invite me to the foxhunt! A deliberate slap in the face. I've had her and Lionel to my house; and she and I are both on the Merriam Country Club board. I have more money and accomplishments than many of their foxhunt guests, and for sure I've done more for this Valley than they or the Krauthammers have, charity-wise, civic-wise, and culture-wise. Case in point: their token contributions to the new firehouse, where I really stepped up.

Okay, my money isn't "old money," and I didn't graduate from a tony prep school or an Ivy League college, and I'm not much of a horsewoman, but so what? The incredible nerve of people whose fathers greased their way to success, who're so proud of themselves for increasing the family fortune! Frankly, if they couldn't manage that they should go back to sucking their thumbs. Balthazar Transport has actually done better since the board forced Lionel out as CEO.

I came from next to nothing, and Veronica did too, but she had high cheekbones and good tits, kept herself thin and divine, and decades ago slept her way to that *Vogue* cover. Eventually she traded up from her Italian first husband to her WASP second. Big deal, huh? She's taken a few plastic surgery vacations, I'll bet. Probably keeps a boy on the side now. Probably Lionel does, too.

I'm going to aggressively short the stock of Balthazar and let a few other people on Wall Street find out and follow suit. That'll shave ten-twenty million bucks off Lionel's fortune in a week.

Maybe then Ronnie Parkford will get my message.

Job-Site Discussion

(thoughts of Andy Borska)

At a quarter to eight, as I'm parking my Borska Family Plumbing chariot at Signet Oaks, the owners are long gone to the Bahamas for a reunion with their yacht and the estate's caretakers have retreated to their separate lodgings, but a half-dozen other tool vans and a Mercedes sedan attest that my fellow Turners Lodge brethren are here. Carpenters, electricians, tilers, glaziers, masons.

This is the second year we're doing a job for the Parkfords. They don't deal directly with us trades, of course; they hire a general contractor—Jemmy Tillotson, owner of the Mercedes—who subcontracts to us. This year it's for a California-style bathroom/solarium with heating coils embedded in a concrete floor and lots of floor-to-ceiling windows so that the place will double as a greenhouse. It adjoins the guest bedroom that was a maid's quarters until we enlarged it last year. Maybe since that time some VIP complained that the utilitarian bathroom wasn't comfy enough. Or perhaps Milady Veronica just had a whim—in these households, every whim, no matter how unwarranted, merits gratifying.

Jemmy, whom I've known since he was an eager young roofer with a nail-gun, has become quite polished and sophisticated; I credit that, and his ability to work smoothly with the sort of architects and interior designers that these wealthy weekenders favor, with his consistently winning these types of contracts. His customers are "MINOs," they for whom Money Is No Object, and who don't blanch at estimates with more than a touch of fat in them. These days the commissioning owners are mostly Gobblers; 9/11 sent us a whole new batch of them, looking to get out of New York. As city-folks they're used to paying through the nose for everything; here they cough up enough for Jemmy to buy off an inspector or two if he believes that'll get the job done faster.

I never do that. I hate that sort of thing. My work is as good as they come, and aways up to code. And I also don't much like that Jemmy, to snag such gigs as this reno, schmoozes with the MINOS at the events they prefer, such as the classical concerts, although I have good reason to say that Jemmy wouldn't know a Mozart from a Mendelssohn.

In the work that we trades do on older homes like this one, we regularly uncover the marks of earlier generations of our brethren, notably in window wells, left over from the era when all windows required plumb-lines and weights. Initials and dates are carved far into the recesses; we read and identify them, then add ours before closing up the cavities. The buildings' owners never see the marks, never understand our historic connection to these abodes in which our forebears plied their trades. But it's of some comfort to us.

Talk amongst the guys, beyond hunting and fishing weekend plans, is about the hot-looking lady of the house, even though, according to *The Country Caller*, she's now 49 and has two grown children. The guys lament that their wives, many around that age (my Stacy, too) are no longer hot. This one drinks; that one is sloppy; a third doesn't give a hoot about her man, only about their kids. I'm tempted to pile on, as Stacy's become a bit bossy in addition to flabby and not always interested in having sex.

Milady Veronica is definitely still a hottie, and for good reasons: she's keeping up her physical appearance so that her second husband won't dump her for someone younger, as Lionel did a dozen years ago when he chose her over his first wife. So Veronica swims daily in the heated pool, uses the exercise machines in the home gym, and has a live-in cook who prepares her diet meals. If our wives had those things, they'd be perfect too, huh?

To be honest, my Stacy runs our office better than I could do myself, and keeps our home on an even keel.

"Hey guys," I say to them. "Stacy's going to have a big-number birthday, and I need to do something grand for her. What d'you suggest?"

Two votes for jewelry, and two for a gift card to a fancy department store. But I like Jemmy's suggestion best: "Take her on a cruise. With lots of music."

Boon Companions

I hang on the north-facing inner wall of Cullen Wilberson's cabin in the endless forest near Jericho's Cobble. We are boon companions. I am his image when he was thirteen. He glances at me occasionally, I gaze at him steadily, when he is awake and when he is asleep. I am stretched taut in a walnut frame, and covered, corner to corner, with layers of oil paint laid down by his father, landscape artist Oregon Wilberson, whose signature I bear in my lower left corner. My colors, after fifty years, are still vibrant, even noble: the foliage's greens and browns and dark berries, the straw of the boy's mop of hair and of the golden retriever's fur; the deep ocher and teal of the dead mallards slung over the boy's shoulder; the gray glint of shotgun and gathering thundercloud; and the startling red rose that flowers in the lower right, counterpart to the faint rosy tinge on the lad's cheeks. Like Oregon and Cullen, I am tough, resilient, watchful, opportunistic, And I take my sustenance and inspiration from the forests, streams, mountains, underbrush, and air. Cullen will never part with me. I am a fixed, focused moment—boy and dog returning from successful hunt—and my stillness and satisfaction contrast for him with the noisy, distracting, scattering, demanding, entangling world beyond our cabin.

Romantic Opportunities

(thoughts of Mary-Beth Flaherty)

At the end of leaf-peeper season things get even quieter in Jericho's Cobble—yes, that is possible! I took the slowing of visitor traffic to the Birdsong House as excuse to return to the Volta dance club in Springfield, promising myself that if Benny was there, and if we clicked again on the dance floor, and if he asked me to stay over, this time I'd chance it. He was there, and we danced up a storm, and he asked, and I did stay over, and it was great!

Benny Steltenham and I are quite compatible. He's not only the hockey coach at Sprouls Academy, he also teaches classics there and is completing his PhD in that field at Amherst. Plus he listens and is very considerate. Learning of my obsession with clogging, next day he took me to a Morris Dancing program put on by a Pioneer Valley Club devoted to it. Being from Tennessee I'd never before seen Morris. The troupe was wonderful! Morris is very much like clogging. Their shoes are more ballet-like than our sabots, so there's less stomping for acoustic effect but there's the same emphasis on rhythm and figures, and I adore how they work with those handkerchiefs. Men and women. They rehearse weekly and are always looking for new members. Benny and I may join them. I invited the troupe to put on a show at the Birdsong House, date TBD.

Since then, Benny and I have become quite involved with each other, and in a way and to a degree I've never felt before; I'm thinking of asking him home with me for Christmas. He already offered a good suggestion for my work, to look for stuff about Eleanor in the Congo church files, and I did and found some. Turns out that in the 1850s, Eleanor, inspired by her heroine, the abolitionist Abby Kelley Foster, wrote the Reverend Horace Butternut that if the Congo church of Jericho's Cobble did not soon take a definitive stand for the abolition of slavery, she was going to organize the flock's women to withdraw support for the church. This pressure helped Butternut become more upfront about his abolitionism and to successfully urge it on the congregation.

Eleanor's active involvement in abolition is something Gertie and I will be adding into the narrative of the Birdsong house.

My new pal Ms. Beresford has had her own new romantic surprise. On unmuting my cellphone after my first overnight with Benny, I found several messages from her.

She really is a dynamo at seventy-plus, a generation older than my mother! In the Sixties and Seventies Gertie was quite the flower-maiden hippie—sex, drugs, and rock'n'roll—and since then has kept that spirit. Twice divorced, and with two grown children whom she calls "lame"—meaning inattentive except when it comes to holding out their hands for money—Gertie has practically adopted me; and while I don't need another mother, I'm happy to have an older ally to advocate for keeping the Birdsong House open.

Gertie's voicemails had something to breathlessly confide.

While I was dancing with Benny, she had gone to dinner a second time with the JCCA's auditor-trustee, Geoffrey Collier, the retired, widowed accounting exec. Eighty-five if he's a day. At the Merriam Country Club. She'd asked him out the first time to try to talk some sense into him about the Birdsong House. He strung her along.

On their second date, he advised her that although the JCCA exec council was definitely leaning toward shutting the Birdsong House, if Gertie played ball with him the closure could be postponed a year or two. She deliberately did not respond. He saw her home. Then, during what she expected to be a routine goodnight kiss at her door, he really embraced her, audaciously reaching behind her and getting her bra half-off before she managed to pull away and send him home.

"What an old goat!" I said, feeling sorry for her.

"Well, it was—Oh, if only he was *seventy*-five and not *eighty*-five. What a time we might've had."

I pray that when I am Gertie's age, I have such an attitude on life.

Gertie, worried that her rebuff of Collier might hasten JCCA's closing of the House, wanted us to redouble our efforts to stave that off by looking for assets to "de-accession" for cash to use for operating expenses. So we've been comparing our holdings to those offered online by antique dealers: while single issues of the 19th century ladies' magazines go for $50 a pop, selling a few of ours won't bring in enough to keep the doors open; however, a complete set of *Ladies' Magazine* is fairly rare and might fetch up to $10,000, so I'm querying an antique-papers dealer as to what he'll offer for ours.

And we'll keep looking for more new material about Eleanor.

One good avenue is her Civil War work to aid the soldiery; this involved the Bucko Whitbred family, as did her work on the Institute for the Wayward. So, this week I'll go to the Whitbred House at The Chancellery and poke around, and Gertie will talk to Pamela (Renwick) Markle and others from the old Cobble families, to see if they know any descendants of the Bucko Whitbreds, so we can get in touch for information and perhaps for assistance.

Far-fetched? Maybe. Desperate? More than we'd like to admit! But Benny thinks it's well justified. Nothing ventured...

A Deuce at Chez Guillaume

(thoughts of Rose Serkin)

When Jerri Schussler, seven-term state representative for Massachusetts' 162nd district, walks into Chez Guillaume she cannot sit down right away at our deuce—what the waiters call a table for two. She nods to me, and I raise my glass of Sauvignon Blanc in acknowledgement as she begins to work the room. She stops to chat with Marc and Martha Posner, doubtless big contributors to her campaigns, who are dining with their neighbors Lionel and Ronnie Parkford, whose horse-farm estate is only slightly smaller than theirs; and then stops to greet Ina Mornay, the international investment-banking senior partner and wealthiest woman in town, who's dining with Dan Romano, owner of Valley Hardware; and lastly, *Country Caller* publisher Pat Tolland, dining with Merl Forstman, former television newsman whose face I recognize from having seen it many times on TV, and who is now on the newspaper's board.

The only patrons that neither Jerri nor I really know are the weekender couple who bought next to the Newingtons, name of Malone or Malzone or Maldone.

No doubt Jerri has memorized all the regulars' backgrounds, children's names, and even their net worths, which are undoubtedly a lot higher than mine. Those Chez Guillaume patrons are all better-side-of-the-tracks people. I was one once, when married to Doc Rusty.

Owner/chef William Beecher comes out of the kitchen to greet Jerri. He wears his monogrammed chef's jacket well and is all smiles, but to my practiced nurse's eye he looks a bit tired, which is odd since the restaurant is closed Sunday, Monday, and Tuesday, and this is a Wednesday. A week ago at Jim's bakery café I asked William why Chez Guillaume isn't doing Sunday brunches, which I said I was sure would be a big moneymaker; he agreed with my contention that brunches would be profitable but asserted that he needed the several days off each week, as he assumed I did too.

He really is quite the charmer. Not unlike my late ex-husband, in that regard.

As Jerri worked the room, she appeared guarded in her conversations, doubtless concerned that a too-hastily-offered opinion or a slip of the tongue might be turned against her. By our gaffes are we hoisted. I hope to never become so overly sensitive to what people think of me. If you treat your every encounter as a transaction, do you not lose spontaneity, frankness, and even reflexive truthfulness?

As Jerri sits down she asks about my daughter Margot, now 26 and living in Bethesda with her husband—they both work at NIH, National Institutes of Health, she in funding and he in the cancer lab—and then Jerri gets on to the reason for our meeting.

It stuns me: She is ready to "step aside" as state representative and to back me to run for that position. She cites, as the qualities that will make me an attractive candidate, my already demonstrated willingness to marshal groups to support the new firehouse, the trustworthiness that I have established as a nurse and as the townhouses leader, my ability to talk easily with both Cobbler and Gobbler factions of the electorate, and my recognition that both are necessary for the future health of the area.

After protesting that she exaggerates my experience and appeal, I express a willingness to explore the idea and to take meetings with people important to the process.

One of those comes right over to us: Ina Mornay.

We have occasionally chatted, though never about anything consequential. Quite hefty and making no attempt to be appealing, Ina exudes toughness, strength, and the sense that whatever Ina wants, Ina gets. Her most recent consort seemed to me not much more than a gigolo; when they separated, he left the area.

Jerri apprises Ina of the still-tentative plan for me to become state representative, a plan that Ina labels "inspired" and to which she pledges support. I am grateful and say so, but her pledge initially puzzles me because Ina is a Republican and I am quite emphatically not; then I realize that she is an immensely practical person, and since this area has become a liberal Democratic one, she is better off backing the horse with the best potential for a win.

But what will she want of me in return? And will I be willing to provide it? I'm not ready to voice such questions aloud, so I ask Ina if she is considering the acquisition of Valley Hardware.

"Ripe for expansion," she allows, with a sort of quizzical new respect for my savvy as she gets up to return to her dinner with Valley Hardware's owner, Romano.

Jerri has an immediate project in mind for me, one that Ina also approves of: obtaining a DSL line for this semi-rural area, which, despite the U.S. being in the era of the Internet, is still accessing the Web via very slow dial-up. To convince the NewTel phone company servicing this area to put in such a DSL line for a mile along East and West Main Street, we'll need at least a hundred separate users to agree in advance to purchase DSL service if and when it becomes available, and even if it costs more than dial-up.

"Let's go to the clipboards," I say.

EIGHT:
THE OWNERS OF EASTLUND COTTAGE

Marc Posner Bears Witness

(thoughts of Marc Posner)

I am a hunter of dead trees. These late fall days, slanting sunlight and thinning underbrush lure me from my "hunting lodge," the old Eastlund Cottage, into the forest of my 160 acres, trodding pastoralists' trails and charcoal-burners' paths with my old dog, old compass, and even older large-format Leica camera. To photograph nature unadorned, I now feel, is what I really came to the Cobble for, offset to my corporate law practice and Manhattan high-rise existence. Out here I don't have to dodge killer attorneys or avoid stepping in piles of dog poop or watch for potential muggers. I can identify, bear witness to, and capture on film multiple images of the fallen trees' fascinating shapes, patterns, and angles, which for me are expressions of the eternal cycle of life, death, and life again.

While those dead trees are my primary focus I cannot avoid noting in them the forensic evidence of their murder: the shearing from the lightning strike, the snap of windthrow on the boles, the drought-compromised roots, the dank and shallow holes made by bark beetles and clearwing moths, the mottling pallor from Dutch Elm disease and Chestnut blight. Trees have so many enemies it is a wonder the forest survives. Further intriguing is that no matter how soon after a tree has fallen that I come upon it, the wood is already stirring with insects turning its fiber into sawdust, mosses and lichens and mushrooms colonizing it, and raccoons and salamanders making it their new home.

Not everyone likes my stark tree portraits. Martha won't allow me to hang them in the great room of the cottage or in the living room of our Manhattan apartment, even though she thinks that my getting out into the forest and taking photographs is good for me. She believes the obsession with dead trees is my attempt to balance out my vicious and unsparing behavior as a corporate legal strategist and enforcer.

Well, you don't succeed at that type of law by playing nice.

So my dead-tree photos are now enshrined in my lodge's den—my lair, Martha calls it—along with a *mezuzah* from Jerusalem and photographs of my parents and grandparents, to remind me that the task of all of us who become fortunate in wealth, health, and companions is, in addition to giving regular *tzedakah* to the poor, to work on appreciating our roots, nature, and art. My friend William Beecher, a Renaissance man—chef/restaurateur, musician, artist, tennis player, ladies' man—has been encouraging my photography as part of opening me up to aspects of life that I should have gotten into long ago but did not, consumed as I have been for decades with steadily upping my billing rate until I was making millions a year and figuring how best to spend them, for instance in buying and revitalizing the Eastlund hunting lodge. It is a comfort to me to own a sizable spread where animals roam wild among countless trees.

Before Eastlund, parts of the area were in pasture, and I occasionally come upon low border walls of loose stones stacked together that used to separate one dairy farm from another. Those dividing walls ceased being cared for in the 1880s and 1890s as small homesteads became absorbed into larger ones—the way of the world! Then, when Eastlund bought up the parcels from the bankrupt heirs of farms, with an eye toward constructing his retreat, he didn't remove the stone walls, knowing that deer, moose, bear, bobcat, and turkey passed easily over such low-lying boundaries.

William and I have disagreed on only one thing: he thinks that some of these acres should become a nature preserve, never to be developed, while I want to maintain sole ownership of my little fiefdom.

I spend two hours locating and photographing a few of the old stone walls before realizing that to do them justice I'll have to return at different hours to record the varying angles of sunlight on them. Maybe Martha will like these photos of inert objects better than those of the dead trees. William, I'd bet, will still prefer the starker images.

Chocolate Fennel Soup

(thoughts of Chelsea Colver)

Sitting in the renovated dining room of the Grey Griffon with my nine-year-old Missy and Sally Melchior (her friend, classmate, and neighbor) out for a "high tea" while Katy, Sally's mother, has her hair done, I'm reminded of a fiasco that happened in this inn a half-dozen years ago, when I was still married to William Beecher. It was then owned by Jess Krauthammer, the "leisure baron" who had made many millions selling everything for the golfer, and who, after scooping up a huge country estate near Merriam, bought the Griff from Fritz Paley's successor. Enamored of all things patrician, he then tried to upscale not only the inn's accommodations but also its restaurant. They remodeled twenty single rooms into a dozen suites that rented for $1,200 per weekend, redid the restaurant and hired a chef whose pedigree included apprenticing with Daniel Boulud and having been head honcho in a multi-star hotel restaurant in California.

April Lasko, editor of *The Country Caller*, for which I was doing dance reviews, knew that William and I had run a restaurant in Brooklyn and asked me to review the new one.

Wow. The menu prices had doubled, and every dish had an ingredient that—despite us being pretty savvy in gourmet foods—was either new to us or being utilized in an unusual way. Case in point, the Chocolate Fennel Soup. Which, I was assured by the young woman *maître'd*, was definitely an appetizer, not a dessert. She told me I'd love it.

It was awful. The rest of the meal was fine but not great, and quite overpriced. I wrote as much in my review, including my dislike of the soup—and I almost expected editor April to spike the article since it was sure to provoke an angry reaction from the Krauthammers. It ran, and Jess and his wife Klara were, as I'd predicted, furious. They took an ad in the next issue of TCC, rebutting and dismissing the review, and pushed April to run an interview with their chef. April and publisher Pat were happy to oblige, since that kept the controversy boiling and sold newspapers.

In April's interview of the chef, she gave him enough rope to hang himself, and he took it by contending that his cuisine had been regularly applauded in a "major metropolitan area"—Sacramento, city of a half-million—and so was perhaps not really appreciated by "rubes a hundred miles from civilization."

Reactions to the chef's diatribe were immediate: every eatery in the Cobble, and for many miles around, put up signs in their driveways and windows saying, "Rubes Gladly Served Here" and "Guaranteed 100 Miles From Civilization." One even said "No Chocolate Fennel Soup Today."

Everybody around here laughed, and attendance at the inn's restaurant dropped sharply. At the same time, its room-occupancy rate did not improve—many a would-be weekend vacationer was deterred by the costly suite rate, as were local diners by the dining room's high prices. Soon enough, Jess let that chef go and offered more ordinary dinners at moderate prices. Even so, few local customers returned.

The last straw was when word got around that the Krauthammers' Christmas bonuses to staff at the inn and the restaurant were $25 gift certificates to Grosvenor's supermarket. How chintzy can you get? The staff drifted away, depriving the supposedly luxurious inn of the ability to pamper its guests. That further dropped its room-occupancy rate.

Jess and Karla, rather than admit their mistake and fight to keep the inn going, took their football and went home—sold the place at a loss.

The closing of the inn's restaurant affected us Beechers, too. Soon afterwards, when the plunging stock market wreaked havoc on William's stash, he decided to open Chez Guillaume, among other reasons, because Cobblers were ready for a slightly upscale restaurant whose offerings were more interesting than the others hereabouts. He hired, as his maître'd, the young woman who had that position at the short-lived Krauthammer restaurant in the Griff. When I found out that she had also become William's mistress, I ended our marriage.

"Paradis Verte" and the Eastlund Legacy

("The Eastlund 'Cottage,'" from *A Brief History of Jericho's Cobble*, by Richard Bond Miller, Town Historian)

From One Panic To Another

During the financial Panic of 1907, the Norwegian-born New York financial wizard Nils Eastlund took part in the famous all-night session in J. P. Morgan's library, a meeting credited with preventing catastrophic decline in the stock market. The next day, unbeknownst to Morgan, Eastlund used his insider's knowledge to short the very stocks that the Morgan cabal chose not to rescue, and reaped an immense reward.

As a result of the 1907 Panic, some small banks incurred such disastrous runs on their cash that they had to permanently close their doors, among them the Merriam National. Its closing catapulted into near insolvency the Berkshire Buttery Cooperative, which collapse in turn compromised dozens of Pequabogue Valley farms, resulting in forced sales at rock-bottom prices. These included the bank-owned Swanton and Burgomeister farms, which had been in their respective families' hands for several generations before being foreclosed.

Eastlund's acquisition of these former farms, and an adjacent forested area, was more than an exchange of money for real estate. Permanently removing 160 acres from agricultural production served to accelerate the decline of the Pequabogue Valley's primarily-agricultural economy that had existed for almost two hundred years, shifting the area toward being more dependent on vacationers and second-home purchasers.

"Born on skis" in Norway, as Eastlund liked to say, he became an enthusiast for the Valley and created in the terrain of his estate and nearby ones cross-country ski trails like those of his youth. After also making preliminary plans for an all-weather cottage and hunting lodge, the perennial bachelor, then forty, went to Europe looking for a young wife to reign over the property that he named Paradis Verte. Meeting in France in 1912 the tennist Héloïse Marcel, then in her twenties, he proposed to her within weeks and brought her to New York, which she enjoyed, and to Jericho's Cobble, which was too rustic and isolated for her Parisian tastes.

So he had the designs for Paradis Verte altered for her to include tennis courts, a swimming pool fed by underground springs, and a playground for their daughter Marcella, born in 1914. Their cottage became notable for its great room, decorated with broad-circumference imported chandeliers and a grand piano, where the couple frequently held soirees and weekend galas for dignitaries from the big cities.

In the early 1920s, Nils endeared himself to Jericho's Cobble by underwriting its public library and by establishing the Valley Long-Distance Ski Association, Valodia, and the first international cross-country-ski competitions. Héloïse's distraction was an affair with George T. Loden, a Great War veteran and Chancellery graduate then serving as the school's tennis coach and mainstay of its Romance Languages program.

What one Panic gives, the next takes away. Despite Eastlund's astute rapaciousness during the Panic of 1907, in October 1929 he failed to adequately prepare for the much more wide-ranging stock market crash, during which the values of stocks, including his, were reduced to pennies on the dollar. It was believed that Nils Eastlund's financial losses from the Crash, combined with learning of his wife's affair with Loden, contributed to his fatal skiing accident just prior to the 1930 opening of the Valodia cross-country competition.

He was buried in Norway. After his death, Mrs. Eastlund rather abruptly abandoned Paradis Verte and her lover Loden, decamping for Florida with her daughter, then sixteen, and what was left of the Eastlund fortune.

The Post-Eastlund Years

In 1936, Paradis Verte and its lands were acquired for a fraction of their Eastlund-era value by Broadway investor Elston Sunforth, who erected twenty small, unheated cabins not far from the main house, refurbished the barn, and turned the estate into a summer retreat for thespians who performed musicals in the renovated barn for paying audiences. Due principally to Sunforth's largesse, the summer theater program existed for seventeen years, until his retirement in 1953.

In 1961, Sunforth's heirs sold the former home and acreage to real estate developers. The new owners' attempts to reconfigure the estate for two-dozen large homes were stymied at every turn by the Jericho's Cobble zoning board.

Twice more the estate was bought and sold for development schemes, its price dropping and its disrepair mounting with each turnover, until in 1997 the buildings and acreage came into the hands of corporate lawyer Marc Posner and his wife Martha. The rotted summer cabins were demolished, all traces of the failed real estate development schemes were removed, the mechanical systems of the main house were modernized, the tennis courts restored, the fabled swimming pool heated, and a new grand piano and chandeliers installed.

In the year 2000, the remodeled "cottage" was featured on the cover of *Architectural Digest*.

The More Idealistic Brother

(Interview with Rev. Aaron Loden by Gertrude Merkin Beresford, for the JCCA Oral History Archives, 1983)

GERTRUDE MERKIN BERESFORD: Aaron, tell me about your older brother George [George T. Loden, 1892-1938]. On his gravestone there are the words "soldier, athlete, teacher."

AARON LODEN: Those about sum him up, Gertie, although I should have added "idealist."

GMB: Idealist? In what way? After all, Aaron, *you're* the one who followed your father Amos into Congo's pulpit.

AL: George had once intended to do so. As you know, in his youth he was a day student at The Chancellery—

GMB: Never the best situation for a student there.

AL:—Agreed, because he was half in, half out, and was looked down upon by some of the wealthier boarders. However! He beat them all in tennis, which they respected; and in his aptitude for the Romance languages, which pleased the older teachers, the ones who had initially come from France to start the school.

GMB: And then he traipsed off to Yale?

AL: Yes, initially to study for the ministry, with the expectation of then coming home and replacing Father; but at Yale he lost his faith in Christ, or at least he told me that he did. He never said just why. It wasn't the academic load. Or the sports. He did rather well there in tennis, a member of the perfect, undefeated Yale teams in 1910-1912; they won twenty-three matchups with rival college teams even though they didn't have a coach!

GMB: Perhaps not everyone requires a coach.

AL: Or a minister betimes, Gertie.

GMB: No fair teasing me when I'm doing an interview, Aaron.

AL: Anyway, when George graduated he decided to take a year abroad, and made his living with his racquets, giving lessons and playing in tournaments. In 1914 he got to the quarterfinals of the French Nationals—lost to Max Decurgis, who won it regularly.

GMB: And then the Great War began a few months later…

AL: Yes; and since in 1914 the U.S. was still neutral, he volunteered for the American Fund for the Wounded, driving ambulances and supply trucks at the Neuilly-Sur-Seine school being run as a hospital by the American Hospital of Paris.

GMB: Well, that is certainly idealistic as all get-out.

AL: Indeed; but he also volunteered because of a woman, a nurse there whom he married and fairly quickly divorced.

GMB: French, I presume?

AL: Belgian, but a French-speaker. Anyway, when the U.S. entered the war in 1917, he enlisted, and at the front he was exposed to mustard gas. Impaired him for the rest of his life. Ended his competitive tennis career, of course, but he had enough lungpower to teach tennis at The Chancellery.

GMB: And the tennis got him involved with The Chancellery's next-door-neighbor...

AL: Héloïse Marcel Eastlund, wife of the Paradis Verte owner Nils Eastlund. She would surely have qualified as an ideal, Gertie. A breathtaking beauty and athlete. George idolized her. I asked him once why he didn't interest himself in other women, and he swore to me that Héloïse was the epitome of womanhood and that she was on the verge of leaving her husband to marry him.

GMB: Which never happened. Seldom does.

AL: True enough! Even after Eastlund's death, when George begged her to marry, there then being no further obstacle to their union.

GMB: This was around the time that you took over for your father at Congo?

AL: I did that in 1930, yes. Father died within the year. It was also near the time that The Chancellery did not renew George's contract. Understandable—the Depression was settling in and they had fewer students. So he returned to Europe.

GMB: "Going back to the past?"

AL: You could argue that, yes; but this time he went to Europe with a difference. By then, George had become a Communist, through and through.

GMB: That, I certainly did not know!

AL: He'd had too much exposure to the rich while being of, let's face it, much more modest means. He was convinced that the poor were being unduly exploited, and that revolution was the answer—just as I was convinced that Christ was the solution to all of our problems. Still am. Anyway! It led him to the International Brigades, to fight the Nazis and Franco and the Rightists in Spain during the Spanish Civil War. Another idealistic cause.

GMB: The Lincoln Brigade?

AL: No, that one was for American Communists. He opted instead to go into the brigade organized by the Commune de Paris. He was among the most seasoned and useful of the volunteers, having fought in the Great War and knowing English and Spanish in addition to French. When that Civil War was over, and the Communists had lost so decisively, he fled to France with many others and was caught and interned at a camp in the western Pyrenees. He soon died there, from dysentery.

GMB: But he is interred in our cemetery.

AL: I did a brother's duty: fetched his remains home in the spring of '39, just before World War II began.

GMB: And that's the end of the story.

AL: Actually, no. But the rest of the story came to me as rumor. At the Valodia games in 1940, a talented young woman came out of nowhere and won the 10K but did not stay to collect her medal; I was told, by people who had once worked for Eastlund, that she greatly resembled Héloïse, and was likely her daughter with Nils. Héloïse had died in 1937. Another clue to the younger woman's identity was that before leaving the Cobble again, she put flowers on my brother's grave.

GMB: Well, that is very darn mysterious. Could it have been in response to her mother's dying wish for her to do so?

AL: Yes, but it could also have been that the young woman and George were once involved. Just goes to show that there's always more to any story than we can ever find out.

A Summer At Sunny's

(Excerpted from an interview of actor Simon Hardcastle, 1997, in *Broadway Blues*, a collection of anecdotes about show-business fiascos)

Sunny's Barn was an artsy-fartsy retreat that was all the rage in the late '40s and early '50s—really until the incident, after which Sunny closed the place. He [Elston Sunforth, Broadway investor, 1902 -1958] was a "stage-door-Johnny," one of those who'd see every single play on Broadway every season. Gay, although he never hit on me. Anyway, the incident: 1953 was my second summer chez Sunny; I'd been the year before because my work had dried up after being listed in *Red Channels* [the do-not-hire list of 151 actors, writers, directors, etc. believed to be Communists, circulated by the TV networks and Hollywood studios]. Those days I was a pinko, a sympathizer but not a card-carrying Party member—the distinction didn't mean [expletive deleted] to *Red Channels*, I was still on the list. It also didn't matter that I'd fought the Nazis, earned a few battlefield medals, and still carried some nasty souvenirs in my flesh.

Sunny didn't give a damn about the *Red Channels* list. No, strike that! It was that he cared *enough* about it to deliberately hire me in spite of it.

Being at his place for the summer was better than regular summer stock because you could spend July and August enjoying his swimming pool, tennis courts, horses, equipment for other sports. Three of us to a cottage, all meals provided, plus spending money. About three-dozen musicians, actors, actresses, backstage people. Most in their twenties; I was the oldest, at 34. We did sets, costumes, everything. Sunny directed; he wasn't very good, but we made things okay. Three different shows in ten weeks in a converted barn seating a hundred. Between rehearsals, we had the run of the place. Great manor house. Terrific grand piano. We got really plowed and leaped from the balcony to swing on the chandeliers.

Sunny liked musicals from the Thirties. That year we did Rodgers & Hart's *Babes in Arms* and the Gershwins' *Of Thee I Sing*. I was John P. Wintergreen in *Thee*—my first starring role. Key to everything I later did on Broadway.

That summer at Sunny's, as you'd expect, there was a whole lot of pairing off and sneaking into the woods. Me and the other straights were after Laura Marvel. Can't remember her real name [Lyudmila Mirlutski, 1931-1993]. Quite the goddess even then, just as succulent and teasing as she'd be in '55 when MGM cast her in the remake of *White Heat* opposite [William] Holden and made her a star. After that she only did a few dreadful movies and then married an exec at RKO who'd knocked her up. Never worked again. Wouldn't even come to the phone when an old friend called.

Anyhow, that long-ago summer I was boffing Laura and in heaven with it; but what I didn't know for a while—seemed long, but it was only a couple weeks—was that she was also getting it on with Jay-Gee Thomas [Jefferson Gill Thomas, first Black actor to be nominated for an Emmy, in 1956, in *Yoknapatawtha County*, the series based on William Faulkner's stories]. Didn't even know Jay-Gee was straight!

So, one Monday I couldn't find Laura and figured she was off somewhere on the property. Me and some of the guys and gals were doing archery practice with haystacks and straw-filled targets. And we were drinking—bourbon in the iced tea—and seeing how good our aim was after a cup or three. One of the girls finally lets on that she's seen Laura go off into the woods with Jay-Gee—and I just lost it: the idea of my incredibly beautiful white goddess being pawed by those black hands and [expletive deleted] by that black [expletive deleted] just enraged me. So I took my bow and arrows ... and "a-hunting we will go."

Long story short: after tearing through the woods like a madman, I find them near the biggest red oak, clothes on the ground beneath. I fire off every arrow in my quiver at him. Fortunately for him, as well as for me, they're not real deer-hunting arrows with razor edges, just with the plain metal tips used for target practice. Most of my shots go wide, stick in trees, but one nicks him on the leg, and another goes right through his arm and stays there.

Sunny's people get Jay-Gee to a guy who's not even a doctor, just a vet, who patches him up, quick and quiet. No permanent damage to Jay-Gee. But the vet calls the police. They come to Sunny's—turns out they'd been waiting years for an excuse. I plead with the cops that I'm a veteran and was drunk and out of my mind because this Black guy's fooling around with my girl. They understand completely! Let me off with just a warning! But in raiding the place they find lots of Mary Jane[23] and coke and evidence of gay sex and other stuff they say's illegal. Costs Sunny quite a bit to get the cops to forget what they'd seen.

He sent us all home. Canceled the rest of the season. Never opened the camp again. Died a few years on.

Took me longer to get my career back on track from shooting arrows at Jay-Gee than it did to get off the *Red Channels* list.

23 Compiler's Note: Mary Jane, an outdated reference to marijuana. RBM.

Afternoon Meeting in a Closed Restaurant

(thoughts of Chelsea Colver)

As William's ex-wife, I could have insisted that whatever business he had to transact with me be done through our attorneys, but I reasoned that he would not be asking to meet in person unless it was important, and I was also persuaded to go along by his tone of voice and insistence that the meeting be just us two.

One inescapable thing about living in a small town is that you can't avoid bumping into your ex at the post office or Jim's café or Grosvenor's grocery, so you are forced to be polite. I've even been to dinner with friends at Chez Guillaume. When William comes to pick up Missy, either at Pelfret Academy, where I teach dance, or at our home on Chariot Hill Lane, we chat. Divorces in families-with-children mandate the parents continuing to deal with one another, post-breakup, whether or not they want to.

At one in the afternoon, Chez Guillaume is closed and empty, though heated enough so that we don't have to keep our coats on. William looks a bit on the thin side but otherwise substantially as he did when we first met, thirteen years ago, when I was twenty-nine, a professional dancer, and beginning to think I'd never get involved with a man terrific enough for me to want to marry him.

William was then forty-seven and fabulous, cultured, athletic, willing to spend his money, great in bed, and considerate of me and respectful of my dancing. For a while our marriage was very good, deepening and satisfying. And maybe if we'd stayed in Brooklyn, we'd still be together, but we came up here. And then eighteen months ago, his latest mistress called me with impossible-to-refute details of his infidelity, and I decided that this time I would not let the matter slide. I did what I had to do. William did not contest the divorce, and frankly, given the monthly tab for our Jericho's Cobble home, which includes quarters for our two horses, my alimony and child support checks are not that high. Since Bert, his son from his first marriage, has finished college, and William's parents are now gone, he has plenty of dough for Missy and me. He's sixty-two now but wears the years easily. It is so unfair that men age more gracefully than women! He's not a bad father, either. Even Bert, who's now making his own way in the world, agrees on that.

At a deuce in the closed restaurant, William's usually-omnipresent smile is gone as he tells me that he has been to the doctor—"to three doctors, actually"—each confirming what the others diagnosed and that has been ratified by tests: "I have cancer, pancreatic cancer. Pretty advanced. Terminal, actually. Three to six months."

I am truly shocked. I've read enough about pancreatic cancer and heard enough from friends and doctors to know that it is among the fastest-moving, deadliest types, usually undetected until it has progressed quite far. Very few patients survive an entire year.

William then asks, quietly and very precisely—he has rehearsed this—if I would allow him to come back into our house and live in the spare bedroom during his final months. He swears that he will be able to stay out of my way, since it is a spacious home and not a cramped Brooklyn apartment; and that he will pay for everything—special hospital-room equipment, visiting nurse care; the works.

Before I can respond he pushes on to inform me that he has redrawn his will so that even more of what he has is going to me in trust for Missy. He hands over a copy of the new document. I take it without glancing at it.

And then he adds that I don't have to give him an answer right this very minute, since he wants me to carefully think over his request. I can get back to him within a few days.

I appreciate that, and say that I will indeed take a day or so to check my own thinking, but in fact my mind is already made up: William is coming home.

NINE:
MANAGING EXPECTATIONS

Horace Butternut

(1811-1869)

The waters that I had to navigate as captain of that ship of souls,
the First Congregational Church of Jericho's Cobble,
were placid on the surface, but hidden beneath it were
shoals, eddies, and other perils.

To get through them I trusted my moral compass.
It was not infallible. Sometimes I ran the ship aground,
as with Oscar and Ementha Dawson,
when my counsel to them, that family conquers all,
led them to reject the idea that professionals
might care for their troubled daughter
better than they could.
Then Celia, "safe" in the bosom of the family, committed mortal sins.

And again I failed when as war began, Bucko Whitbred's eldest
asked my blessing to volunteer
and I gave it willingly, not consulting his parents,
which sin of omission became indelible to me
when that young man returned home in a coffin.

And a third time, when I advised poetess Birdsong that
what she described as unrequited love
was her cross to bear
and would be tonic for her verses,
she advised me to give up my own burden,
my love for fire-and-brimstone chastisement,
and she never again set foot in our church.

From such failures the Good Lord eventually allowed me to learn
that the right path through the difficulties of this world
is seldom as straight or as obvious
as my fellow pastors and I were once certain that it was.

Yet our generation was indeed fortunate
in having had an absolute moral choice to make:
between the righteousness of abolition
and the "societal necessity" of slavery.
I came to acknowledge that the original sin of mankind
was not murder, it was slavery.

We in the Cobble knew that the willingness to push
for slavery's abolition would trouble the nation;
I did not believe it would hurt us at home as much.
Nor that too many innocent and useful lives would be lost,
and that survivors would still need to inculcate
the most difficult of the war's lessons,
to abandon the evil at the heart of all slaveries,
economic, familial, and religious.

Some lessons have to be taught to us over and over again
before we allow ourselves to learn them .

Forgiveness is never easy but is always necessary.

Trying to follow that moral imperative is what got me killed:

Four years after the war's end, two veterans, both maimed
and both desirous of the same young woman, clashed.
I tried to get in the middle and stop it.
A pistol shot, intended by one man for the other, claimed me.

As my breath and blood slipped away and I knew I was dying,
I felt bitter about ending thusly.

Not now.
In my grave, I know my earthly demise was fitting conclusion.

Dialogue Under the Writing Desk

(Mary-Beth Flaherty and Gertie Beresford)

SETTING: *The Birdsong House's second floor bedroom with adjoining small sitting room and writing desk, once the province of poetess Eleanor Rummet Birdsong, kept intact since her demise. Standing near that desk are MARY-BETH FLAHERTY, 26, Executive Director of The Birdsong House, and GERTRUDE MERKIN BERESFORD, 72, trustee in charge of The Birdsong House for the Jericho's Cobble Civic Association.*

TIME: *The present; mid-afternoon on a late fall weekday.*

MBF: Gertie, you know that antique desks like this one are a hot item; some go for thirty-forty thousand bucks. Maybe Eleanor's would fetch that—it matches the catalog descriptions of eighteenth-century Rhode Island designs ...

GMB: You think selling it would keep the Birdsong House open as a museum—?

MBF:—for the next couple of years, yeah. But I'd hate to see it go.

GMB: Me too. But we at least oughta look at it more closely.

(They jointly move the desk away from where it abuts the wall. Then GMB drops to her knees and her back, and starts edging her way underneath it.)

MBF: Gertie! What're you doing! At your age! Lemme do this!

GMB: I'm fine, girlie. Just hand me the flashlight.

(A flashlight is passed down to her. She flicks it on, and it illumines the undersides of the desk.)

GMB: AH-HA!

(Pause)

Come on down. This, you gotta look at for yourself.

(MBF gets on the floor and wriggles her way next to GMB under the desk, and looks at its undersides.)

GMB: Do you see what I see?

MBF: Dark spot. Means there's something above it. I think it's a hidden drawer.

GMB: To which there must be a key!

(They scramble upright and begin to look closely at the desk's other parts.)

MBF: This here's the front of the hidden drawer. Desk would have been pushed up against the wall, so nobody would've ever seen it but Eleanor. And it is locked, of course.

GMB: Of course! Only a dummy leaves a hidden drawer open....

(MBF is at the desk's front, and reaches inside its open front drawer ... and comes up with a key, shows it to GMB.)

GMB: Well, that's handy.

MBF: I knew it had to be close by. You want to do the honors?

GMB: No, you go ahead, Mary-Beth. My old hands might tremble.

(They turn the desk around so that they can fit the key into the "hidden" drawer. It opens easily with the key, and MBF reaches in and comes out with a series of ancient white folded notes.)

GMB: Oh, good Lord!

(MBF rifles through them as GMB peers over her shoulder.)

MBF: They're all addressed to "E."

GMB: Which must be Eleanor ...

MBF: Right! And they're dated from 1863 to 1877 ...

GMB: When Eleanor died!

MBF: And the signature on each one is "S."

GMB: S! So the rumor about Bucko Whitbred being Eleanor's lover is ... all wet. Musta been some other fella.

(MBF continues to read the notes, briefly, then whistles in admiration, passes one to GMB.)

MBF: This is pretty hot stuff, Gertie.

GMB: Yer darn tootin'. "No greater love than ours."

MBF: Remember Eleanor's gloss on the Hamlet poem? "To love or not to love, that is the question/Whether 'tis nobler in the main/ to suffer yearn, and sob oneself to sleep/ or to pursue what one must not obtain/ court disdain, endure scorn so very deep?"

GMB: Echoes in some of these love notes, yes. That poem was 1862, if I remember rightly.

MBF: Yup—her "yearning" poem. And these notes start in 1863! And in them the yearning is ... to put it mildly ... slaked.

GMB: D'you think Eleanor left these here so that someday somebody who cared for her would find them? And would really understand her at last?

MBF: Now that you put it that way, I do, yes. Who better to have found them?

GMB: You should write a paper about them!

MBF: Ab-so-lute-ly. Doctoral theses have been based on less. This is a breakthrough, Gertie: Proves that our Eleanor wasn't just some poetry-dabbling spinster in a backwater, she was a sensitive, sophisticated artiste involved in a long-term, clandestine love affair ...

GMB: And maybe getting some inspiration from that lover, who according to these mash notes, was no slouch with a pen either.

(They look at each other.)

MBF and GMB: We really have to find out who "S" was.

Judge Thornton's Law-Enforcement Poker Night.

(Excerpt, interview of Rev. Peter Hickle
by Gertrude Merkin Beresford, 1993,
for the JCCA Oral History files)

GERTRUDE MERKIN BERESFORD: Now I'd like to ask you, Peter, about the Tuesday night, no-women-allowed "law enforcement" poker night at Judge Thornton's [Alonzo Thornton, Merriam Superior Court, ret'd. 1989]. How was it you took part?

PETER HICKLE: I asked in. The game was already an institution, started in the early Seventies by police brass and court figures, as a way of letting off steam. By the time I joined there were seven or eight regulars—not everybody showed at every session—and Alonzo was hosting it in his finished basement, with pizza, beer, and sodas on hand. He only wanted players connected to law enforcement but he'd already made an exception for Rusty [Dr. Sandor "Rusty" Serkin], so I asserted that I qualified because my patrol beat was also enforcement—enforcement of God's laws!

GMB: Did you enjoy the game and the company?

PH: Oh, yes. It was one of the few periods in my week when I could laugh and even make jokes without being tut-tutted by someone in the community. All of us card-players knew that feeling—cops, lawyers, judges, doctors, ministers: we're all expected to be on duty and serious one hundred percent of the time. Poker night for me was an opportunity to let off steam. For a couple of the guys, it was a good alternative to seeing a psychiatrist—

GMB:—Or a minister!

PH:—Yes. We probably saved a marriage or two, although we never spoke directly about our wives; mostly it was general stuff about how to accommodate to maintain an even keel.

GMB: What else did you talk about during the sessions?

PH: We stayed away from politics, since not everyone was of the same stripe. Mild grumbling about life was allowed, but not deep grousing. In this beautiful, calm setting, among a congenial group, the world's troubles can be held at bay for an evening.

GMB: Any male jousting?

PH: You mean the sort of locker-room stuff where the guys are all constantly goading one another? Trying to get in zingers? Scoring points?

GMB: I see you're familiar with the practice.

PH: All of us were in high school once upon a time. Well, in the poker game, some guys would try that stuff, but when the rest of us didn't respond in kind, the jock-jesters would get the message that the behavior was too juvenile, and also that in the outer world there's enough competition so that on Tuesday nights we didn't need an extra helping of it.

GMB: Any occasions at the game when conflicts came up?

PH: None for me. But there were a few.

GMB: The embezzlement at FIND? After all, the judge and Rusty were on that board.

PH: Definitely. That was in '87. As you've implied, Gertie, for eight years Alonzo, Rusty, and the other FIND board members had ignored the signs that former FIND client Delia Middleton, the single mom who they'd put in charge of the books but underpaid, had diverted a total of about $100,000 to her own pockets.

GMB: Delia was quite the sad sack, I remember that about her. Still in prison! What bothered me and other Cobblers, Peter, was that the FIND trustees never got taken to task for inadequate oversight of the period when Delia was embezzling. Clearly they hadn't been fulfilling their obligations. Any talk of that over the poker table?

PH: Not even in a teasing way.

Delia A. Middleton

(1955-1999)

I'm glad my gravestone is simple and conveys no lies, good or bad;
    there were plenty of both about me.

At Stillwater Mountain High, Mr. Miller told me I was smarter
    than I gave myself credit for.
I wasn't so sure about that, and meanwhile my parents were too busy
    arguing with Welfare to stop me from getting pregnant.

When my husband Gil got fired and stayed drunk for a week
    I finally upped and left, taking the kids, a "female in need" for sure.
FIND helped me with food, shelter, medicines,
    and let me volunteer in the office to get some work experience.

I did such good work they hired me: fulltime bookkeeper, smalltime salary.
A couple board members hit on me;
    I shooed those flies away, but they never went far.

To make ends meet I took money from the organization.
Not much; an extra thousand a month
    —peanuts to them!—for eight years, until the dolts found out.

It was what they should've been paying me, and I needed every penny:
    for a car that wouldn't break down once a month,
    for my daughter's graduation dress,
    for a doctor to heal the thing in my gut.

But no board member paid attention, too busy to see what was right there.
    Complicit in my crimes, that's what they were;
    and yet when I got caught
    no board member copped to being responsible in any way.

In prison, whatever sin I'd done on the outside, I paid for, double.

By the time I got out, my kids, raised in foster homes, didn't want to return to the Cobble or to me.
I kept hoping I'd be forgiven, and not just for embezzlement.

I became a counselor in a halfway house.
I loved it and was finally doing good and using my God-given smarts.

Two years on, when I wouldn't give up my purse, a "client" shot and killed me.

The Size of the Sailboat

(thoughts of Duke Duhamel)

Old age is a series of retrenchments, only some of which are predictable. Marla and I are selling our home and moving into a cottage at Moorehead, a planned downsizing. We know it's time: while we're in relatively good health—not using walkers. But then, as my duchess reminds me, I've always had a sense of when it's time to move on, e.g., after the war I left *Stars and Stripes* for the *Chicago Tribune*, and a quarter-century later, left the *Trib* for *The Country Caller.*

The retrenchment going on at TCC was not as foreseeable, or perhaps I just missed the signs because the new board, led by Merl Forstmann, who's now put several of his wealthy friends on it, has lessened my residual say in the paper's oversight; I don't like that, but then I do grant that I'm a dead-tree-media guy and this new world is a fast-moving, increasingly-digital theater of operations. And to stay in this new world, the Cobble has to change along with it.

There are also upheavals in how one remembers the past, in my case caused by realizations of having missed something important on one's watch. An alarm was rung for me by an obit in *TCC* of retired former police sergeant Claude Zoldano, whose personality I thought I knew from many exchanges with him during the decades before he retired, mostly in regard to putting away the Kleckos.

His daughter sent in the obit and paid for it. The verbiage was about Zoldano's award-winning career as an officer, his loving family, his community spirit, etc., and the information that he died of a heart attack while out on his motorized sailboat, off Dunedin, on Florida's West Coast. So far, so standard. Then I looked closely at her snapshot of him that we printed alongside the obit, one with his sailboat behind him. The boat is 35-40 feet long, about the largest sailboat one man can handle. And a thought nagged at me: this boat is too expensive for an ex-cop who retired at age 57. Nobody on a modest state pension could afford a boat like that, even a second-hand one. How had Zoldano managed to buy it?

Fearing I'd missed something important during our years of coverage of police activities, I began asking around. Many old Cobblers had a Zoldano story to tell, none of them admiring. These spurred me to ask state rep Jerri Schussler to find and copy for me a state report, almost completely unknown to the public, regarding allegations of corruption among the state troopers. To my amazement, what I learned from the report was that it hadn't only been the Klecko brothers stealing in the Pequabogue Valley! After the Kleckos were shut behind prison walls for long stretches, Zoldano and his police pals moved into the power vacuum they had left. With fellow sergeants from the Merriam barracks who covered similar small towns in the Valley, and colluding with the troop's lieutenant, they extorted monthly payments from the higher-volume businesses, ostensibly for providing them with protection from the criminal successors to the Kleckos. The money changed hands as contributions to a sham police benevolent organization—and it did so for the better part of a decade, so quietly that I never even got a hint of it!

What eventually shut down the sergeants was that the actual Massachusetts Police Benevolent Association got wind of the scheme and complained. But by the time the investigation into the complaint got up to speed, Zoldano, the other sergeants, and the lieutenant had all retired and moved out of state, and the statute of limitations soon expired—it's just three years for theft, or for any crime that doesn't involve physical violence! The officers' pensions couldn't be blocked—union contracts assured that. Steps were taken to make sure such extortion-by-cop would never happen again; as one such step, troopers were thereafter reassigned every few years to a different jurisdiction.

A big story—a scandal!—happened in my town and on my watch, and I entirely missed it. Bad on me. Goes to show that 1), One mustn't be too cocky about one's level of knowledge about one's hometown; 2), a key to being comfortable with aging is to be clear-eyed about one's own past.

A "Thursday Girls" Save

(thoughts of Liliane Griswold)

The incessant yapping of Sadie's mutt GoFetch gets to a neighbor, so he knocks on her trailer's locked door. When he can't hear her inside or open the door, he dials 911.

My volunteer ambulance crew for the last eight years, the Thursday Girls, is on call. We get to the trailer fairly quick and force the lock. Being as I know Sadie better than my mates, since she often comes into the bank just to chat, I go in to make the assessment, see what equip we'll need. She's on the floor in the shower. It's still running. I shut it off. Crumpled but breathing; probably a heart attack. Lucky her face isn't in water, or she'd have drowned.

I lift her out, set her down, cover her with a bathrobe and blankets before letting my crewmates come in with the stretcher and put an oxygen mask on her, etc. She revives enough to recognize me, and to remark—through the mask—that she's glad it's me, Liliane, as found her, because she really doesn't want strangers seeing her "naked as a jaybird."

That's Sadie for ya!

Actually, I was a bit amazed on viewing her in the shower, because while in full gear she's formidable, when she's bare-assed and in a heap she's really tiny, seventy-five pounds sopping wet, as they say. And eighty-plus if she's a day.

The neighbor takes the pesky GoFetch, and I ride with Sadie in the back of the bus to the hospital because she needs her hand held even if she wouldn't ever ask.

I hang around the ER until I get a report from the duty nurse: Sadie's stable and should recover well enough after a few days in the hospital and a stint in rehab.

This is a pretty good save for us Thursday Girls, the best since we scraped Sam Newington off the roadway couple months ago. Sam's still on the mend but he's coming back strong.

I don't know how far back Sadie can come—she's at least twenty years older than Newington. She can for sure be counted on to fight pretty hard to get better, but her trailer's not the place for it. She shouldn't be returning there after her rehab, though she keeps it neat as a pin. Big recliner, big TV, small everything else. So I ring up Jane Milch of Moorehead, my class of '73 buddy, and explain to her what's happened and offer my idea on how to fix the problem. Jane thinks it is a good one. She's not in Sadie's poker game but will phone the hostess of it, Jane's boss, the assistant manager of Moorehead.

Next day, Jane reports that Beetle and the rest of the poker-game crew will take turns visiting Sadie in the hospital, and during their visits will lay the groundwork for Sadie first to go to Moorehead rehab, and then to transfer to one of the Moorehead studio apartments; they keep a few available for visiting VIPs. Sadie might kick a bit about the move, since—to put it mildly—she loves her independence, but like the rest of us she sometimes needs assistance, and this is one time she'll need to admit that. Her friends'll make it easy for her: bring over her recliner, her belongings, and her dog. Monthly fee and meals at the Moorehead complex will be within her monthly Social Security check, and she'll be able to rent out her trailer for a bit of spending money.

But her poker pals will warn her that they won't ease up on her during the nickel-ante sessions.

Snow, the Mother of Reminiscence

(thoughts of Sam Newington)

The Cobble's first snow of the season:
not a blizzard, just a few-inch coating,
yet a coverlet so majestic, so basic,
that it completely subsumes
and transforms forests, fields,
and all of mankind's arrangements.

Snow, the mother of reminiscence,
evokes that tranche of childhood
recalled in contrasting pairs:
the brightness of the snow blanket
and the darkness of the night;
the frigid air and the cocoa's warmth;
the icy glide's sleek thrill
and the stuttering of deceleration.

Mid-way through our lives,
increasingly faced with contrasts
that are less starkly juxtaposed,
and answers not as clear as crystal,
we remember the snowbanks as higher,
the days as flying by much more swiftly,
the air as stimulating, never as chilling.

Snow asks of us what we owe the past.
To meet its exacting standards?
To be bound by all of it, good and bad?
To bury unwanted parts 'neath its blanket?

Softening all boundaries, snow
forces us to revise our notions
of what is owed, what is forgiven,
what we can and cannot change,
and what we must no longer postpone.

The Hailstorm and The Revival Camp

(from *A Brief History of Jericho's Cobble*
by Richard Bond Miller, Town Historian)

In New England in July of 1816, what was already becoming known as "the year without a summer" was reaching its climax. An amazing twelve-month, it was characterized by a persistent dark hue to the skies during daylight, intense purple dawns and scarlet sunsets, too many snow- and lighting-storms, and a winter freeze that continued through spring, killing newly planted crops. And this, during what was also an odd time in the "second Revolutionary War" (later dubbed The War of 1812): the fighting had mostly ended, but a peace treaty between the U.S. and Great Britain had not yet been signed.

While most Americans then knew the causes of the war, hardly any could imagine the true origin of the terrifying skies and the distortion of the seasons: an eruption of a volcano, a year earlier and half a world away, Mount Tambora on the Indonesian island of Sumbawa, and consequent torrents in the upper atmosphere that carried the debris around the world. Not until a century later would that eruption be recognized as the most powerful in recorded history, dwarfing the Roman-era Vesuvius that suffocated Pompei, and ten times larger than the 1883 eruption of Krakatoa, which would become much better known because by then the telegraph (only developed in the 1830s) efficiently spread the news of it to areas far from the Indonesian islands.

But in New England in 1816, the weather's strangeness added urgency and impetus to religious revival meetings then being held in the region's small towns—for verily, the distorted atmospherics easily qualified as the wrath of God, ample reason for the unexpectedly large flock at the Jericho's Cobble revival camp. Ours was among the first of hundreds of such meetings during what became known as the Second Great Awakening. Such religious revivals, historians note, frequently occur in the aftermaths of wars. Fifty years earlier, after the French and Indian War (1756-1763), one such revival had spurred the establishment of Jericho's Cobble's First Congregational Church.

The 1816 Cobble revival meeting in the Cobble, drawing hundreds from miles around, was led not by a Congregationalist but by a Methodist, the Very Reverend Mordecai Meacham, a disciple of Methodist Bishop Francis Asbury, who had just died after forty-five years of service. Meacham's preaching style, like Asbury's, was to make Christians tremble for fear lest God wreak His vengeance on them.

At the Jericho's Cobble meeting, Meacham re-baptized two hundred people, from infants to Henry Merkin, a wounded soldier on the verge of death.

Some who attended were then motivated to establish a new, Methodist church in town, a rival to the Congregational one that had held sole sway for generations. Other attendees took the two churches' sometimes bitter rivalry, and the horrible weather, and the failure of their farms' crops, as reasons to leave town altogether. During the next year, many wagons crossed the Hudson River on the new Union Bridge and continued on toward the setting sun.

The loss of a hundred out of three hundred Cobbler families was a disaster far worse for the town than any crop failures. It would take twenty years, and an economic upheaval, for the Cobble's population to recover and stabilize.

Henry Oliphant Merkin

(1795-1816)

Here I lie, last of the Merkins, my Da having died leaving just me,
and then me passing without a son.

My Da was in the Revolution, though he never fired a shot,
an army supply depot man for three years.
Yet on coming home in '81 he was greeted as a hero!
In 1812, I wanted the same applause, so I joined up,
because the Brits were coming at us again.
Seventeen years old. Left behind my sweetheart.
Mustered in Tom Jesup's 25th under Major-General Jacob Brown.

Cavalry gets all the credit but infantry does all the work.
We had us a slew of victories—Second Battle of Sackets Harbor,
Fort Erie, Chippewa near its river.
Then come the Battle of Lundy's Lane, not far from those Niagara Falls
you can hear from miles away.
We snuck up on the Redcoats; they thought they'd no need to fear us
because we wore our own clothes, not uniforms like the regulars.
Joke was on them.

We had them Brits on the run, retreating in their bright target coats;
but then two bullets tore up my gut.
Almost died right then and there.
Felt I was floating. Saw the white light.

Don't know why the Lord spared me, but He must have had reasons.
Could've died too in that field hospital, where they dug out the bullets
and told me I was lucky.
Didn't feel lucky, just alive and hurting.

The Battle of Lundy's Lane was a wash, they said,
    nothing gained, nothing lost—like the whole damned war!
But those Brits'll never bother us again.

Was more dead than alive when they loaded me on a wagon
    heading east.
I walked the last ten mile to home.
Hoped I'd get better in the Cobble.
Most days, for more than a year, I sat out on the porch
    with my sweetheart, bigbellied with Celandine,
my sisters Ellie and Jeannie and Trudy
feeding me meat whilst they ate cabbage and potatoes.

In August '16, terrible skies tell us Hell's opening a branch near us.

Then news come of a Revival Camp,
    and of the famous Preacher Meacham to speak in the Cobble.
We pray he has the healing touch.

I felt the preacher's hand on me and 'twas indeed the hand of God.
    After that, I no longer needed to hold on so tight,
    knowing as the Lord would accept me just like I am,
    warts, wounds , imperfections, and sins of all kind.

Not long after the revival camp tents come down, I died.

My family brung me here, to lie near my Da.

Never got to hold my little daughter Celandine in my living arms.

People always putting flowers on Da's grave
    because he's a Revolutionary War Hero.
They don't bother much with flowers for me or for my war.

Apostles and Farmers

Nov. 21, 2003
Dear Rev. Trainor:

As I was cleaning our attic today—part of our preparations as we try to sell the Murtaugh-Lydner farm—I found this Hymnal. It has the church's bookplate; my father probably brought the hymnal home by mistake. I'm returning it herewith.

I'm also enclosing a copy of a paper that fell out of it. (I'm keeping the original.) It is the handout for Sunday, November 23, 1975, a celebration of the life of my grand-mother, Christine Alford Murtaugh, prior to her burial in the Jericho's Cobble cemetery. The program insists that I spoke from the pulpit at the occasion, and I must have, but I've no memory of what I said! Granma Chrissy was a lovely person. Anyway, the notes on the back of the program are in my father's handwriting, complete with his underlining and his 'Amens;' and since they refer to the terrific sermon preached that day by your predecessor, the Rev. Peter Hickle, I thought that these notes ought to be in the church's archives.

Best regards,

Kelly Murtaugh Lydner

(notes from Rev. Peter's homily)

"How many of Jesus Christ's disciples were farmers?"
Answer: None that we know of.

Several fishermen or employers of fishermen; one tax collector; one thief. Others, professions unknown.

Why no farmers with the Christ, at a time when so many people were farmers?

Because the farmers were too busy! Couldn't just abandon what they were doing and follow Jesus, like the fishermen could. Then as now, farms have work to be done every single day, rain or shine, weekday or Sabbath. (Amen!) Yet the vast majority of the populace then, and for most of history since, were tillers of earth/herders of animals.

Eden didn't start out that way—"No tilling required!" "Bounty provided by The Lord, free of toil!" But by time of Cain & Abel's growing up, all have to be farmers or shepherds ...

Today's small-farm families, like the Murtaughs, still have a great deal to do, each and every day. (Amen!) There are no members of this congregation more devout or as stalwart as individuals than our farm family members, who cannot use their Sabbaths entirely for well-deserved rest but must do chores before and after they attend our services.

So let us be thankful, on this forthcoming Thanksgiving—this most American of holidays—for our farmers, on whom we depend more than we know, and surely more than we usually acknowledge.

Do I hear an echo of our similar relationship to The Lord? On Whom we depend yet do not acknowledge often enough or deeply enough?

'Tis the season to be grateful."

“Reorganization” at Valley Hardware

(memo from VH, and thoughts of Harvey Galter)

MEMO: December 12, 2003
FROM: Dante Romano, CEO
TO: Harvey Galter, Mgr., Contractor Supplies

Message: Thank you for your years of service to Valley Hardware. Because of our ongoing reorganization, your position has been eliminated as of today, and your services will no longer be needed.

Danny Romano, CEO

Ten days before Christmas, a pink slip from my employer of the last fifteen years. No ‘Goodbye and good luck,’ no ‘You’ve been a stand-up guy,’ just “Go away.”

I’m in shock.

I’m 54 years old, I’ve been through a bankruptcy, and I’ve worked at VH since before I turned 40. What am I supposed to do? Start all over again?

Asking around, I learned there were other pink slips among the hardware-side’s twenty-five employees: a secretary, a bookkeeper, Chad Stucnowicz (Starker’s son) and two other guys from the DIY division that caters to homeowners. All of us, long-term employees, let go two weeks before Christmas! It couldn’t have waited until after the holidays?

What nasty bastards.

This would never have happened under old Sal Romano, who started VH. He wouldn’t have done this to people who were neighbors and lifelong acquaintances.

The "reorganization" is doubtless the result of Ina Mornay's investing in VH, her money being used so that she and Danny Romano can buy out stand-alone hardwares in Merriam and in Ruttleford, and make them all into Valley Hardwares, a coup announced before Thanksgiving, to take effect in January '04. Ina is no doubt trying to trim costs so that the VH mini-chain can better compete with Lowe's and Home Depot.

Well, firing me won't help with that. I not only know the VH inventory and what's available from the wholesalers, but I also have the confidence of the Valley's indie contractors, since I used to be one. They trust me, and because they do, I actually bring in a lot of business—much more than what's covered by my salary. Ina and Danny probably decided I'm redundant with some younger, cheaper contractor-relations guy in the Merriam or Ruttleford stores, and plan to use the guy to buy for all three. But according to an authority on wholesale buying, Ernie Melchior, regional v.p. for wholesaler Harwin House, three stores doesn't get you much of a discount. If Ina's and Danny's new buyer makes just one ordering mistake, it'll cost VH more than Danny's been paying me per year.

I blame Danny for this firing more than Ina. What a coward—couldn't even tell me in person. The second-generation owner of VH, having inherited it from his father, Danny never learned how to say 'no' to power. He could easily have argued to Ina that he needed to give the six of us until after January first. How much will VH save by firing us before year's end? Twenty-five thousand bucks? On a twenty-million-dollar-a-year enterprise? Couldn't Danny have taken $20,000 less for himself and still felt rich after being paid millions for his company? This is morally wrong. And not the Cobble way, no, not at all.

What am I supposed to do for ten years until I get Social Security and Medicare? What about Chad, who's much younger? Maybe Starker can get his son hired on the town crew, if there's an opening—a big "if."

At least VH didn't fire my wife Beth or anyone at her

division, Valley Fuels, which is a good moneymaker, so the Galter family will still have income. I'll file for unemployment—God knows how long that'll last, probably weeks or months, certainly not years.

This stinks.

The Geminids Peak

(Grace Newington, notes of a star-lit dialogue)

Thanksgiving was wonderful: all hands on deck, our children and grandchildren, and Sam's mother and sister—"the starting eleven," we called ourselves. The snow was gone, here, but our oldest granddaughter, just ten, was impressed by the darkness of the night, a hundred miles from New York and surrounded by forests with few lights. "Great for stargazing," she said, and advised us that just before sunrise on the 14th of December, according to what she was taught in school, the heavens would align for some magical moments.

Sam wants to see them. "Time to learn from the kids," he says. Although still quite impaired and anxious to get back to the city to resume his stock analyst's job, full-time, scheduled for after the first of the year, he insisted we now do something new together.

So we set our alarms, dress warmly, go out on the open porch an hour before dawn, lie down on our backs on our deck chairs, and focus in an easterly direction—according to a NASA online bulletin, it takes half an hour in that position to fully adjust your eyes to the dark, which will enable us to best see what is crossing the heavens.

The moon is a crescent.

"A scythe in the sky," say I.

"A skinny croissant," says he.

Then, appearing in mid-sky near the Gemini constellation, a small but noticeable white spot, one that NASA has primed us to recognize as the planet Jupiter, moving slowly toward the crescent. A second dot in another quadrant, we're informed, is Saturn.

"Makes me wish we had a telescope!"

"Christmas is coming," is Sam's response.

Then the meteor shower takes over the sky. Cascading pips

of yellow light floating down towards us at a rapid rate, two or three bunches per minute, attracting our newly widened eyes. They come out of near-sheer blackness and travel as though upwards—an illusion, of course, since we know it isn't 'up' but 'across.' What they're really doing is coursing through earth's upper atmosphere, visible because the particles are flaming up in the oxygenated air. Even one as small as a grain of sand can be seen when it lights up.

"Better than fireworks," I observe.

Geminids are believed to originate in what is known as the Object 3200 Phaeton, supposedly an asteroid, not a comet—most other annual meteor showers are from comets. '3200 Phaeton' was discovered fairly recently, in 1983. Phaeton was the Greek god who drove Helios's chariot, in which the sun traversed the sky daily.

Each time we think that the meteor shower is over for the night, another flurry appears.

"I wish dawn would hold back for a while so we can continue to enjoy the show," Sam says.

"Yes. I wonder how many people in history have had that same thought? Millions, probably. Just a bit humbling."

"But also exciting."

"NASA says that the precise word for burning up in the sky with oxygen is 'ablating.'"

"Our new word for the day," Sam opines.

"Don't know that it works as a metaphor for anything, but it's very precise. I like it."

"Meteor-watching is an activity that—not unlike sex—can be done alone but is best done with a partner," says my partner.

"Best not rushed through," I agree. "Rises and falls and rises again."

"Abating and then ablating."

"Hmm. You reckon we'd best go back inside now?"

FIND Incident Report:

Dec. 24, 2003, 2:08 AM

From: Louise Gutkind
To: FIND Exec. Director Sally Hartbush
Dec. 24, 2003
Subject: After-action report.

I was in the hotline swivel chair for the midnight to 8:00 a.m., having agreed to take it since The Chancellery's students have gone home for the holidays, and because I'm not travelling this year while other FIND volunteers are.

In the past, on overnight duty, I never had a real tough case. Most nights I was able to read my junk book or watch TV and the phone did not ring. Twice it did, but I was able to use my training to defuse the caller's immediate fears, figure out that the situation wasn't dire, and schedule her to come in to see you the next day.

Like most FIND volunteers, I am personally acquainted with abuse. My father was lousy to women, and so was my ex-husband, supposedly a gentleman—fortunately he left me before verbal abuse escalated into physical abuse. My history helps me with such calls as the one from a youngish woman named Tina Gabianco that came in at 2:08 a.m.

I had to strain to hear Tina since she was whispering. She had locked herself and her two-year-old and four-year-old in the bathroom of her home because John-O, her husband, was so drunk and violent that he had broken her arm, and now she didn't want him to hear her making this call. Until midnight he'd been at work, getting overtime at the Mulroney Marmalade factory, shipping out last-minute packages for Christmas—the big post office in GB takes packages until that hour for guaranteed Christmas Day delivery anywhere in the U.S.—and he'd come home frazzled, and started drinking. Tina was terrified that if he now heard her on the phone he'd try to smash in the bathroom door to get at her and the kids.

As we learned in training sessions, I kept the caller talking while on the other line I dialed the special number to connect through the 911 system with police, fire, and ambulance crews. Tina was frantic for someone to spill to, so I even said hello to the kids when she put them on the line. Meanwhile, her arm was getting worse; she couldn't hold anything with it, yet the kids needed to cuddle.

The state cops had most of their units at a three-car accident in Merriam and said they couldn't get to Tina's for at least twenty minutes. Our Cobble ambulance and fire crews were also at that gory scene; thirty-minute ETAs to Tina's.

Fearful for her and the kids, I told her to hang on, that the emergency services people would be there in probably fifteen minutes. She started to cry.

"Tell me about your job before your marriage," I said, to keep her talking. She'd had a job that she loved, at that Cornucopia Garden Center halfway to Merriam, minimum wage but steady. When her first child was born, she had to give up the job, and since then her income had fallen to zero, making her totally dependent on John-O. Miserly in doling out the money, he spends too much on cigarettes and booze. Food stamps keep the four of them from starving, and Tina is also a regular at the MFA (Meals For All) pick-up on Friday nights, when she can get the car away from John-O to make the run. Her own car broke down and they don't have the several thousand bucks to fix it, so it's sitting on blocks. Her mother moved to Florida and is of no help, and her mother-in-law, she says, is as much of a drinker as John-O.

The more Tina talked, the harder I had to work to

keep myself from crying. I couldn't help but think of the contrast between this hard-working, barely scraping-by young mother, no more than 24, and the spoiled-brat teenagers at The Chancellery who blow their pocket money on CDs, fancy sneakers, alternate-reality headsets and other stuff that nobody needs.

What an unfair world this is.

By the time the cops got there—2:47 a.m.—and pushed in the door, John-O was passed out on the sofa with the TV blaring. He'd almost set the place on fire with his last cigarette. A pathetic scene, the patrol guys told me, a small Christmas tree sitting there with electric lights on but no presents beneath it.

The cops easily cuffed John-O because he was out cold, and then woke him and marched him to the car and took him to the cells at the barracks in Merriam. The ambulance crew was about to ferry Tina and the kids to the hospital to get treatment for the arm. Before she left she thanked me and asks whether she and the kids could come to the FIND facility for a few days because she didn't want to return to the home—John-O would get out of the drunk-tank before long—after all, it's Christmas!—and she didn't want to be there then. I told her to phone me when she's done at the hospital and I'd pick her and the kids up and bring them to our shelter.

God willing, by the first of the year FIND should be able to get her into alternate housing.

I'm now going over to the hospital to get her. I'm relieved that the situation didn't get a lot worse, and I'm completely exhausted. Even so, when the stores open, later in the morning, I am going to have to go out and buy those kids a couple presents.

keep myself from cringing—I couldn't help but think of the contrast between this hard-working, barely scraping-by young mother, no more than 24, and the smoke-bra [illegible] teenagers in The Chronicles, who blow their pocket money on CDs, fancy sneakers, alternate-reality [illegible] and other stuff that nobody needs.

What the [illegible] word this is.

By the time the [illegible] got there—[illegible]—[illegible] [illegible] [illegible] John-O was passed out on the sofa until the [illegible] [illegible] He'd almost [illegible] the [illegible] on the way to [illegible] [illegible] a pathetic scene, the [illegible] [illegible] [illegible] [illegible] [illegible] is [illegible] there with [illegible] [illegible] but no [illegible] bandages.

The [illegible] [illegible] [illegible] John-O because he was out cold, and then woke him and [illegible] him to the [illegible] and [illegible] him in the cells at the [illegible] in Merriam. [illegible] [illegible] [illegible] [illegible] [illegible] and the kids to the hospital to get treatment for the arm. Before she left she thanked me and asked whether she and the kids could [illegible] to the [illegible] for a few days because she didn't want to [illegible] the house—John-O would get [illegible] the [illegible] before long—[illegible] [illegible] [illegible] He didn't [illegible] [illegible] there [illegible] I told her to [illegible] me when she's done at the hospital and I'll pick her and the kids up and bring them to our [illegible].

[illegible] by the [illegible] the [illegible] John-O [illegible] able to [illegible] into alternate [illegible].

I'm now [illegible] to the hospital to [illegible] her. I'm relieved that the situation didn't get a lot worse, and I'm [illegible] [illegible]. Even so, when the stores open later in the morning, I am going to have to go out and buy the kids a couple presents.

TEN:
NEW YEAR, NEW PLANS

Binocular Vision

(thoughts of Sam Newington)

Through these high-power binoculars,
my wife's Christmas present to me,
counterpart of the reflector telescope
I gifted her for starry nights,
on our first walk of the new year I spot,
where barren fields meet the woods,
a snow-frosted bobcat, waylaying turkeys,
all, dark silhouettes against the white.

Too rapidly for me to share the lenses
the tangle-furred assassin attacks,
the fatal assault on a straggler complete
before the prey's distressed squawks
spur the rafter to hop, flap, and hiss,
feathers shedding in comic riot.
Then a baring of teeth in their direction
spurs them to lurch and flee,
albeit in proper pecking order.

The event is too stark for metaphor
yet I cannot help but think
that in my stock-brokerage's terms
it was a 'non-zero-sum' game,
a transaction benefitting each player—
the lone bobcat, obviously,
since she has her next few meals—
but also, a naturalist might argue,
the Valley's population of turkeys,
which have multiplied more rapidly
than these environs can sustain.

I detest such rationalizations.
May that bobcat choke on a bone!

Hugo's Announcement

(thoughts of Hugo Borska)

The new year's begun, time to get it done: I'm announcing to Dad and Mom that Hugo Borska, slamming rock guitarist, is going to stop being Hugo Borska, live-at-home pharmacy clerk.

Our band, the Nasty Globalizers, is known around Great Barrington and the Southern Berkshires, from our frequent (but low-paying) gigs as being a bit edgy, a bit Goth, a bit spacey, a bit wild. Now we four are heading for the mucho bigger time, New York City, to be seen and heard by people who can help us make it.

Out here in the sticks, that'll never happen.

We saved money from our day jobs. Put a deposit on a far uptown Manhattan two-bedroom that's affordable because we'll split the rent four ways. There's a nearby subway station so we can easily get downtown. We've applied for day-jobs as bicycle messengers—whatever it takes! I'll even work in a pharmacy, so long as it's in the center of the universe.

My Dad and his pal since high school, Zach Galter, my supe at Prince's, will label me stupider than dirt for leaving this paradise, but if I don't make my break at 21, when will I? Gotta give my music a chance. Yes, it means that much to me.

Dad and Zach have this default view of me staying in the Valley, going to pharm school, getting my diploma, and then taking over at Prince's so Zach can go fish in North Carolina. Not gonna happen. Ina Mornay, who owns Prince's, is smarter than the two of them put together and it's crystal clear to me she values Prince's mainly as a piece of real estate, to go with her other holdings in town. She's already figured out, as I have, that with increasing competition from the drugstore chains and the Internet cut-pricers, stand-alone pharms like Prince's are goners. In five years, there wouldn't be anything here for me to take over, even if I wanted to, which I don't. Ever. I'm going to be a rock star.

In New York, there's at least a chance of that happening.

Not guaranteed, of course. I know that the Nasty Globalizers could flop. Or that one of us could go on and become big and leave the rest of us eating his dust, even though right now we're very tight. I'm giving myself until I'm 25 to make it in the music scene in New York or maybe L.A. After that—well, I don't know. Nobody does.

But I do know that my future's not in Jericho's Cobble.

In re: The Red Lasses

January 2, 2004
Ms. Louisa Ralston Stafford
765 Bush Street
San Francisco CA 94109
Dear Mrs. Stafford:

We are writing to you in regard to your great-grandmother, Lisa Whitbred Ralston and a painting sent to her in San Francisco in the 1890s from Jericho's Cobble, an oil that we hope is still in your family.

In 1871, Lisa, elder daughter of Selwyn and J. C. ("Bucko") Whitbred V of Jericho's Cobble, married Yale graduate Humphrey Crennell Ralston and moved with him to San Francisco. In 1895, according to California public records, Lisa and Humphrey's daughter married Sidney Stafford, scion of another well-known Nob Hill family, and in 1903 your mother, Melinda Ralston Stafford was born. Is this all correct?

After Selwyn's death in 1890, an important 1853 oil portrait of Selwyn and her two daughters, Lisa and Anna, painted by the latterly famous Ammi Phillips, was reportedly shipped across country to Mrs. Ralston. Known as *The Red Lasses*, it was the complement to a similar Phillips portrait of her father, Bucko, seated with her brothers, the couple's sons. *The Green Lads* still hangs in the great hall of Whitbred Manor, now the administration building of The Chancellery preparatory school. We are including a photograph of that painting with this letter.

Might *The Red Lasses* still be in your family's possession? We are hoping that it survived the earthquake and fire of 1906. If so, please send us a photograph, along with any information about your great-grandmother's life in San Francisco. We are particularly interested in letters from her parents or from other members of the Jericho's Cobble community such as poetess Eleanor Birdsong, known to have been involved with the Whitbreds in various endeavors.

Unfortunately, we must also take this opportunity to inform you of a groundswell in Jericho's Cobble that is attempting to remove the Whitbred name from our grammar school, whose previous building, erected in the 1880s but replaced in the 1950s, had been constructed and donated to the town by Bucko and Selwyn Whitbred. We and many other responsible Cobblers, including most though not all of the members of the local school board, oppose any such change but at this moment cannot assure you that the Whitbred name will survive on the school. There is similar pressure on The Chancellery to alter the name of Whitbred Manor.

We thank you, in advance, for any information you may be able to provide.

Mary-Beth Flaherty
Executive Director, The Birdsong House;

Gertrude Merkin Beresford
trustee, Jericho's Cobble Civic Association

A Day of Give and Take

(Alice Hadley Morely, diary entry, Jan. 4, 2004)

We had quite a work crew, & quite a Sat. @ the X-country trail, portions of which I've been jogging/walking regularly. We were there as part of Valodia's push 2 clear & mark all trails prior 2 the Feb. games, now just 5 wks off. We needed 2 do this on a day w/o snow on the ground.

R crew could C a very lovely sight, the seasonal lights @ in-town houses. Also beautiful: ice formations @ the edges of the river, sparkling in sunlight; + the briskness of the air.

2 of us = my former students: Laurie Milch, now a sr. at Stillwater; & Chuck Mulroney, who was in the 2nd class I taught at Whitb. Elem. Now 45! Got gray hair 2 prove it! I also recognized & was glad 2 see Harv Galter, & Eddie Griswold the septic fields instructor who's a fellow Val. trustee. Vinny Djere, early 20s, I didn't know B4, sent by The Chancellery since some of the biathlon course is on their property. Reason I didn't know Vin is b/c he was in Merriam's grade school B4 his family moved 2 Mackenzie Rd. Recently saw service in Iraq. Uncle works @ The Chancellery.

In charge today is Harv, husband of Beth G, a Valodia trustee; Harv brought tools 4 all (had them in his garage from last yr.) & assigned tasks for ea. Guy knows what he's doing!

It was a day of much give & take.

Using shovels, rakes, hedge clippers, small chainsaw,

garden-waste bags & little flags, we went over every inch of the course, clearing fallen twigs + overhanging branches, marking the turns on the 5km. route. The longest event is 20 km = 4 laps of the course, the biathlon also has 4 stops 4 rifle shooting, ½ taken prone, ½ while standing. There is also a biathlon penalty loop trail, 2 B skied if U miss w/1 or more of the 5 rifle shots per stop.

We had very nice weather for early Jan., in the 30s with not much wind 2 make it feel colder, & we all dressed warmly enuf 2 enjoy the tasks + being out of doors—& it led 2 our doing a lot of chatting while we worked.

Harv was the neediest, recently fired by VHardwr. Still shaken up, & hasn't a clue what he'll do next. Chuck Mulroney is not long out of his mother's Small Luxuries firm, altho he has a new job which he says is 1 hour ea. way & where he's "low on totem pole."

None of us knew what 2 say 2 Harv but we encouraged Chuck 2 give the new job a chance & definitely 2 enter the 'Young Srs.' 20K (ages 45-60); as a former winner here—"But that was so long ago," he protests, "I was 17!"—he'll probably do well. After all, as we pointed out, he'll be 1 of the few contenders @ his home course.

Laurie 2 is hurting, which is why her mother Jane (knows a thing or 2 from Moorehead @ physical/mental problems) has permitted her 2 take what they refer 2 in their family as a "mental health day" off from school; Laurie, who as an 8-yr old was quite bright, is feeling down @ Stillwater because they "teach 2 the norm"—do they ever!—& she doesn't know how 2 utilize what smarts she's got 2 transcend the situation.

"I'm tired of ppl asking me what I want 2 do in life," she told us. "I can't answer that question yet."

"What do you do well, then?"

"Read."

Huzzah! 2 me, being good @ reading means U R eager to learn, but I didn't even have 2 say that 2 Laurie because the guys all jumped in, urging her 2 read more + seek challenging books @ Eastlund Libe if her teachers won't suggest them. I piped in 2 say that she should also write more—& that I'd help her w/that & w/laying out a plan @ snagging a state scholarship 2 UMass or a community coll. for after she graduates Stillwtr.

"I've never planned anything that far ahead in my life," Laurie laughed. None of the rest of us had either, we confessed, but we're all agreed that she'll be the better 4 having an objective 2 work towards. I could see the Vinny kid nodding, probably regretting he hadn't tried harder 2 get at least a year of community coll. Or maybe it's just that he thinks Laurie's cute, which she is.

Seeing Eddie, Harv, & Chuck talking serious, I avoided the 3 so as not 2 overhear. I could guess it anyway: a caution, based on Harv & Chuck's recent probs, 4 Eddie not 2 leave his secure state job 2 quick even tho he's understandably fed up w/it. Use more of yr sick days, accumulated vacay days, whatever; ease yr time there, but don't ditch it. Eddie pondered this. As he should. When such good advice is offered 2 U by a neighbor who shares yr circumstances—as was done not only 4/Eddie but also 4/Harv and Chuck & even 4/ Laurie—U must listen & understand b/c it comes from those *who share a lot of yr world. That's how we do it—that's the Jericho's Cobble way!*

As for me, everybody urged me 2 say 'yes' 2 the Valodia board's request that I take in a boarder or 2 during the event, now that I'm retired + my house is otherwise empty. I never aspired 2 having a B&B, as some ppl around here do; & as a very private person I was on the fence about boarders, but the gang's encouragement has decided me.

I'm going 2 agree 2 it.

The Artist In His Lair

(a letter from Cullen Wilberson)

January 6, 2004

Dr. Arthur Fleidermanns, director
The Semafor Museum
Eugene, Oregon
Dear Dr. Fleidermanns:

Thank you for your letter inquiring about my father, Oregon Wilberson, to obtain background material for use in the retrospective *The Semafor* is mounting next fall, which I hope to travel to see. You pose an important question: Why did a leading artist, already recognized and rewarded, settle in a backwoods part of a small town a hundred miles from New York?

The short answer: A love of nature combined with a deep distrust of what he labeled "the un-civil aspects of civilization."

That love and distrust are reflected in his landscapes, which do not celebrate monumental shapes or magnificently broad skies, but rather the universal in the small: beavers and mallards sharing a pond; the remains of a charcoal-burners' pit overgrown by lichens and mosses; the lad bicycling a country lane that stretches to eternity. All these my father honors and investigates; not for him the monoliths of mountains or skyscrapers.

I see similar love and distrust in his portraits, both the commissioned ones of college and prep-school leaders, industrial tycoons, and trophy wives, and those done for his own pleasure, the children of local merchants and workmen, paintings that aptly reflect the individuals' characters and their semi-rural setting. In town here there is an older woman who posed for him as a young girl, about to roll a hoop down a valley road—and today you can still recognize in her aged visage the spirit of eagerness for the adventure that the portrait distilled. For another example, at 63 I am still the 13-year-old he painted, with his hunting rifle and a brace of mallards slung over his shoulder, accompanied by his faithful dog, coming home to his cabin in the woods as the rose of summer fades.

By the by, neither of these paintings are for sale or loan.

My father came to Jericho's Cobble after his World War II service—which he never spoke about—and after post-war years of trying to make it in Manhattan. This was initially a summer retreat but it soon became our only residence and remained his after my mother divorced him and moved back to the city once my younger sister had gone off to college. My father hunted and fished and grew vegetables and reveled in his ability to provide for his larder. I believe he chose this area of the country, rather than return to the Pacific Northwest of his youth, because twice a year he could easily truck his recent work to the Gaia Gallery in Manhattan, buy art supplies, and be back home that evening.

The people of Jericho's Cobble respected his art and his uniqueness and even his celebrity, but rather than treat him as royalty they called him "Robby"—a nickname he preferred but that had been too ordinary for the first gallery that showed his work—and they chatted with him just as they did with each other, about the weather, the slowness of the mail, the recalcitrance of teenagers. He much preferred such affectionate, neighborly give-and-take about nothing and everything to the chatter of his city-based artistic peers, who treated him as a rival seeker after fame, entangling him in their debates over realism vs. abstractionism and whether or not the Museum of Modern Art would ever buy their work. That two of his paintings ended up at MoMA, my father believed, was due to collectors donating them to raise the value of their other Wilbersons.

Robert Obregon "Oregon" Wilberson lived in Jericho's Cobble because here he could be who he wanted to be, and could associate with those he wanted to be with, and in many other ways could do precisely what he wished to be doing.

As we all should.

Sincerely,
Cullen Wilberson

Aimee and Rose on *FM in the AM*

(transcript of radio broadcast on WCBL)

AIMEE BISHOP: My guest this morning on *FM in the AM*, Rose Serkin, RN, an old friend, a kindred spirit—a fellow Pisces!—who has some important news. These past weeks you've probably seen Rose and her clipboards at her folding table, perched in front of the post office on Main Street, collecting signatures on a petition to the phone company—you may even have signed one! Rose, is that the subject of your 'important news?'

ROSE SERKIN: Yes. At the request of State Representative Jerri Schussler, I have been—as you've pointed out, Aimee—collecting signatures requesting that NewTel provide our town's Main Street corridor with a working DSL line—Digital Subscriber Line—that will allow us to ditch our molasses-slow dial-up Internet service and obtain faster access to the world wide web. So I'm here today to announce that we've turned in the petitions and that within sixty days NewTel will begin installing the new capacity on our telephone poles along Route 29, where most of the in-town houses are.

AIMEE: And that's just a start, right?

ROSE: The hope is to steadily extend the coverage zone in the coming years.

AIMEE: Will extending it be a priority of yours when you're the state rep?

ROSE: Let's not put the cart ahead of the horse! With the help of Jerri, who's retiring, I've obtained the endorsement of the Pequabogue County Democratic Party—but there's an election to be won in November before I can truthfully say that 'this' or 'that' will be my priority in the legislature. The long-term goal is Internet *accessibility* for all, everywhere in the county, so we won't get left behind in this new, digitally-enhanced century. An intermediate-term goal is better connectivity, and for more people.

AIMEE: That's a bit more achievable, I think, than the 'health-care-for-all' and 'workforce-housing' goals that you and I have discussed in previous sessions on these airwaves ... goals that we won't give up on. But Rose, tell WCBL's audience, please: Has running for state office changed your life very much? I know you've chosen to reduce your schedule with the Visiting Nurse Association.

ROSE: Can't be in two places at once! I'm still working as a nurse, and hope never to give that up! But yes, Aimee, campaigning is very different, and I'm having to adjust.

AIMEE: For instance?

ROSE: Needing to have an opinion ready on every issue, and a considered opinion at that, meaning one that's benefitted from my doing some research before I open my mouth to speak about it.

AIMEE: And you must also be prepared to defend your position, since not everyone will agree with the one you've chosen?

ROSE: As we both well know!

(They chortle)

AIMEE: Such contentious issues as?

ROSE: Oh, whether the state should mandate that small employers must provide health insurance plans for employees who work at least 20 hours a week—there's not an easy answer to that one.

AIMEE: And what about the proposed motorcycle raceway on the old Dawson House property? The public vote has been postponed, but is scheduled for February 12.

ROSE: Well, now, we all know *your* feelings on *that*. But my private opinion now must defer to what a representative of the public—even an aspiring one—must consider, which is to try to reconcile the competing interests. What's open-and-shut for me is that a decision on the site's use must wait for the environmental-impact studies to be completed.

AIMEE: Very nuanced of you. Aren't you a committed environmentalist?

ROSE: You know that I am, yes, but—

AIMEE: Are you giving in to the moneyed interests?

ROSE: Not at all! But a public servant—and that's the point-of-view that I'm coming from here, Aimee—has an obligation to see all sides and to take into consideration economic realities as well as ideals.

AIMEE: Politics as the art of compromise?

ROSE: I like Jerri's definition: Politics as the art of the possible. Deals will always be made in back rooms, Aimee, but you don't get to participate in such back rooms until you've spent lots of time in *front* rooms, in constituents' living-rooms and on their patios, listening to donors and to people with axes to grind and agendas to push.

AIMEE: Which you have been doing.

ROSE: Yes. And I must confess: I have a hard time asking for money for my campaign rather than for such causes as MFA—Meals For All—as you and I have done for years. I want to listen to people willing to donate to my campaign, and to thank them personally, but also to listen to those who may not be able to donate. I'll be representing a large geographical area and a full spectrum of incomes, from the very wealthy to the quite poor, and I'm making it clear to everyone that as their rep I'll be concentrating on people in need.

AIMEE: In a sense, Rose, expanding your patient base!

ROSE: Not exactly, but I know you can't resist a metaphor, Aimee.

AIMEE: Guilty! Now tell me, old pal, will you still be as sweet a person? Will being out in public toughen you up too much?

ROSE: I hope not too much, although I must admit to now being less candid than I have been, both in private conversation and in public; a bit less trusting; and, of course, much more diligent about apportioning my time and not letting others waste it.

AIMEE: Now there's an exit line if I ever heard one!

After the Nightmare

(thoughts of Louise Gutwind)

Jericho's Cobble, although a wonderful place, suffers from a condition common to rural towns, a lack of adequate resources for those in need. Which means that around here if you really want something to get done you must be prepared to do it yourself.

After Tina Gabianco's nightmare of a Christmas Eve, when husband John-O broke her arm and threatened further harm to her and their two small children, FIND did provide temporary housing, but we have a three week limit on any one-time stay at our facility, and that period is about up for Tina. What next?

For the moment, John-O is still cooling his heels in the Merriam lock-up. Tina has been to see him—courageously, in my opinion. He apologized profusely and swore he has gone cold turkey. Tina decided not to press charges, knowing that a felony conviction would negatively impact her husband's ability to get work and provide support for her and the kids, whether or not they live in the same household with him. The prosecutor agreed to downgrade the charges to Disorderly Conduct if Jon-O's behavior in jail was considered satisfactory. So far it has been, and he's due out in a few weeks.

More important to Tina is that currently she and the children have no home to return to. Their landlord has canceled their lease because of non-payment and cleared out their belongings—even Tina's old jalopy, which was up on blocks, he hauled away for the junk fee, which he kept in lieu of unpaid rent.

Tina's actions in response to all this have been so reasoned and so sensitive that they inspired me to invite her and the kids to live in my 'mother-in-law' apartment, and to buy her a used car so she can take the children to daycare—FIND clients get a reduced rate—and commute to her job at the garden center until John-O gets out of jail.

It is only a little bit disconcerting to have her kids calling me Gramma Lulu.

But I'm getting used to it.

"'Inspiring' Messiah at Congregational Church"

BY DOUG FLIPKENS, *The Country Caller*, ISSUE OF JANUARY 15, 2004

An exhilarating performance of George Frideric Handel's *Messiah* was presented this past Sunday afternoon at the First Congregational Church. Under the direction of choirmaster Victor Leighton, it was sung with the enthusiastic participation of a large audience, estimated by the Reverend Vernon Trainor at two hundred. Many in the seats joined in with the choir on a dozen passages, the church having furnished everyone with the sheet music.

According to Leighton, this is true to history. Handel's *Messiah* "purposefully does not feature soloists as Jesus or Mary like most oratorios and was not written for operatic voices but for those more used to singing hymns." Usually, however, audience participation in the *Messiah* is limited to the famous "Hallelujah" chorus and the final "Amen" section. The choir director, wanting additional sing-alongs, transposed some of the music and put it "within the vocal range of ordinary folks."

Reverend Trainor attributes the success of the performance to director Leighton, who transposed and rearranged the music and led the choir while simultaneously playing the accompaniment on the organ. Leighton, in turn, credits Reverend Trainor for "first-class, open-handed support" of the enterprise, and also the community, for responding so well, "especially in the sing-alongs."

Choir members Grace Newington and Alice Morely reported being "happy and hoarse," and opined that doing the *Messiah* had brought the community together, a sentiment echoed by former First Selectman Pamela Markle, who attended with two van-loads of other Moorehead residents. She pointed to the presence in the audience of many weekenders, who in order to attend, had evidently postponed the time of their usual Sunday return to New York.

Confabs at the Grey Griffon

(thoughts of Jane Milch)

We had not set a gang-of-six lunch at the Griff for January, but one was hastily convened at the behest of Louise Gutwind. As secretary to the Dean of The Chancellery, part of her job is opening the dean's mail each day, so she was the first to see (and to quickly rifle through) the lengthy report of the New York law firm, Rounsel, Waterson and Peters, regarding the sexual molestation allegations against the former women's athletic director, Casimir "Chip" Garuzelski, and others. After putting the report on her boss's desk, Louise needed to tell us about it.

She has done so—and we are, as she was when she first read it, appalled.

According to the report, between 1983 and Garuzelski's retirement in 1996, he forced at least a dozen female students to engage in sexual acts and a few to actual intercourse. For years The Chancellery admin either ignored the teenaged victims' complaints or accepted the s.o.b's denials without challenge—until six months ago, when a major donor turned up the heat because his daughter, a Garuzelski victim, was still having mental problems. The donor threatened to sue unless The Chancellery commissioned a thorough, outsider-run investigation. The school hired the big-city-firm RWP to look into sexual misconduct complaints over the past quarter-century.

The Chancellery's admin and board of trustees are currently trying to figure out how to deal with the lawyers' findings and recommendations. Louise says they'd like to keep the whole shebang hush-hush until the school is able to reach settlements with the Garuzelski victims. Eventually the report will have to be made public, but it will be done quietly.

Clearly, we realize, the interval between now and that publicizing of the report is a window of opportunity during which we can and must Do Something. Not in regard to Garuzelski, though; none of us cares a fig about Garuzelski. But we have great interest in two others identified in the report whose purported activities occurred further back in time.

One is the late Dr. Sandor Serkin. Even though none of us is surprised at the report's mention of him—his reputation as a lecher was well-known even to those of us who did not use him as a physician—we still found the details quite awful: unnecessary vaginal examinations of at least a dozen girls and pushing several of them even further.

That behavior, carried on for a decade, only ceased when The Chancellery's nurse, who one day happened to be in the examining room with him, objected to his doing a pelvic exam on a teenage girl who did not report any symptoms. Rusty squelched the nurse by saying that he was the medical expert, not her; the nurse reported him to the admin anyway, and her report couldn't be ignored like they ignored students' complaints. When the Dean confronted Rusty about these pelvic exams, Rusty kept him at bay with the same bullshit he'd given the nurse. Thereafter, according to the lawyers' report, the nurse insisted on being in the room for such exams, so Rusty ceased doing them, and the following year The Chancellery did not renew Rusty Serkin's contract to provide medical services.

Not much we can do about that one except to quietly notify Rose Serkin, Rusty's ex, who will need to know in case she gets asked about it at a campaign event.

The other named person in the lawyers' report was a terrible surprise to us: Victor Leighton, Congo's choir director. There was only one incident. In 1981, a male student charged that Vic, then the music director at The Chancellery, had engaged in a "homosexual assault" on him. The law firm could not verify that the event actually took place because that former student left the school shortly after the incident and had since changed his name and place of residence. Also, at the time of the incident Vic, when interviewed by the Dean, said, according to the record, "I was completely drunk. If the boy says that's what happened, I can't remember enough to deny it." No legal action was taken against

Vic, but his contract, too, was not renewed, after twenty years of previous regular renewals.

Vic is a person of great value to this town and to us. As I am the only one of us six who's in the choir, the gang tasked me with acting on this info at the Congo church. I suggested starting with my fellow female choristers. Everyone thinks that's the right way.

So I set up another confab at the Griff, with fellow-choristers Glenda, Grace, and Alice, even though I was nervous about this little old high-school grad—me—trying to convince these three college-graduate professionals to do anything.

They were terrific with me, agreeing with my conclusion that we could not reject out of hand the possibility that Vic Leighton might long ago have engaged in homosexual activity, but equally that Vic's subsequent behavior at the church had been "unassailable" (a word I worked hard to have ready for them). We all admire what he's done for the Congo—most recently, the *Messiah*—and for us in the choir, and we applaud what he did at the time of the incident, accept responsibility rather than protest that the incident couldn't've happened or that the accuser wasn't credible.

First thing to do, we agreed, was alert Vic that this stuff would come out. Then we'd need to let Reverend Vern know, and to request of Vern—indeed, to demand!—that Congo be absolutely supportive of Vic or else we'd all quit the choir and publicly say crappy things about the church. Only after doing that, Grace said, could we take Step Three, visit *The Country Caller*, and try to convince them that when The Chancellery report does eventually surface, the newspaper must not use it to malign Vic.

Rose's Visit to William

(thoughts of Rose Serkin)

William Beecher in his home hospital-bed is surprised to see this particular Visiting Nurse, having expected and I'm sure also anticipated a younger woman, rather than one nearer his age and known to him as the friendly neighbor at Jim's, sipping a latté at the next table or as a patron of his now-closed Chez Guillaume restaurant. I apprise him that I claimed this VNA appointment so as to give him and Chelsea the chance to ask of a neighbor the sort of questions they would not as readily put to a nurse who is more of a stranger.

William looks smaller and older, propped up in bed by pillows, surrounded by vases of flowers and recently gifted books, diminished not only because of his advanced pancreatic cancer but also because he is not daily out-of-doors playing tennis or swimming. Pallor very quickly replaces color.

I take his pulse and other vital signs. Fortunately, I find no bedsores, whose absence I attribute to his insistence on getting out of bed and keep on moving, although ambulation is now clearly difficult. The health slope he is sliding down is as yet not too steep but will shortly end in a cliff that he cannot avoid. Four to six weeks, he's been told. He seems philosophically prepared for death, as are many folks who know that they have lived a full life—which William, although not that old, certainly has done.

His wife Chelsea—his ex-wife to be precise, although the term 'ex' now seems moot because of her caring for him—politely stays out of our way. I am thrilled at her courage and magnanimity in performing the onerous task of shepherding through his last days the husband who cheated on her so flagrantly that she had to divorce him. I don't know that I would have been as helpful to my late ex-husband Rusty, who was as much a charmer and a cheater as William.[24] Chelsea is smiling and positively responsive to William, which is good for both of them. She understands that doing her tasks without rancor is a blessing for herself as well as for William. In bad circumstances, people like to feel they've done the best they can.

ROSE: Getting lots of visitors?

WILLIAM: Yes. It's like having a chance to attend your own funeral and hearing people say nice things about you … some of which are even true.

ROSE: I'm sure that most are. But, you know, William, I hate it at funerals when everybody at the podium feels they have to tell a funny story.

WILLIAM: Me, too! You're right, Rose! I'll decree that at mine, everybody has to be serious, keep wearing the long face …

ROSE: Your vital signs are reasonably stable. If you continue to fight the decline, you'll have a slightly better time than if you just lie there and let it happen.

WILLIAM: Tell that to Chelsea, please.

ROSE: I shall. What do you want from your medications?

WILLIAM: To remain lucid but free of pain—although I'm sure those two objectives are close to mutually exclusive.

ROSE: My recommendation for you is the same as I'd

24 Compiler's note: At this point in time, Rose Serkin had not been apprised of the still-private report containing allegations of her ex-husband's assaults on young female students at The Chancellery. RBM.

want for myself: opt for lucidity over being pain-free—for William to remain William, not some pale shadow of himself.

WILLIAM: Will you say that to the doctors for me?

ROSE: Absolutely.

WILLIAM: Thank you.

ROSE: Don't know whether they'll listen to me, though.

WILLIAM: They will, Rose—and so will the voters. Run hard for that state rep job, Rose. It'll do you good, and you'll help Jericho's Cobble.

ROSE: Flattery will get you anywhere.

Actually, I sense that William's more-usual pose of slightly looking down upon those not as suave nor as accomplished or as well-off as he—which categories encompass almost everyone in town!—has been replaced by the awareness and sensitivity that sometimes comes to the dying once they accept their obligation to those they will leave behind.

This guess about this change in William's attitude is affirmed by the arriving Marc Posner, his quite close friend, who according to Chelsea visits every day when not at his office in Manhattan. "He was never snobbish when it was just us two," Marc tells me in the foyer, out of William's earshot, "but now he treats all visitors as welcome and interesting, I think out of the realization that it costs people quite a lot to come here to see him, because no one really knows what to say to somebody who's dying. William, understanding that, uses his charm to put them at their ease. I'm more admiring of him now than ever."

27 Inches!

(thoughts of Polly Maldone)

The forecast yesterday was 24 to 30 inches of snow by sun-up this morning, and the radio puts what we actually have as 27 inches! Outside our windows: mountains and mountains of snow, so much that it does more than soften contours, it entirely obscures them, disappearing low bushes, tree stumps, flowerbeds, and a lawn chair that we forgot to take in. The entrance to the garage is blocked. So are the house's outer doors. It takes me quite an effort to push one door open enough to use a shovel to bite into the snow. So it takes me a while before I can step outside to do more.

Jonathan and Cecily are of course home from third and second grade and itching to play in the snow. Cavorting outside is not easy, though, since the snow is well above boot-top level, making movement turgid. In ten minutes they tire of being outdoors and are eager to return inside. Thank goodness for a mudroom in which to ditch their sopping snowsuits and boots. Former farmhouses like ours generally have ample-sized mudrooms.

The town roads are rapidly being cleared. Our Volvo is safely dry in the garage, but I can't get it out by myself, even with all-wheel drive designed for tough roads and conditions, because there is too much snow atop our driveway and the garage is a long hundred yards from the street. I can't even contemplate approaching the old barn, which is even further back on the property, now home to a nesting pair of barn owls, their feather coats almost as white as the snow.

In the summer we loved being this far back from the main road and its traffic noises. Now that distance is a hardship for us.

Well, at least we didn't lose power! During the first blackout, this past August, we camped out on the property, which was sort of fun, but the second blackout was not fun. We stayed one night with our next-door neighbors, Grace and Sam Newington (before his accident), and then bought a generator like theirs and had it installed. Another $5,000 spent. But it helped us weather last night's storm.

I had expected that Steve, who works for the small firm that does our mowing, would show up here this morning with a plow on his truck to do the driveway, but he did not. The truck broke down, he finally calls and says, and all of his snow-jockey friends who might have covered for him are busy with their own customers. He hopes to get to us by sundown—tomorrow morning at the latest.

I'm feeling very trapped by the snow. And I'm also missing New York's museums, theaters, and restaurants. Along with their benefits to society, these provide wonderful occasional escapes for parents who are raising small children. But I'm not making any such escapes, just now. Nor is Walter, though he's in the city during the week, in a studio apartment.

The children like the excitement of the snow but I'm no longer sure that we Maldones made the right move in coming up here after 9/11, or that I am at all suited to living year-round in an often-isolated New England town, subject in the winter months to snowdrifts, blocked roads and driveways, and more. Maybe Walt should seek a transfer to one of the company's offices in the sunbelt.

I'm thinking Atlanta.

ELEVEN:
COMPLICATIONS

Muted Spotlights

(thoughts of Sam Newington)

Pallid, blurry, low wattage,
the mid-February sun rises low
and scuds close to the horizon,
not challenging the heavy air
nor offering solace to aging bones.
Soon, even before darkness falls,
the full wolf moon rises,
ivory, vivid, sharp-edged,
glistening in the resplendent snow.

Pity those people who take no joy
in knitted woolen mittens
or snug thermal underwear,
nor cherish the rosiness of cheeks
after a brisk walk to the village;
who are insufficiently astonished
at crystalline embellishments
to the underfoot and the overhead,
snowy outlinings of trees that reveal
the extraordinary in the everyday.

How ingenious of the trickster-in-chief
to inspire us while also plaguing us
with the seasons' seismic shifts,
their angles so acute and emphatic
that as they satisfy they also unsettle.

To be present, truly present,
winter's muted spotlights teach,
is to aspire to become
the author of one's life-script,
not just its featured speaker.

A Very Bad Date

(diary entry, Laurie Milch, February 8, 2004)

This is the hardest thing I ever had to write: Stewie and me broke up forever, and its mostly my fault.

It happened last night (Sat.). We're out in his car—his Dad's car—with Barb Arnold and Jed Cavendish, and some pot from Jed's brother Herb's stash. We're smoking the weed, me for the first time—wow, on steroids! Anyway, while waiting for the high to come on full, me and Stewie are talking, serious-like, about what we'll do after graduation in a couple months, and I'm saying how Mr. Miller is telling me I'd do fine at college, and Mrs. Morely is helping me so much, to study to get a state scholarship, like at Holyoke Community.

Stewie says his grandfather, who runs the carting trucks around here, and his father Horace Globus, who's the Number Two there, are after him to take over the garbage-hauling business, and he's thinking it can be good money—and I respond (it's the pot talking) that that's a dead fucking end, and if Stewie does it he'll never get away from Jericho's Cobble.

Well, that upsets Stewie big-time, but instead of ragging on me, which he could have done legit, he takes off on his Dad, saying he'll never again let his father whup him or swat his mother—Stewie's big and strong, football team, hockey team, bulking up at the gym.

"At least you've got a dad around," I say.

Probably shouldn't've.

By then Jed and Barb are going at it pretty heavy in the backseat, and Stewie's trying to get me to unzip my pants so we can do the same. The pot has definitely put me in a weirdly relaxed mood, a 'who cares?' feeling, which is so good! But at the same time a little bird's whispering in my ear, 'Laurie, Don't Be A Fool!"

So I slap Stewie's hand away from my zipper, and when he tries it again I slap the hand harder.

He's pissed, and accuses me of looking down on him because his family works with garbage; and I say, 'No, it's because you're stupid.'

Then he looks so hurt and so sad that I apologize, even though it's true he's kinda dumb. But I'm not giving in: the zipper stays zipped.

On the way home, coming down from the high—now there's a steep slope!—and even though I'm angry at myself for having called anyone stupid—I was once accused of that, and it hurts—what pops into my head is that if I really want to make something of myself I can't have a guy tying me down just now; and so I tell him we can't see each other anymore.

He lets me walk up to my house alone, without a goodnight kiss.

Even though I know that come Monday Stewie'll diss me all over Stillwater Mountain High, I'm not changing my mind. If they ask for my side of the story, I'll smile like it's none of their damn business.

Tale of the Delegations

(thoughts of Glenda Trainor)

As we four choristers gamed out in advance how we'd deal with the threat to our choirmaster Vic Leighton, my admiration for my singing sisters Jane Milch, Alice Morely, and Grace Newington grew. Doctors like me usually deem ourselves superior to everyone around us; the choristers' discussion showed me that's not so.

Just after the service on Sunday, and while still wearing our robes, the four of us traipse into Vic's office. Per our agreement, Alice goes first. She lets Vic know that we have learned there's a Chancellery report coming out on old sexual abuse allegations, centering on someone else but mentioning him.

Vic seems startled but then goes impassive, as though he's been expecting this for a long time. He listens intently as Alice tells him that the New York law firm doing the report for the Chancellery could not verify the old "homosexual attack" charge because the alleged victim has changed his name and otherwise vanished. Jane then chimes in to emphasize that we all believe this past incident has no bearing on his current work, which is terrific, and that we much admire his acceptance of responsibility for that event when it was first reported. I add that we are prepared to defend him and his position at the church. What we don't need to say out loud is, 'We've all done things we regret and don't want to dredge up'—Vic gets that. He does say that he appreciates our concern and our method of conveying the news; he's long feared this day might come, and that there would be repercussions. "Not on our watch," I insist, and tell him we're next going to see Vern.

Still not having doffed our choir robes, we then troop into my husband's office, where it's my turn to take the lead. I lay it all out for Vern, with my three robed sisters as silent Greek chorus. Vern too is bit taken aback by the news, but after hearing it says he not only agrees with us that Vic is terrific as a music director and as a person, but also, that having read the late Rev. Peter Hickle's file on Vic, he can attest that there is no hint of anything "untoward" in it, even going back twenty years.

Vern announces that he will do two things: 1) apprise the Congo council of elders that allegations against Vic might surface, and 2) recommend that they reaffirm their commitment to Vic and to the church's music program "without delay, quibble, or caveat."

"That's very heartening to hear," I say. My companions nod agreement.

Sometimes men are better at this than we women give them credit for.

The following Wednesday, to protect the source of the information (Jane's friend Louise Gutwind), Jane does not come along when Grace, Alice, and I visit *The Country Caller*.

There it is Grace's turn to lead. The week's issue of TCC closes on Tuesday, so Wednesday is the slowest day of the week and we have no trouble corralling publisher Pat Tolland and editor April Lasko for a brief sit-down, even without an appointment. Grace announces why we're there—that we've learned of a forthcoming hush-hush report to The Chancellery about sexual matters that nails Chip Garuzelski.

Pat interrupts to say that the paper is already aware of the allegations, and also that a law firm's report to the school is in the works.

We are surprised by this but try not to show it, and Grace counters by asserting that we have no interest in Garuzelski but do in two others named, first among them the now-deceased former columnist for *TCC*, Dr. Sandor "Rusty" Serkin.

At the mention of Doc Rusty's name, both Pat and April just shake their heads, as though to say, "We should've known." Which is just what we want them to think!

Then, after they've been softened up, Alice feeds them the stuff about Vic Leighton, advising them that we're here as choir members to speak about the choir's and the Congo church's determination to take no recriminatory actions on Vic for this long-ago allegation.

Pat and April's faces grow grim at this news. So Grace suggests that the paper, in reporting this stuff, concentrate on Garuzelski, whose actions are not yet beyond the legal statute of limitations, and on the now-deceased Dr. Rusty, whose violations were pretty darned disgusting. Then, as planned, I jump in. My description of what the report identifies as Doc Rusty's unnecessary vaginal exams of underage girls makes the newspaper duo blanch. Grace emphasizes that while the shocking stuff about Garuzelski and Serkin is well documented, that about Vic Leighton is not, so the paper ought to be very cautious about reporting "unsubstantiated" allegations against a venerated member of the community.

"We can't make such a promise," publisher Pat Tolland says, "but we can be very, very judicious about our reporting on this, because we don't want anybody suing *The Country Caller*."

“80th Annual Valodia Competition Held”

BY APRIL LASKO, *The Country Caller*,

ISSUE OF FEB. 19, 2004

The 80th Valodia Cross-Country Ski Competition on February 13, 14, and 15, was a rousing, if chilly, success.

Forty-eight competitors from five countries, ranging in age from 15 to 72, took part in the 10 and 20-kilometer races and biathlons, in front of a crowd that steadily numbered more than a hundred, according to Eddie Griswold, spokesman for Valodia. He thanked them for coming out in the cold weather—and it was quite frigid: while during the first two days the average temperature was around 32, on Sunday, for the finals, the high was 19.

Among those braving the icy blasts for that last day of competition was former selectman Herman Murfrees, who recalled taking third place in the 10-K race in 1980; retired third-grade teacher Alice Morely, who is boarding a competitor; Kelly and Corey Lydner, whose farm is temporary quarters for two families of out-of-town spectators who want horse-drawn sleigh rides and big farm breakfasts in addition to lodging; Harry and Horace Globus of the Supraclean Garbage Hauling Company, watching grandson Stuart Globus win the 18-and-under competition; and Mary-Beth Flaherty, executive director of the Birdsong House, to cheer on her boyfriend, Benny Steltenham, hockey coach at Sprouls Academy, who was competing in the men’s 20-K.

A full list of prizewinners will be found on page 14.

It is estimated that the three-day competition brings in $50,000 - $100,000 for the area's businesses.

Begun in 1924 by Norwegian-born Nils Eastlund, the Valodia games have been held every year since, even during World War II, and are funded by donations, bequests, and entry fees. This year, the Senior Handicapped Race trophy has been renamed for recently-deceased veterinarian Jonathan "Doc" Nash, who won that competition several times and who left a bequest for the benefit of Valodia.

In the 45-60 age group, the 20-K winner this year was the Cobble's own former youth division champion Chuck Mulroney, who expressed both chagrin at reaching the required age to be eligible and delight at winning a competition that he first won as a teenager in 1974.

Competitors, times, results, commentary, and interviews were broadcast live at the site by WCBL, the local public-broadcasting affiliate. The station's anchor Maurice Carter and entertainment editor Aimee Bishop set up an outdoor studio-table not far from the biathlon finish line.

Bishop, also a columnist for this newspaper, had no comment on the recent Selectmen's decision to postpone until May the scheduled Feb. 12 meeting on the sale of the Dawson Property.

The broadcasting pair also served as the emcees for Friday evening's Valentine's Day/Valodia dinner-and-dance at the Grey Griffon Inn, one of the competition's corporate sponsors. This year, the “Val-Val” dinner featured a special treat dreamed up for the early competitions of the 1920s but that had been absent from area menus for many years, the “triple-O,” the Olive Onion Open-face tart.

Future Planning

(Alice Hadley Morely, diary entry)

I really don't know how else 2 put this: by sheer happenstance or mayB by fate, an interesting man has come in2 my life.

Valodia asked me 2 take in a boarder-participant 4 the '04 games, & it turned out 2B a competitor in the 65+ races, Basily—Baz—Mikulski. 70, he said he was a widower @ Milwaukee, formerly a regional mgr. 4 the Piggly Wiggly supermkt chain, HQed in the south but also big in Upper Midwest. After his wife died 3 yrs. ago, Baz retired rather than take a x/fer to Mobile, Alabama, & has been spending part of his time @ the X-country ski circuit.

Anyway, as a boarder he was so nice, so charming & polite, & I was so embarrassed by the money that he paid me for the lodgings, that I spent some of it 2 take him as my guest at the Val-Val gala at the Griff, where we danced a bit, & after coming back to my house talked into the wee hours, until he had 2 go 2 bed 2 rest before his race.

That next afternoon he won the 10K in his age group!

That night we had a bit of a celebration, w/some champagne, &—well, it just sort of "happened!"—as my teenage pal Laurie Milch would say. A bit awkward 4 me, & not B4 I used a little dab of olive oil ...

The last time I lay w/Arthur must've been 17–18 yrs. ago, B4 he ran off w/his sec'y. Since then = just me in bed. At

1st, after Arthur vamoosed, I missed having sex, but it had been intermittent B4 he left, so I don't 'zackly recall when I became conscious @ the lack of it. I do know that after being alone 4 a time I didn't miss it that much...or at least told myself I didn't.

But w/ Baz, the love-making was a breeze. So natural! So X-citing! After it, I was so awake & filled w/sensations—happy; exhausted; thrilled; + sad that 4 so long I had not had a man in my arms & in my caring thoughts—that I almost cried.

Anyway, we tried it again in the morning, w/our eyes open & in daylight & not befuddled by darkness/drink—& again it felt good.

Baz then went on 2 Montpelier VT, where there was another X-country the following wk, and then 2 Maine for 1 after that...but he wanted v/much, he said, for us 2 keep in touch—easier these days, w/e-mail—so Laurie's shown me a few email trix. And thru correspondence Baz & I have agreed that the 2 of us will take a Mediterranean cruise together in Apr. A test drive, Baz says, B4 we make any further decisions @ a relationship.

I'm already on a diet.

The Triple-O Tart War of 1928

(Interview, Vance Youngblood,
by Gertrude Merkin Beresford, for the
JCCA Oral History Archives, 1985)

GERTRUDE MERKIN BERESFORD: Now Vance, please tell us about the 'triple-O tart' war between the Grey Griffon and Dawson's House inns in the 1920s. Before my time!

VANCE YOUNGBLOOD: Oh, you would have enjoyed it, Gertie; it was a lot of fun. In *The Country Caller* for months even made it into *The New Yorker*, a squib about a 'tempest in a teapot' in a New England town. Looking down the magazine's collective nose, you can be sure. 'How quaint.'

GMB: I prefer 'old fashioned' to characterize us. Which inn was the originator of the Olive Onion Open-face tart?

VY: I hired a chef—a cook, really—from Italy, and he made this special *crostata* that became very popular. Everybody who came in wanted one. A dish for two people, cut in half—thus, open-faced. Really a pizza before Americans knew anything about pizzas, except it didn't have tomato sauce. At about the same time, the Griffon started making a very similar tart and called it a *galette*—which is the same thing as a crostata, except in French! Their chef accused our guy of stealing the recipe, and there was even a threatened lawsuit by the Griff. Lots of shouting and hoopla.

GMB: Over such a petty matter?

VY: You know the old saying: 'The level of acrimony is so high because the stakes are so low.'

GMB: Certainly in small towns! And the war was unwinnable, of course?

VY: There you go—there was no patentable recipe. Galettes and crostatas had been made all over Italy, France, and Spain going back to the Middle Ages. The lawsuit went away. But the 'war' about the tart gave people something to gossip about, and it was good for business for both inns. And no harm done to anyone.

GMB: What distinguished one tart from the other? Some secret ingredient?

VY: People said ours had a special tang, or zest, or zing, depending on who was describing it. The secret? White balsamic vinegar, pretty much unknown here at the time. On the other hand, the Griff one's uniqueness anybody could see—came from putting goat cheese on top, not mozzarella.

GMB: Almost anything's better with goat cheese on top.

VY: There you go.

GMB: But eventually both Inns stopped making it?

VY: Well, sure. During the Depression the Cobble wasn't getting as many tourists or travelers staying over, and the locals couldn't afford to eat out as often. So I closed the Inn. Then in the Forties, when a new owner re-opened Dawson's Inn, he didn't bring the triple-O back on the menu, and neither did the Griff. I think that was because during the War nobody wanted to be reminded of the old carefree days.

"The Un-Thermometer"

BY GRACE NEWINGTON
(submitted to *The Country Caller*)

When my husband and I first came to the Cobble, being city-born and city-bred we installed a mercury-filled thermometer outside our bedroom window, to alert us to how cold or warm the day was and likely would be.

Now and then a few of our Manhattan-based friends who are up visiting us chortle at that thermometer as old-fashioned and urge us to replace it with a new, digitally aware machine, the sort of micro weather station that provides hyper-accurate time, date, humidity, wind speed and even "misery index" numbers in addition to temperature.

No, thank you; because in the Cobble we already have a temperature-teller provided by nature, a non-mechanical, non-mercury indicator that you don't often see in the city but that's in my garden and that infallibly tells me what I need to know. A rhododendron bush.

My wonderful un-thermometer.

One of the lessons the Cobble teaches is that we should rely less on technology to interpret the world for us and more on what nature itself has available to teach us.

The rhodo leaves' angles, elevations, shapes and furls all change in reaction to the temperature. When we reach above the freezing point of water, 32 degrees Fahrenheit (zero degrees Centigrade), as we are increasingly doing these days, those leathery, tear-drop shaped, slightly waxen leaves are extended laterally, very gently curved and normal-appearing, even hosting light burdens of snow, but when we drop below that freezing point, as we do by late afternoon, the leaves fold in on themselves, the more so the further down the temperature goes. When the "temps drop into the teens," as the TV weather chatterers put it, the leaves become tight little green pencils, elongated curls dangling from branches like sets of chimes. In the single digits, the leaves become tighter, more like matchsticks.

My rhodos and I are looking forward to warmer days, after the March solstice, when during high daylight the temperature in Jericho's Cobble edges into the stratosphere of the Low Forties and allows the green leaves to unfold and stretch. Sometimes the change is so rapid you can see it occur over a ten- to fifteen-minute period of time.

Part of the thrill of looking forward to spring and summer, in the Cobble, is sharing the eagerness of expectation as to what will happen to the rhodo leaves when much warmer temperatures make those leaves point upwards, like arms upraised in supplication of the sun, as though offering thanks for their full recovery from their wintry, traumatized state and ready for their wonderful though short-lived blossoms.

No wonder that in cultures around the world the rhododendron has always been the symbol for endurance, for getting through difficulties.

But I must also report that the rhodo has historically been employed as a warning sign. That, I believe, is because every part of the rhododendron plant is toxic, root, trunk, branch, and leaf, and while the toxicity does not seem to bother bees and other flying pollinators, the taste and touch of it for human beings and even for dogs is awful and bad-hallucination-making. That may explain why, during the Victorian era in England, people would send rhodo blossoms to a friend who was about to make a wrong decision, usually one regarding a potential mate who was deemed unacceptable.

Keepers of the Night

(thoughts and dialogue, Maria Delacroix, RN)

"Am I going to die tonight, Maria?"

"Told you many times, Mrs. Markle: Not on our watch. Try to get some sleep now."

My husband Jack and I, overnight-shift nurses at Moorehead's Rehab center, have pledged to each other, and to our patients, when they ask us Pamela Markle's question—as most of them eventually do—that we will keep them safe through the night. Moorehead hasn't lost anyone at night in several years. Daytimes, yes; nights, no.

From nine in the evening until seven the next morning, from Wednesdays through Sundays (and into Monday mornings), Moorehead Rehab is ours. We love this shift because there are no visitors and no well-meaning volunteers, and by eleven p.m. the last of the moppers and supply-cabinet stockers have clocked out, leaving us alone with the residents, who call us "Maria and Jack," presuming that we're a pair even though they think us oddly matched.

Well, Jack Stoltzfus and Maria Delacroix are definitely that—him tall, lanky, and mostly silent, and me short, bubbly, quick to talk and laugh—yet we mesh well, which is much easier for us to do now that the last of my kids from my earlier marriage have grown up and gone on their own ways, so Jack and me can work the same shift, the overnight, which we like because it's more about nursing and less about paperwork.

Both of us born elsewhere, we nonetheless consider ourselves real Cobblers even though we don't get to see the town much in daylight. Now and then, after work, we do go to Jim's for coffee and his divine pastries—it's breakfast for most people, post-work refresher for us. There are times when I'd prefer a life more like that of our neighbors, awake during the whole day and asleep when it's dark, but that's not in the cards until I retire. Which I don't plan on doing any time soon.

A few of this ward's patients, sent over by the hospital after surgery, are improving enough to return home soon, but most, like former First Selectman Pamela Markle, will never do so, and they're the ones we take special care of, as we are for them the intermediaries between this world and the next. Beyond the chores of assessing the patients' health, plumping the pillows, emptying the bedpans, doling out the scrips, and updating the records, we chat at length with those whose eyes beg us for company, who find the dark hours harder to bear than the daylight ones, since when the TV is off and the corridor halls are quiet and the lights have been dimmed, fears and regrets come out to bedevil them. Often they keep themselves awake just to talk with a person like me or Jack who doesn't make judgments on the behavior of the very old and the very infirm; these patients aren't afraid of death, but they do seek comforting on their last journeys.

Horizontal Dialogue

(In bed, in the caretaker quarters of the Birdsong House)

MARY-BETH FLAHERTY: … so I'm not sure what Gertie and I ought to do about what we've found: verification, of sorts, of a long lesbian affair between Eleanor and Selwyn Whitbred.

BENNY SHELTENHAM: Why do you say 'of sorts'?

MBF: Because the documentation is iffy. Oblique at best. You know that skirt of Eleanor's, the one in the cedar closet? The tartan? With insets of dark purple? Actually, it's a German tartan, a Coburg, which is why she had it—the Vogelsangs originally came from that part of the empire. Well, we found three photos of Eleanor wearing it, one of them in Gertie's family album, different photos taken on different occasions, but more-or-less the same pose in each: the two women standing right next to each other, Eleanor in that skirt. Gertie and I think the skirt is a signal—"Coast is clear, let's get it on at my place."

BS: Could well be.

MBF: Just to think of how difficult the affair had to have been, a hundred years ahead of the time that women having sex with each other became socially OK! On the other hand, maybe the forbidden aspect was what turned them on.

BS: Who made the first move?

MBF: Eleanor, we think. She was twenty years older, and probably already had some lesbian experience among her literati gal-pals in New York. But Selwyn—well, she'd been married off at seventeen to Bucko, and pretty quickly after that had four kids in eight years, maybe with miscarriages in between...

BS: And was quite isolated at Whitbred Manor, seeing to all those children...

MBF: Exactly. So she was likely the more naïve one. We're pretty sure the affair began after the burial of Selwyn's firstborn, Joshua VI, in 1863. He died at Shiloh the year before, and they re-buried him in the Cobble cemetery.

BS: And Eleanor paid a condolence call...

MBF: That turned into something more; yes, that's what it feels like. The first note from "S" to Eleanor is a week after the burial. After that, they were thrown together, or they arranged to be together, in war-related activities—making bandages for the troops, and in the board meetings of the Institute for the Wayward. And eventually they planned to run off together.

BS: No kidding!

MBF: Yes, in 1870. Just for a while, with the excuse of a convention, and then they'd come back. But it never happened. That was because the older Whitbred daughter, Lisa, had just been jilted—the guy just about left her at the altar!—and Selwyn needed to stay home and console her... so she and Eleanor mothballed their getaway plans.

BS: Lisa did eventually get married, didn't she?

MBF: Oh, yes. Bucko doubled the dowry, and then there

was no shortage of suitors. A Yale grad named Alston stepped right up.

BS: Your dowry… is your natural endowments.

(Interlude)

MBF: Anyway, there's a lot we don't know. Did any of Eleanor's paramours—ha, that rhymes!—visit her during the summers? To what degree did the affair inspire her late poetry, which is gutsier than her earlier stuff? There are no extant notes from Eleanor to Selwyn, although there surely were some. Did Bucko find them? Did anyone else know?

BS: So you can't figure out where to stop, hmm? Well, that's what PhD theses are for! To find and tell the whole exhaustive story. Actually, Bets, not all mysteries have to be solved. Leaving some unsolved but needing investigation might help you with the JCCA, to keep the house open and functioning for at least another year or two—

MBF:—and keep my salary going, so the house can open for visitors on the weekends—

BS:—Exactly!—while you continue working towards your doctorate at UMass. And you can counter the JCCA's objections to airing the 'forbidden love' by pointing out that your paper will bring more visitors and more interest in the poetess of Jericho's Cobble, that there'll be more tourism money …

MBF: I like it. Gertie will like it, and we might even succeed in bringing the Cobble into the twentieth century, if not into the twenty-first!

TWELVE:
RETRENCHMENTS

The Coming Evolution

(note from Patrick Tolland to Duke Duhamel)

Dear Duke:

Well, the die is cast at *The Country Caller*, and with breathtaking quickness.

Merl Forstmann, that former network news anchor with a face recognized by millions, whom I lobbied to join the TCC board, has taken it over and become the catalyst for serious change. Once made fully aware of our financial obligations, meager income, annual losses, and of the decreasing viability of rural newspapers, he pushed for *The Country Caller* to "evolve" from a regularly unprofitable commercial business into a nonprofit that won't have to worry as much about the bottom line. He's pledged himself and his board pals to annual donations and to raise the remainder of the budget through paid subscriptions, ad sales, $100-a-ticket bashes, and memberships in the nonprofit. His argument: that the paper will be better off relying on donors than on ever-more-scarce advertisements. Well, it is increasingly true that the sort of printed ads we once profitably ran are instead being put online, and for a fraction of what a print ad costs the advertiser. Can't fight that math.

Anyway, according to what you told me eight years ago, the paper hasn't been in the black for more than thirty years. And the current owners are perfectly willing to have a stop put to its annual drain on their bank accounts. Or at least to get a charitable deduction that can reduce their tax obligations.

The public relations line is that while the ownership structure will change, the paper will not—it will appear physically as it always has, with its mixture of reportage, commentary, and local ads, so that readers and advertisers will not notice the difference in ownership. Only the financing of the operations will change.

But in reality, that won't be the only change. Even as the rejuvenated board claims to love me and the work I've done, I can sense that it is moving toward the conclusion that the job of leading a nonprofit is very different from that of leading a for-profit-though-unprofitable enterprise and therefore will seek a different publisher—one half my age.

As for that, also ending in this evolution of *The Country Caller* is the era in which a small-town cub reporter, assistant editor, or publisher's aide could sharpen their skills at the local weekly, as I did here under you, before moving up to a big-city daily. In 2004 there are far fewer major urban papers for a cub reporter to graduate to than there were twenty-five years ago, and today's urban dailies are even more subject to increasing competition for readers' attention from Internet journalists, with every would-be Clark Kent and Lois Lane posting his or her own scoops and tidbits on the World Wide Web, and getting paid by the click—accuracy, fairness, verifiability of facts and sagacity of news judgment not necessarily included!

Will *The Country Caller* still be the newspaper that so well reflected Jericho's Cobble? I don't know, Duke, and frankly neither does anyone else, but I worry that it won't.

I've loved this job, even with its constant heartaches and worries, because in small town New England, as you conveyed to me, being a journalist is as much of a calling as being a minister or a physician: the critical factor in all of those jobs is a belief in the absolute necessity of what we do, and the fundamental satisfaction comes from knowing that we toil for the benefit of the community as well as to earn a living, and that our work is vital to the community's health and survival. We are the priesthood of thankless tasks.

The word "evolution," in the popular mind, is synonymous with forward progress; but for me personally, in this instance, "forward," "progress," and "evolution" are definitely not interchangeable terms.

Maybe I'll channel my frustrations at being let go into writing that novel about star-crossed young reporters that I never have had time to work on. And we'll have lunches more often.

Best regards,
Pat

Redefining Home

(thoughts of Sam Newington)

Time was, we cherished as ideal home
our well-curated five-room apartment
in a good Manhattan zip code,
launching site for forays in culture,
indulgences, and extravagances;
our retreat and comfort zone
after difficult days at our offices.

Still impaired, still tentative,
after having returned to work
in my cubicle and at my screen,
in an office overrun by vampires,
hollow, and looking at me askance—
I agree with Heraclitus, who held
that one does not, cannot,
step twice into the same stream.

Is it only the waterflow that changes?
Or is the stepper-in also altered?

Manhattan is awash in too-much-ness,
profligacies, garbages, sprawlings,
relativity as a substitute for clarity,
needless complexity for exquisiteness.

Yet for us city-bred it is not easy
to cotton to a semi-rural existence
once valued mainly as offset
to urban intensity and edge.

To redefine for us what is home
we must-re-think the meanings
of neighbor, of gnostic, of stimulation.

In the Cobble, as it once was all over,
neighbor remains a term of respect
born of shared circumstances
that override all differences,
economic, educatory, and social.

Awareness of the divine?
As much in the ordinary as in the awesome,
and in a closer embrace of the past
in all its flaws and excesses,
and with nearby sentient beasts,
and the vagaries of the weather—
this setting being a paradise
only for those who accept it as such,
who thrill to the heightened breeze at dusk.

Stimulation? Mostly by neighbors
met at the post office or coffee shop,
not too task-burdened to chat;
by time and room and quiet enough
to read books that require much of us,
do chores that are their own reward,
encounter nature that makes demands
of us yet is particularly amenable
to midwifing thoughts that span the world.

A Terrible Bad Run

(by Liliane Griswold)

Even though when the Code 3 call came in—lights and sirens on!—I didn't recognize the street address, I somehow knew it would be a terrible run for us Thursday Girls, because I had a suspicion it involved Chad, Starker's son.

A neighbor heard a gunshot and called 911.

The freezing rain, of the sort that's worse than snow, made every bend in the road dangerous and every step on the ground slippery. It was 2:13 p.m. when the ambulance left the garage. That's before schools let out for the day, I remember thinking. And when the transfer station is still open for the day. Grosvenor's supermarket too.

We get to the place. Sign says Stucnowicz. Door's locked. No cops—nearest one is five, seven minutes out, he says on the radio.

We force the door. It's worse than I feared. Multi-car accidents have nothing on this. Blood, brains, bone, spattered all over. Chad's slumped back in a chair with half his head blown off and the deer-hunting shotgun on the floor.

A latex glove on, I feel the carotid.

Nothing. No pulse.

Somehow, even though I'm looking at the mangled face of a guy I've been aware of all his life, I manage not to throw up. A new man on our crew does, and none of us blames or razzes him.

I won't let anybody take photographs. Cops can do that when they get there.

"Somebody's got to tell Starker," my colleague murmurs. She's crying, and so am I.

"And Chad's wife, Sheila."

"The cashier at Grosvenor's?"

A neighbor who comes to the door—we won't let him in—shouts to say Sheila's taken herself and the two kids to Florida for the week to visit her parents because her father's in bad shape.

Now I'm sure that Chad planned this suicide, down to the minute, for when his family's away and when his father's at work. What pushed him to this? Being fired by Valley Hardware? That there were no town job openings, even though Starker pleaded for one? Chad's probably late on his mortgages—us bank people can sense that—and God only knows what other kind of debt he's in. A man in his early thirties! Maybe some life insurance?

There's a note addressed to Sheila. I won't read it and won't let anyone else do it. Another thing for the cops to decide on. But I know what the note will say because this is not my first rodeo: "I'm sorry. I can't take it anymore. The pain's too great. I apologize, but it's better this way. I love you very much." Jesus, how pathetic we all are in such awful moments, when we're so overcome that we want to die just to get away from the insane pressures. Life's too complicated sometimes. It can get to you.

"Starker's parking his truck and's he's gonna run in."

"No!" He must not see this! I leave the house and with my colleagues form up to prevent the big guy from coming in. Fortunately a cop arrives, instantly understands what needs to be done, and with some effort all of us together manage to keep Starker away from the carnage.

There are days when we as an ambulance crew do good by making a save. This afternoon we're performing an equal service by preventing a Cobbler from seeing how his son has destroyed himself.

Chadwick Stucnowicz (1972-2004)

The deed's done and I'm glad of it. Now I'm where I need to be.
Peaceful here, that's for sure; and the world can't hurt me anymore;

Maybe God can hurt me, and maybe God will hurt me,
but maybe not,
because He'll understand,
having made the weak as well as the strong.

I couldn't face thirty-forty more years of drowning
in debt, dirt, and disdain,
unable to live up to my Dad,
who's so terrific, so perfectly himself,
who never screws up, never makes a mistake.

Wanted to be near Mom in death but of course the Catholic Church
won't let me into sanctified ground;
that's only for those who never despair.

They say despair's the worst of the mortal sins; I think that's not so:
The Lord knows that despair is as common as love,
and that failure's more usual than success.
What sort of God would only love winners?

Left my sincerest apology for Sheila, but Dad will get to it first.
A father known for his good deeds on behalf of neighbors, even strangers,
but when it came to his only son,
'Throw the kid in the swimming hole, let him sink or swim.'
I sank, over and over again.

Never smart enough to figure out how to get away.
The insurance'll help my wife and kids.
My dying's not Sheila's fault.
I hope she'll find a better man.
one that'll raise my kids right and gentle,
and do it someplace else.

Questions That Have No Answers

(Starker Stucnowicz)

Two weeks. I'm now back at the transfer station. After we close for the day I go to the firehouse and just sit. They know enough to let me be. Drink beer and watch TV quietly until it's time I went on home to bed. Hasn't been a call on our watch while I'm there, thank the Lord; don't know anyhow if I'm ready to go out with the truck.

I can't get shut of Chad's killing himself, him saying he couldn't take the pressures, that he was worth more dead than alive, and that he hoped his wife and his Dad and his long-dead Mom would understand. I don't understand! Probably never will. All these questions—how a young man like that, with a sweet wife and adorable kids, could do this? So what if he'd lost his job—I didn't raise him to give up that easy, did I?

He'd been planning this, for sure. Kept up the life insurance payments even after he fell way behind on the mortgages. Now Sheila's selling the house and moving herself and the kids permanent to Florida.

Can't shake the feeling he killed himself to get back at me for being an overbearing, in-your-face s.o.b. of a father even though I was tough because that's what was needed in that situation, as it is in most. Is that enough to kill yourself over? If Chad wanted me to feel hurt, he's done it! I'll stay wounded for the rest of my life—which might not be that long, according to the VA docs. That cancer thing in the lungs they saw on the X-rays and gave me meds for. All those cigarettes I smoked. No reason to stop now!

If I'd told Chad about my having only a year or so to live, would he have hung on? For the satisfaction of dancing on my grave? I got insurance, too. Would've gone to him. Don't know and will never know how much of his killing himself is on me. Or on Sheila. Or on his mother's dying when he was 18. Or on the town's not being able to put him on the payroll after overspending for the new firehouse.

Maybe I'll drive down to Florida to visit the grandkids. And tell them what? That their Daddy really did love them but skipped out anyway? How will they live with that? Maybe, Lord willing, they'll forget and even forgive.

All my life I've known what to do. Not now. Confused. I hate that, but it's where I'm at right now.

Don't understand neither these people coming to the transfer station to see me, people I only half-know, women especially, just to give me a hug—like that Rose woman, used to be married to Doc Rusty. Tall, skinny thing. I let her put her arms 'round me and nodded a 'thank you' at her condolences and took the plum cake she brought. My fridge's already full of bakings and dinners, and I don't hardly know what to do with them because I can't really eat now.

Nobody knows what to do for people like me, left behind by suicide.

St. Catherine's isn't open every day like it used to be—the diocese cut back on Father Gregory's time with us, him having to shuttle between us and two other parishes—but I look after the place like a janitor, so's I have a key, and each day before coming to work I go in, just me there in the church, nobody else there but Christ up on His cross.

Lord Jesus, you died for our sins. Did Chad die for mine?

I pray for Our Heavenly Father's guidance .

Don't get answers to my questions, but I'm keeping on praying, anyway. What else can you possibly do?

From The Thinnest of Connections

(thoughts of Beth Galter)

Out of the blue, Harv got a new job! At The Chancellery. From the thinnest of connections, that young Army vet, Vinny Djere, who worked with him on the Valodia cleanup. We knew that Vinny was in the Chancellery grounds and maintenance department and that his Uncle Angelo was in it, but didn't know Angelo had any clout there. Angelo also served overseas, like my Harv—who was in Vietnam in '74, though he never talks about that. Anyway, when a graybeard on the Chancellery maintenance team took early retirement and left before the end of the school term, there was an opening, Vinny got Harv in there and he aced the interview with Angelo like we all knew he would. Harv is perfect for The Chancellery to be in charge of buying supplies for maintenance and repairs—window replacements, that sort of stuff—and as liaison to small contractors. Having been an indie GC himself, and for the past ten years at VH in charge of buying supplies, he's just what The Chancellery needs. Salary's below what he had before, but the benefits are better and there's room to advance.

One question is, can Harv stop The Chancellery buying supplies from Valley Hardware, and even should he, seeing that if he does it might be bad for his former fellow workers? Harv'll figure out a compromise; he's good at that.

I'm so proud of him and so relieved for him. He's not yet ready to accept that he'll be far better off at the Chancellery than he ever was at VH, able to stay employed simply by doing his job well, which he has always done and which he loves to do. But I point out to him that he won't have to worry about kissing the asses of Danny Romano and Ina Mornay, which I still have to do, because either one of them, Danny or Ina, could fire me at any moment for any reason at all, or without providing a reason. That's their privilege under Massachusetts state law, it turns out. Harv and me are definitely going to church this Sunday. We have a lot to be thankful for, and a lot of protecting to pray for.

Coping with the Unforeseeable

(thoughts of Veronica Parkford)

Lionel and I had always assumed he would be the one to deteriorate and I'd be the one seeing to his care—after all, he's 64 now, and I'm 49. And for years I worked hard at keeping myself healthy and in shape, doing huge amounts of fitness stuff—personal trainer, daily swims, proper diet, everything! Back when I modeled I was actually too thin, but since last being on a runway, ten years ago, I haven't put on more than ten pounds.

My fitness didn't help me much when push came to shove. According to my New York cardiologist, my "arrhythmic event" in the Bahamas was virtually unpredictable. Nor could anyone have foreseen that it would cause me to faint aboard our *Very Veronica* off Freeport, and as I collapsed to break my left hip. In the Freeport hospital, where they replaced the hip, they told me that the cardiac "event" had not been too bad, and that it had come with an upside, since it enabled the docs to identify the underlying heart weakness and to begin to treat it in time to prevent worse damage.

At least it wasn't my worst nightmare, a stroke that would make me lose control of half my body.

My cardiologist wants to put in a pacemaker. Good God! I'd never again be able to wear a two-piece bathing suit! So, I've postponed getting a pacemaker to first try to control this heart thing through meds and exercise. Not stinting on the painkillers, though, since exercising the new hip comes with plenty of pain!

I used to pride myself that I was able to have everything I set my sights on, ample wealth to buy whatever I felt like and go wherever I wanted to, continuing good looks as I aged, a well-mannered second husband, successfully-launched children, social status, a yacht named for me, a home in the country with horses, similarly-positioned friends, a young lover.... Well, the fact now is, I can no longer have *all* of these; my future expectations must be more dove-tailed with reality. It's time for a few adjustments.

After consulting with the docs, Lionel persuaded me to do my rehab at Signet Oaks rather than in Manhattan, since the countryside is more restful and I have more room for myself—that main floor guest bedroom suite with the big bathroom that I just had renovated, and all the equipment that a personal physical therapist might want to use. And so far, the country has been great for my recuperation! Calm and quiet. Wonderful vistas from my windows. A nurse who comes in daily. The PT, three days a week; he's quite good and knows how to work well with women.

As important is that my illness has brought out the best in Lionel; he has been incredibly kind, anticipating my needs—devoted to them, really—sparing no expense, keeping me entertained, bringing in a jazz trio to cheer me up. He even quietly removed the oil portrait of me, done ten years ago, from our living room, so that visitors would not see it and compare my current appearance to that ideal; he has hung it, instead, in his office.

He is exceeding what I had any right to expect, and so I must reciprocate and am eager to do so. As a start, I'm giving up my young stud, the fitness instructor at the 59th Street gym. I suspect that Lionel either knew about that lover or presumed I had one in the city and didn't hassle me about it so that I'd have no grounds to chide him about his affair with one of my best friends. I know that he hasn't seen her lately, because since our return to Signet Oaks, Lionel hasn't spent a single day in the city. I'll leave a voicemail telling my stud to find another sugar mommy; he'll have little trouble doing so. I'd alert my city girlfriends that he's available, but they haven't bothered staying in touch during my time of difficulty…

Rehab will continue to be tough for me, including the part that nobody outside of me can teach, learning how to properly co-exist with my husband as we both age.

Actually, I'm grateful to have such a goal.

Pellets in the Barn

(thoughts of Polly Maldone)

Jonathan, my third grader, is in love. Not with a girl, so far as I know, but with the pair of snowy barn owls nesting in our barn. They've been there forever, I'd bet; the nest looks old enough to have hatched at least one of the nesting pair. The birds are eerily beautiful, snow-white in winter, with no visible ears or tufts like horned owls have, and with their head feathers as flat as a Marine's crew-cut and beaks so small you can hardly see them. On the floorboards beneath their nest, Jonathan found little black balls of stuff that he took into school for help in identifying them. His teacher, Miss Helen (the last name is unpronounceable by eight-year-olds), a Merriam housewife just returning to the workforce after her children became old enough to be in school six hours a day—hint, hint, to me—is more STEM[25] oriented than the former teacher Alice Morely, whose retirement everybody lamented. Jonathan learned from Miss Helen and from Internet sites that the balls are called pellets, and are what the owls disgorge after eating but before sending the food down into their stomachs—fur, hair, bones, that sort of thing. Then she advised Jonathan that he might be able to figure out exactly what the owls were eating based on a microscope-aided analysis of the pellets, and steered him to the class microscope—well, it was like a light had been turned on in my beautiful boy's head! It sent him to the barn daily, to observe (but not to touch!) and to write in his little notebook—he's pleading for a digital notepad for his birthday—what's happening in the nest as the eggs begin to hatch. There are four eggs, and Miss Helen cautions him that not all of the hatchlings will survive and grow up to be adults. Jonathan and his lab buddy Darius Melchior have gone deeper

25 Compiler's Note: STEM = Science, Technology, Engineering, and Mathematics. RBM.

into the science, learning that the barn owl's ears are "asymmetrical," meaning not in the same location on each side of the head, and that this contributes to the barn owl's fabulous ability to hear—best on the planet, he assures me—and track their prey through a covering of snow (our 27 inches is finally almost all melted).

Jonathan and Darius got an A+ on their report, which included their photographs of the nest and the birds, featuring the owlets—very dark and awkward-looking compared to their parents. Jon was very proud, and galvanized. Now he checks the calendar and the thermometer every day and is talking about how he and Darry plan to fish together when the trout season opens.

It's all delightful, and my daughter Cecily is enthused too. Her desire to catch up with her brother on this nature stuff is helping her in reading comprehension.

And then there are the buds shooting up around the periphery of the house and in the nearby field, identified for me—I'm an amateur at this—by our neighbor Grace Newington in her recent column, "Everybody Ought to Get a Spade," regarding which particular foliage emerges at what point in the spring—the crocuses and irises first, for instance—and about the urge to get out and plant or at least Do Something in the Garden. Grace told me privately what she didn't want to put in print, that there's a divide in the Cobble's newcomers between those who do their own gardening and those who hire others so as not to dirty their own hands. The former are more likely to become permanent residents and not re-sell their houses after a few years. She thinks I'm the willing-to-dig sort—a 'spade-in-hand' type. Even though I haven't done it much, I'm inclined to give it a try. Grace looks forward to the first time I am able to put cut flowers from my garden on my dining-room table, since doing so, she says, had been her inflection point.

Maybe we shouldn't put our house on the market just yet. I can't wait to see how Miss Helen will do with our Cecily next year. Plus, I'm hearing that Atlanta can get quite sweltering in the summer and I'm less comfortable with excess heat than I am with excess cold, because here at least I can come indoors to escape the cold. I'm going to ask Walt if we can buy a snow-blower for the driveway for next winter. Should be able to get a bargain on one, now that this winter's about over.

Conversation on a Doorstep

(Aimee Bishop, thoughts and dialogue)

On one of the first really warm days of April who should show up on my doorstep but Cullen Wilberson, that determined recluse, habitual stepper-on-toes, gleeful ne'er-do-well, and fortunate heir of a successful artist father. Cull is closing in on sixty-five, although he looks younger, tanned and leathery, not much the worse for wear than when we had a brief fling in my post-Ade doldrums—and he's dangling a pair of mid-sized speckled trout.

AIMEE BISHOP: Pour moi?

CULLEN WILBERSON: First of the season. Thought you'd like something fresh.

AB: Merci, Cullen. You shouldn't have…unless there's—I'm guessing, here—something that you want from me in return?

CW: We're grown-ups, we negotiate. May I come in?

AB: No; the place is a mess right now.

CW: I'm sure I've seen worse—at my abode!

AB: No comment.

CW: Well, you know, the cabin after a long winter—got to air it out…. How's the Dawson Property fight going?

AB: More of a struggle than I bargained for. The motorcycle-racing people and Ade Castelmara have a lot more resources than the Pequabogue Protectorate—but you know this, you're on our mailing list.

CW: I don't pick up my mail that often. But I do listen to "FM in the AM" all the time.

AB: Nice to know.

CW: I'd like to be a guest on-air with you again.

AB: Yes, but—and it has to be a 'yes but,' Cull, because I can't be seen or heard as too radical these days, when we're fighting a foe that's already shown they're willing to get nasty if we give them half a chance. And you *are* notorious for irking people even without an obvious reason, right?

CW: Guilty as charged.

AB: So none of this 'tear down the establishment stuff,' OK?

CW: What I want is to get a plug in for my kayak-training sessions. Whitewater season is upon us. I need to appeal to the 'kayak virgins' among us.

AB: Ha! Well, okay, we could have you tell a few wild-river stories—but Cullen, aren't you getting a bit long in the tooth for this? And surely with your inheritance, you don't need the money from it to—ahem—stay afloat?

CW: It was never about the money—for either of us, Aimee. Look, beautiful: in these kind of fights it behooves us to remember who we want to be, the sort of lives we wish to lead, the kind of town we want to be in. It's about following one's instincts, Aimee.

AB: That's not so simple for me to do anymore.

CW: I disagree. Why don't I just pan-fry these trout for us, and we can talk over strategy on the Dawson property? Ought to qualify as a refuge for the purple-blotched bog turtle. Splotchy fella's going on the feds' endangered-species list soon.

AB: How on earth do you know that?

CW: I'm an amateur chelenologist, you know—turtle-ologist.

AB: What you are is incorrigible.

CW: Working on it.

AB: Just dinner—no dessert.

CW: Wouldn't think of it.

THIRTEEN:
PROGRESS

Spring's Imperatives

(thoughts of Sam Newington)

These are the known imperatives of spring
for flora and fauna:
absorb sun, water, and nutrients;
prepare the young for solo flight;
consolidate the inner essence;
entertain grand goals
rather than elucidate them,
which, as all inherently sense,
is best left for high summer.

For a man entering his autumn,
spring is fit subject for study:
to emulate its assuredness,
sample its smorgasbord of potentials,
embrace its naïve enthusiasms,
so joyously dismissive
of quality, purity, and uniqueness.

For spring's greatest wonder
is not its hatchlings, cute or ugly,
nor its progression of flowers
from pastels to primaries,
but new growth on old trees:
from gnarled branches and thick trunks
seemingly incapable of innovation,
fresh leaves, primed for praise and glory.

Please post in a prominent place
spring's bullet-point directives:
Appreciate more.
Complain less.
End well what has begun less so.
Close some doors
and open others.

Selling the Farm

(thoughts of Kelly Murtaugh Lydner)

February is the toughest month of the year in Western Massachusetts, so after the Valodia games Corey and I escaped to Florida, confident that our employees, the Paredeses, could handle any problems that came up on the farm, and that if they needed to, they could reach us by phone at my parents' home.

Not a peep from them! We spent three glorious, uninterrupted weeks in Palm Harbor, on the Gulf Coast, with Mum and Pop Murtaugh, basking in the sun, fishing, walking on the beach—just lovely. No cares, no chores to do at every moment. Time to contemplate. So nice that we looked into buying a condo nearby. We would have stayed on in Florida but did not want to be away from the farm too long while trying to sell it. So in early March we came back. Wow! The contrast between the balminess of Palm Harbor and the frostiness of Jericho's Cobble gave us the shivers.

No doubt it also softened us up for an unexpected pitch from Angel and Jorge Paredes, as articulated in English for them by Father Gregory of Our Lady of Mercy in Merriam. Their offer is based on knowing us pretty well: an immediate down payment of $25,000, which they've saved from their wages over the past five years—I'm amazed they've been able to do so—and another $200,000 once they obtain a bank mortgage, which Our Lady of Mercy will help them get; and then to pay us an additional $250,000 over the next ten years, which would mean, in effect, our taking back a no-interest mortgage. The sweetener: We would be able to remain in our house for six months of the year and to spend the other six months, including the long winter, in Florida.

Corey had hoped to get a million dollars for the property. The prospect of only half of that occasioned a real disagreement between us. I was all for it, but he was unwilling to even consider the Paredeses' deal until we found out whether Ina Mornay would actually offer us a million—in village sidewalk conversations she had often said that our property was certainly worth that. So we had a real estate agent advise Ina that we had an offer on the farm, but that if she would go the whole $1 million, we would likely take that.

She said yes immediately and was ready to put down a binder, with the provisos that she might replace the farmhouse with one more to her tastes, and could not guarantee to maintain all of the acreage in agricultural use.

I was reluctant to accept Ina's offer because I want the farm to continue as a farm, and don't want to shaft the Paredeses, who have been so helpful in keeping it alive. So I asked the agent to ascertain from Ina whether she had in her employ any seasoned farm managers. She did not and was willing to consider hiring ours. Which allowed a complex set of negotiations to begin involving us, the realtor, Ina, Father Gregory, and the Paredeses.

Long story short, we worked out an unusual deal that comes close to satisfying all the parties and that definitely saves my marriage. Ina will buy outright 65 of our 80 acres and most of our farm stock, for $750,000. The remaining acres and livestock will be bought by the Paredeses for $150,000, through a combination of mortgages, and the Paredeses will thereafter be employed by Ina as farm managers and have the right to graze their animals on all the acreage of the farms that's in pasture. And vice-versa for Ina's animals.

I'm okay with this arrangement, though chagrined at the permanent loss of the farm and my former way of life. Not sure what I'll do with my leisure time. But the arrangement is good for my husband, who was really overworked, and the money will enable us to buy outright a condo near my parents in Florida and still have some dough left over to live on.

Ina gets quite a lot for her money—the big estate she always wanted, and a place for her dream house. The Paredeses get to own a small farm and to increase its value through use of adjoining acreage. The Cobble will benefit from not losing another farm to McMansions. All positives. Our children, though, won't be able to benefit from the sale of their parents' family farm, at least not right away, because we'll be using the money to buy a condo and to live on. But that can't be helped.

Tag-Teaming the Stuffed Shirts

(thoughts of Gertrude M. Beresford)

Mary-Beth and I tag-teamed at a bevy of meetings this week. We met, in turn, with the Selectmen, then with the JCCA, and then with the admin at The Chancellery. Stuffed shirts, all of them, very taken with their own importance and wisdom! Which we praised lavishly.

Massachusetts laws forbid any town's Selectmen from meeting together except in public, so we met with them one by one. I was more insistent on that than M-B—I've more milage on my tires and more experience with officials' public bluster. We presented to each Selectman the letter from Louisa Ralston Stafford of San Francisco, a great-great-granddaughter of Bucko and Selwyn Whitbred, a letter written in response to our inquiry to her about the long-lost *The Red Lasses* painting, by Ammi Phillips, of Selwyn, Anna, and Lisa. Mrs. Stafford let us know that the painting did survive the San Francisco earthquake—yay!—and sent along a photo. That clinched our belief that *The Red Lasses* is indeed the counterpart of *The Green Lads* portrait of Bucko, Junior, and Chum at The Chancellery.

And here's the beauty part, we told the Selectmen: we had alerted Mrs. Stafford of the controversy regarding a proposed renaming of the Whitbred Elementary and the supposed reason for dumping the Whitbred name—their alleged usurpation of native land, and later, slavery—which historian Richard Bond Miller has refuted in *The Country Caller* and elsewhere; in response, Mrs. Stafford is proposing to permanently loan *The Red Lasses* to Jericho's Cobble, if and only if the town will bind itself to maintaining the Whitbred name on the elementary school.

Open-handed bribery is the best, isn't it? The Selectmen

agreed that the Whitbred name ought to be kept on and will so inform the school board. There's no guarantee, of course, that that board will agree, but seeing as in the past they've asked the Selectmen's opinion on the subject, the board should. Fingers crossed.

Then we were on to the JCCA exec committee meeting, to present our case for the Civic Association's keeping open the Birdsong House as a museum for at least another fiscal year beyond the coming July 1st. We anticipated the fulminations of Geoffrey Collier, my would-be lothario, the outgoing JCCA treasurer, who was indeed still foaming at the mouth over the cost of upkeep, $36,000 a year including M-B's salary. Fortunately, Sam Newington is scheduled to soon replace Geoff as treasurer-trustee.

M-B opened with the tidbit that paid attendance at the Birdsong House has been on the rise, and ought to continue to do so as the House becomes a "feminist destination."

Why would it become such a destination?

Oh, Mr. Collier, thank you so much for asking!

Now M-B let out the zinger about the romantic relationship between spinster poetess Eleanor Birdsong and Mrs. Selwyn Whitbred—yes, she of *The Red Lasses* painting, mother of four and wife of the wealthiest man in town!—a lesbian pairing that began in 1863 and lasted for thirteen-plus years! As documented by the love notes that M-B and I found in Eleanor's desk, and as augmented by M-B's research in archives in Boston and New York in pursuit of her doctorate! M-B showed them a preliminary draft of her scholarly paper, which is a condensed version of the doctoral thesis, a paper scheduled for publication at year's end and that is already getting buzz on the Internet as it circulates for peer review.

While the JCCA trustees were reeling, I hit them with the numbers, that the JCCA endowment, now hovering between $2.5 and $3 million, is blossoming due to the post-9/11 recovery in the stock markets—and therefore that the $36K tab for the Birdsong House upkeep, offset partially by admissions fees and other House income, was a modest fraction of the annual JCCA operating budget, and was more valuable than the outlay in terms of positive publicity for the Civic Association and the town of Jericho's Cobble.

Our plan: to have the Birdsong House remain open as a museum, with M-B as live-in paid executive director while she commutes to UMass/Amherst to complete her doctorate. We'll rewrite the House visitor-welcoming speech to reflect the new information about Eleanor and Selwyn and will set goals for the House's earned income and for a forthcoming conference on "American feminist life, love, and literature in the mid-19th century."

The counterpart of the open bribe is the unspoken threat. Gotta love that, too.

Left unvoiced by us to the JCCA exec board was that our proposal was an ultimatum, accompanied by the obvious but not uttered-aloud threat of what we might do should the board say 'no' to the plan: publicize the information about the "Birdsong-Whitbred dyad," as M-B's boyfriend Benny calls it, and in doing so embarrass the heck out of the JCCA for shutting the Museum to avoid the taint of a very old and very minor scandal.

The JCCA exec committee should readily understand that it will be better and easier for them to get out in front of this information, and to celebrate the deep though untraditional affair of Eleanor and Selwyn, than for the trustees to look like old cobwebbed fools for attempting to hide it.

As we wait to learn what sort of stuffing is in their shirts, I almost hope they'll say 'no' to us and to the plan, so we can make them regret that decision.

Our third meeting was a breeze. It was with the vice-administrator for The Chancellery, and we were ushered into the inner sanctum with a wink by Louise Gutkind, my occasional bridge partner. M-B spoke of the imminent return of *The Red Lasses* painting and asked if The Chancellery would agree to loaning *The Green Lads* to the town, to display at Town Hall alongside its counterpart. He said he would have to check the idea with his superiors, but he thought it a very good one, and that The Chancellery looked forward to the opportunity to work more with the town.

Don't know if we'll pull off this triple play, but I am so grateful to have been summoned to this good fight.

Foursome on the Fairways

(thoughts of Chelsea Colver)

Quite the foursome, convened for a 10:45 a.m. weekday tee-time at The Merriam Country Club's golf course: Martha Posner, Ina Mornay, Lene Mulroney, and little old recent-widow me. They are frequent golfers; I'm not. Martha invited me, ostensibly to help me back into circulation after William's death, a month ago. Marc was a superb friend to William in his last years, and through the guys' connection, Martha and I have come a bit closer.

Ina and Lene ask in a solicitous way about life without William. I confess to still missing him but to also feeling content at having done all I could to help him through his final months. By the end, he and I were closer than we had ever been. And he bequeathed me and our daughter a quite comfortable estate.

Fortunately my mental health is not the main agenda for this outing. Rather, it is the planned renovation and expansion of Eastlund Library, which Martha is championing—she will shortly become president of that board. She and Marc are both pushing on the charitable-civic front, her with the library and him by acceding to William's vision and putting half of his 160 acres into a nature trust to prevent their future development. I applaud Marc's willingness to do so, but as for Martha's project, am not convinced that the library needs expansion, although the 75-year-old building surely deserves a renovation.

What Martha wants from us golfers is to commit $25,000 apiece to the project, which she has already done. It is immediately clear to me that I'll need to ante up if I want to play in this town on this level—which I think I'd like to do. Using my money to make the Cobble a better place for people to live and learn, rather than spending it on a more lavish lifestyle is a goal I never entertained before. But it feels right.

I sign on, and Lene Mulroney agrees to, as well.

What Martha asks from Ina, though, is more than the $25,000. It is for Ina to chair the board of the project and, commensurate with doing so, to make the sort of leading gift expected of such chairs.

This, I believe, would be the first time in this town that Ina takes on a public leading role in anything. She is regularly hit up for money, and has responded well, but has not previously been solicited to take a position of authority. She does not immediately answer Martha, just smacks another drive down the fairway; and then, when we're in the midst of that fairway, our balls not far from one another, Ina outlines a deal: she will take on the project and commit to a big seed-money gift if the board is limited to us four.

Martha does not instantly agree, and I wonder why. Then, while Lene and I are moving our carts together along the next fairway, Lene gives me to understand that Ina's most likely reason for the condition is to exclude Veronica Parkford from joining that board, likely because, as is well known, Ronnie did not invite Ina to last fall's foxhunt at the Parkford estate.

On the putting green the matter is settled. Since it would be petulant of Martha to turn down an Ina pledge of $75,000 plus having Ina's presumably aggressive chairing of the fundraising committee, Martha says yes. We applaud.

Clearly this is how big things get done in this town. And it's not such a bad deal, right? That this agreement will effectively blackball Martha's neighbor Ronnie Parkford from being on a board that the recovering Ronnie would doubtless like to be associated with is a pill that will just have to be swallowed. No doubt Ina and Martha will try to get a hefty pledge from Ronnie and Lionel anyway.

I regret only not being able to tell William about this moneyed nonsense. He would've gotten a kick and a laugh out of it.

Skipping the Weekly Breakfast

(thoughts of Chuck Mulroney)

Eight on a Sunday morning, I'm driving over to Peyton's Corners for a meeting —and for the first time in quite a while, skipping Mass because I really must be across state at a meeting of my group of stores that I've convened—it has to be at this hour because later in the morning the proprietors will have to be at their stores, tending to the full Sunday traffic. I regret that missing Mass will further distance me from my family, but I've learned that few of life's big choices can be made without there being a downside.

I'm taking my store-owners to IHOP for a frank discussion of shared problems and to introduce a new campaign.

The first-quarter '04 results, which I've culled from the data that the nine have individually reported to me, show an average 5 per cent year-over-year above inflation jump in sales, which I can partly attribute to my instituting the cooperative-marketing ad plan that they initially resisted but that has brought results and also got me kudos up the ladder at Kinshauzer Malls. To build on the momentum, I'll propose a new push centering on a trend in the wider world: in-store pick-up of items ordered online. Customers agreeing to pick up merchandise are already avoiding shipping-and-handling costs, and we can sweeten that with discounts for on-site purchases made at time of pick-up. Such discounts should more than pay for themselves, because as is known from surveys and in-store robo-camera feeds, when customers come in to collect already-bought items, they are likely to linger and buy on impulse.

A year ago, at Small Luxuries, if I'd had a similar big idea, I probably wouldn't have brought it up, not having enough confidence to believe I could sell it well enough.

Leaving Small Luxuries was very tough for me, but I must admit that it has been liberating. Would I have gotten myself into athletic shape and won the Valodia biathlon in my age group had I stayed in the family firm and in my rut? I doubt it. Would I have thought harder about how to innovate in the business had I continued on? Or been rewarded for innovation? I don't know. We Mulroneys had always been a close-knit family, and that closeness sustained me for many years. I've now lost that daily intimacy with my parents and siblings, and its absence is painful. Yet the positive things that have happened to me in the months since the breach has shown me the truth of the old adage, what props you up is often what also holds you down.

Today, at my meeting with nine store owners, my overarching task is to convince them that in today's world what affects one small retailer in a defined geographical area affects all nearby ones, and therefore that we must all work more so as to keep abreast of the rapid changes in retail and to share helpful ideas that will keep us all profitable, such as the in-store pickup discounts...and the monthly breakfast itself.

Pretty sure they'll go for the whole package.

The Demands of a Country Pulpit

From: Rev. Vernon Trainor (MDiv.)
To: Dr. Glenda Trainor

Glennie—check out the below, a terrif oral history intvu w/1 of my predecessors, Aaron Loden, done in 1983. Provides a good way to look at issues we've been chewing over.

Vern

GERTRUDE MERKIN BERESFORD: Now Aaron, we spoke before about your brother George, but not enough about yourself! You were Congo's longest-serving minister, from the year I was born, 1930, until you retired in 1974.

AARON LODEN: Just shy of 45 years, yes. I was twenty-six when I replaced my father as minister at Jericho's Cobble's First Congregational Church.

GMB: It must have been difficult, succeeding your father, and shortly after that, having to deal with the Depression years.

AL: Replacing a previous, well-revered minister was not so difficult, Gertie, because everyone in the Cobble expected less of me and so cut me some slack! As for the Depression years: granted that the Thirties were terrible times for the U.S., but for us here they were a little less so because we could grow our own food. From the pulpit I only cautiously spoke of hope, because realism and championing the various ways to make do were what was needed, much more so than some vague promise that everything would be okay.

The Second World War? The same, from a country minister's point of view. So I have to conclude that the harder the times for the community, the more straightforward the pastor's task. That's why I also contend that for me, from the 1960s on, the pulpit was much more demanding than ever.

GMB: In what ways?

AL: More complexity. Having to deal with many more possibilities of spirituality, temptations, experiences. Stimulations. Drugs. LSD. Rock 'n Roll. Free love. Rebellions of all sizes, shapes, and kinds. The rising number of infidelities, divorces, communal arrangements, sexual orientations. God tests our faith in many ways.

GMB: The new tugs and pulls made me feel young in those years. I loved them. But I hardly remember going to church during that era.

AL: It wasn't only you—attendance was way down. Contributions, too. Nobody wanted to celebrate the past.

GMB: How did Congo survive? How did you?

AL: Well, the church survived because it adapted. And so did I. I learned that there are many ways to take the Word to the people rather than wait for the people to come to the church. The more complicated the world is, the less obvious the country minister's task. So you adapt. You search for what you can help with, rather than what you can't ameliorate.

GMB: Twenty years on, you retired early because Peter Hickle became available to replace you?

AL: Precisely! And my wife and I wanted to see the world a bit before we got too old.

GMB: And perhaps you'd had enough of the simple country life by then, as I had in those years? My parents had passed, and I was in my glory on my own.

AL: Yes; but you came back to the Cobble, and so did we. My guess? You, like us, had seen as much of the wider world as we needed to.

GB: Did you find, once back here, that things had changed?

AL: Yes and no. 'Yes' in many surface ways: new telephones and faster cars, fewer small businesses, more weekenders. But also 'no,' because there were no major changes in the slow and steady Cobble way of life. In some ways, Gertie, the Cobble is the most forgiving of surrounds; that's readily visible and audible in the coffee shop, the post office, the drugstore, Congo's community hall after the service on Sunday mornings—even in the poker game over at Moorehead.

GB: Any other thoughts on being the minister in a country setting?

AL: One needs to be aware of being the latest in a long line of Congo shepherds, dating back 200-plus years. I read extensively in the files of my predecessors' struggles, their attempts to deal with crises—the Civil War, in which so many of the area's young men died; and in the early part of the twentieth century, the supposedly 'good-old' days. The files showed me that even the most independent-minded people are always in need of spiritual counsel. Problems today are less about how to meet basic life-needs than they were in the past, and more about lifestyle choices, but the overarching task of shepherd and flock alike is still about making peace with what's around you, with meeting your obligations to your neighbors and your world and your God.

Another Fine Mess

(thoughts of Beetle Oostendyck)

"Another fine mess you've gotten me into!" That's what Ollie Hardy used to say to Stan Laurel when they landed in a terrific jam that they'd have a hard time getting out of. I loved those 'Laurel and Hardy' films. And that line. But what happened today is not a fine mess, it's a bloody and awful mess.

At our family Easter dinner, held this year at my eldest sister Aleida's on Dugout Road, in the home I gave to her, there was an altercation in the kitchen that ended in an accident and a knife stuck in Allie's arm. The arm bled terribly and all over the floor before the EMS crew got there and properly tied it off and took Allie to the ER. Greitje—Gree—cried so terribly that she almost ended up in the hospital too.

Now I'm in the hospital's waiting room with Allie's husband and her son, my nephew, while the docs sew up his mother's arm. We're hoping she hasn't lost too much blood, and that in a month or so she'll regain full function in the arm.

Were my sisters drunk? We all were, except the children, and I'm not too sure about the older kids—wouldn't be the first time in my family that a juvenile managed to sneak a snoot-full at a holiday dinner. I'd certainly had plenty to drink, relaxing with the only family I'll ever have: three sisters, two brothers-in-law, five nieces and nephews, and my last surviving aunt, our dead mother's sister.

And of course, money is at the root of the problem. My money. I gave Allie and her shiftless husband one of the houses in the Valley that I own because they really needed it. But Allie getting a house from me, free and clear, bummed out Gree, who moved to South Carolina years ago with her husband, and who I only gave $20,000 to, plus more to help their kids finish college. Did the same with all the sisters' kids, though some of them haven't always been nice to Uncle Beetle. Twine—my youngest sister, Toine—didn't complain, but then she seldom does, a very sweet woman, now a single mom and dreading the future moment when her kids stop living at home and abandon her to loneliness.

For thirty years we Oostendycks have mostly had these family Easters without this level of uproar. I won't say there were never flare-ups, but none this bad, certainly not for the last twenty-five years since my sisters stopped competing with each other for the same men. For a long time my money wasn't really a problem for the family because they knew that I lived very modestly and that my assets were mostly tied up, not liquid. Any money I gave to them, back then, I did so one by one and swore each to silence, which they mostly kept to. But my deeding Allie a house could hardly remain private. Now Gree's upset that I didn't do the same for her; but I don't own property in South Carolina, where she lives, or in New Jersey, where Twine's at.

Benevolence ain't easy, I'm finding.

Which makes me realize that in order to get this mess resolved I'm going to have to do what I should have done years ago, pay off the mortgages for Gree and Twine, which will enable them to stretch their own money further each month. And I'm going to have to set up an actual family scholarship fund for the nieces and nephews.

To underwrite all that I'll need to sell two more Cobble-area properties. There'll be less for me to donate to organizations like MFA and FIND, but family's first.

"100th Anniversary of Country Caller Celebrated"

BY FELICITY RINGELL

***The Country Caller*, ISSUE OF MAY 6, 2004**

To mark the 100th anniversary of *The Country Caller* and the opening of a retrospective exhibit on the newspaper's history, a party was held on Saturday, May 1st at the Jericho's Cobble Civic Association's headquarters on Main Street.

The weekly was begun in 1904 by Marlon Fitzhugh and his family. The display cases feature such milestones as Fitzhugh's interview of a retired Bucko Whitbred stablehand in that year; the paper's 1913 coverage of the fiftieth anniversary celebration of the Battle of Gettysburg; the 'Triple-O tart war' between the Inns of 1928; the lone triumph of the Stillwater Mountaineers in the Division II state football championships in 1939; the devasting flood of 1955; the countrywide recognition of artist Oregon Wilberson in the 1960s; the ownership-editorship of Malcolm Duhamel that began in 1969—Duke Duhamel and his "duchess," Marla, were at the reception—and the burning-down of the old town hall in 1981, among other panels chronicling the technical changes in printing technology, the use of color photographs, and plans for an online edition. The weekly is currently in the process of changing to a non-profit supported by donations.

Benign weather allowed the crowd to spill over from the interior of the JCCA building to its grounds outside, where a bar was located.

Publisher Pat Tolland estimated attendance through the evening at a couple of hundred people, most of them subscribers to the paper. Tolland will be relinquishing his post as publisher as soon as the board, led by former television newsman Merl Forstmann, identifies a successor with appropriate experience in the non-profit sector.

Editor April Lasko, who like Tolland is proud to have begun her journalism career at the *Caller* as a reporter under Duhamel before going to Boston and rising in the ranks at *The Boston Clarion*, was pleased to see so many weekenders as well as full-time residents at the event, mingling with the reportorial staff and the paper's columnists, who included gardening writer Grace Newington, entertainment editor Aimee Bishop, dance critic Chelsea Colver, and frequent guest editorialists Rose Serkin of the VNA, currently the Democratic candidate for the 162nd state district, and Martha Posner, incoming president of the Eastlund Library.

The exhibit at JCCA will remain open through the July Fourth weekend.

In September, Forstmann plans to host an invitation-only event for donors to The Country Caller Foundation, for which he hopes that one or more of his senior colleagues in television news, such as Peter Jennings, Tom Brokaw, or Dan Rather, will attend as special honoree.

Do I Dare?

(diary entry, Alice Hadley Morely, May 10, 2004)

My Mediterranean cruise w/Baz was great, even tho I mostly paid 4 the 2 of us since he was short of $. Basily Mikulski is better than me @ chatting w/strangers & new acquaintances/ other ppl on R cruise. He was also quite complimentary 2 me, @ how I encourage everybody 2 learn + enjoy.

By mid-voyage, I deemed us 2 B in love—as we did whisper 2 ea. other in bed (when quite drunk). Were we 22 & similarly inclined—even 44!—I said to him, I'd follow U anywhere, just so we 2 could B together. But as he pointed out, we're both 66-plus & well-rooted, me in the Cobble & him in Milwaukee's South Side. We must B thankful 4 mutual attraction + enjoyment of ea. other's company, but also B very aware @ ea. of us needing NOT 2 overthrow life routines & homey-homes & strong senses of B-longing 2 communities; & so we agreed NOT 2 move in 2gether, much less 2 think @ getting married, at least not now. I 'spoze we could both someday leave where we R & jointly begin anew in a 3rd loc., but neither of us has suggested that.

T. S. Eliot's aging J. Alfred Prufrock asks, over and over, "Do I dare?" Baz Mikulski, reciting that poem 2 me on board, opined that we must dare if we R 2 make the most out of R elderhood. "We're 2 old not 2 take risks," I quipped back to him that evening, as we gazed out @ that glorious sea in moonlight.

Since returning to the Cobble I haven't heard from Baz, & I'm beginning 2 question whether he really felt 4 me as

I felt 4 him. Was I literally taken 4 a ride? Don't know; but I'm not bitter, maybe because I really agree that at my age it is indeed important to take risks. Which means occasionally failing, or—in this instance—my possibly having been conned.

So 2day, on this bright/warm morning, I decided on a different risk, 2 do something I'd never done, 2 stray from my fixed walking route 2 go down 2 the river, & amble along the Pequabogue's northern bank while it is swollen & rushing w/snowmelt—w/what they call a freshet, an annual spring phenomenon. In 1 hr. of being very still/observant, I saw 6 adult deer + 2 adorable fauns, squirrels w/o #, a couple hawks & rabbits, & 1 raccoon, all interested in the racing/raging waters or in what's swimming thru them. And again I felt, as I did when I beheld Skanaska's moose, that these creatures R somehow connected 2 long-dead local ppl.

Just a passing thought!

In low-lying areas I spotted clumps of flowers I'd only previously seen in garden books: saxifrage, the stone-breaker plant, w/its burst of ground-hugging off-whites and pinks; & the shad-bush, its squatting little branches w/their similar off-whites & a few already-intense purple berries. How could I have never B4 seen these in situ? I definitely need 2 explore more. Maybe I could induce these 2 grow in the lower-lying area of my ½-acre. I bent 2 gather samples, stuffing them, roots and all, into a pocket of my parka. By then I was @ the edge of the turbulent stream... & I slipped and fell into the waters! Panicked for a moment, and feared I was in danger of drowning... but soon stood up. Wasn't really imperiled, b/c the stream @ that point was only 2 ft. deep—but wow! was I ever chilled! Lucky to be able 2 get home w/o freezing 2 death. Ached & sneezed & let out a few cuss words along the way.

Then I realized that this was just like my adventure w/Baz: It hurt, but I wouldn't have missed it 4 the world.

Outcomes Toasted

(thoughts of Liliane Griswold)

Today's meet-up of the Gang of Six at the Griff is to welcome back former-farmer Kelly Murtaugh Lydner from her several-months stay in her and Corey's new Florida condo, and for us all to debrief on what's happened regarding the awfulness at The Chancellery.

According to Louise Gutwind, the prep school's board, going all out to avoid civil suits on the Garuzelski accusations, has authorized payoffs to victims but has rejected the idea of forcing them to sign NDAs in exchange for the payoffs, so as not to hamper them should they choose to testify against Garuzelski. They have also referred the former athletic director to the state authorities for prosecution despite his threat to incriminate the school if put on trial. These are good, tough actions on the part of The Chancellery, and we toast them with our colas and iced teas.

Jane Milch reports that choirmaster Vic Leighton and the Congo church have come to an understanding about the old allegation in the prep school's report. Should there be any mention of it in *The Country Caller* or elsewhere, Reverend Vern will put out a statement saying the church has every confidence in its music director, and hopes that Vic will stay on for as long as he can, given his age and the advancing medical condition of Mrs. Leighton; then, in the fall, or whenever the storm has blown over enough, Vic will retire to take care of Muriel, and a new music director will be hired. However, Vic will still be allowed to use the church's pipe organ whenever he feels the need. We toasted that arrangement, too.

Other stuff. Louise's guests, the Gabianco mother and children, have now moved into a new apartment and John-O is back with them and sober; the kids are still referring to Louise as Gramma Lulu, adopting her like she's adopting them. And Stacy Borska announced that she's going to be working as a volunteer with Rose Serkin's campaign for state rep. Last, I reported that the rumors going around about my Eddie were true, that he's decided to retire from his job as a state septic-fields inspector. Barkeep, another round!

FOURTEEN: COUNTRY OF THE SECOND CHANCES

Interlude on the Nature Path

(Sam and Grace Newington)

SAM: Let's rest on this bench here for a spell. Last night was really a perfect Manhattan night, wasn't it? Concert at Lincoln Center, followed by a late light meal at a new bistro, with friends from the concert—fine food, fine wine, fine conversation about the music, the children, the state of the world—then an easy taxi ride back to the apartment.

GRACE: Quite restorative for you after your bad days in returning to the office.

SAM: It's taking me a lot longer than I'd hoped to get fully up to speed at work.

GRACE: And you're not entirely sure that getting up to speed is worth doing.

SAM: Did I say that?

GRACE: You've been implying that your enthusiasm for that office is waning—

SAM: Well, that's so.

GRACE: —while your attachment to Jericho's Cobble is waxing. As is mine.

SAM: Who would not want to be here when the earth is greening up so beautifully? It's just wonderful! But "the country" is where ambition goes to die.

GRACE: Maybe it's time for ambition to be left to others, Sam. Mine as well as yours.

SAM: Don't know if I'm capable of giving it up.

GRACE: Put it another way: It's time to re-assess ambition. What is its aim? To accomplish things? To become rich? To win?

SAM: Those are pretty good aims—they'll do.

GRACE: The city is where things are accomplished; the country is where life is lived.

SAM: Not entirely. Culture thrives in the city. Museums, concerts, libraries, galleries, Broadway shows, scads of interesting restaurants and shops—the stuff we like. Out here, they're few and far between.

GRACE: Okay, so let us grant that the city is the locus of, the fountainhead of, the treasure chest of, the divertissements that we love. On the other hand, in the Cobble, as we are coming to understand, accessibility to nature and warm personal interactions with neighbors are as beneficial to us as, or possibly even more than, sophisticated culture is.

SAM: Okay...

GRACE: Do you hear those birds? I think they're blue jays. The cardinals make a different trill. Definitely not woodpeckers.

SAM: All part of the symphony?

GRACE: Well, you're the one who's been writing poems.

SAM: Because my restless mind needs an outlet and I couldn't do my regular work. Years ago, I put aside such childish urges because of the imperative to make a living.

GRACE: And to amass money for a good life. Now you have! You could say, "Been there, done that!" We've gotten past the major expenses: college tuitions, caring for aged parents...

SAM: To move up here permanently would mean quitting the stock brokerage—a huge loss of income for us.

GRACE: Yes, but selling the apartment, which we'd also do, would produce money we could use to erase our mortgages. You could do some trading from here, be freelance too, like me. If we're not profligate, we'll get by, here. And within five years you'll also be receiving a monthly Social Security check.

SAM: You're implying that resolving the matters of where to live, and in what manner, and what to do with our time, depends on our deciding how much is enough?

GRACE: Amen.

SAM: I don't know about that. We who have adequate education, money, and expertise need to do something with those gifts. Part of our obligation to the world.

GRACE: And you have done! But going forward, what are your obligations to yourself? At sixty? After almost being killed?

SAM: That's what I'm still trying to figure out.

(They resume walking.)

Bench in a Shaded Niche

Many, many humans daily walk, jog, bike, or ski past me,
and most days some stop to sit and rest on me. I'm a wooden
bench over iron hoops and a concrete base, set back a bit from
the Cobble's main nature trail, and always in the shade. Every
few years, they replace this part or that part of me eaten
by ice, moss, or insects, and I am like new again. Man-made,
I am also of the forest and enjoy partaking of both
and being a bridge between. Unlike the trees, or the deer
that now and then gaze at me with big eyes, or the bugs that crawl
on me ceaselessly, or the birds that take a temporary perch on me,
I am aware of what humans really need: rest, shade, time to gaze
about and above without watching where they have come from
or are going to, space and sunlight and air in which to ponder,
to look up at the trees and clouds, to look across at the marsh
as the breeze ruffles it, to follow the glide of the purple
martin to its nest; to listen to the soughing of the trees and the
murmur of the lower-lying plants, to smell the air. I provide all that.
And more: for whomsoever among humans rests upon me for a while,
when they rise to return to more civilized paths they take something
of my spirit with them. If they do not sit, if they always pass me by,
they never gain that benefit; but those who do spend time with me
take a bit of my peace with them.

Lobsters at the Lodge

(thoughts of Andy Borska)

It's the first lobster sale of the season for the Turners Lodge, and the first Lodge-sponsored event since Stacy and I came back from the Danube music cruise that we took for our fiftieth birthdays.

This is an odd moment and place for an important thought to crop up, although its origin is really the cruise. That reconnected us, allowing us to enjoy each other's company and the music too, daily and nightly concerts, opera, lieder singing, all excellent, even though very little was Chopin. Now we're both on diets—those Viennese pastries were irresistible. And we've begun to push a bit to do more of what we like, for instance, to get to Tanglewood a couple times this coming summer. We're already planning a music cruise for next spring, on the northern European rivers, where there'll be mazurkas for sure. And Tracy's volunteered with Rose Serkin's campaign and is generally getting more involved in helping this area prepare for the future.

I applaud that idea, but until today hadn't found a way to act on it. Now, maybe I have. This Lodge has been part of my life forever. I joined because Pop was a member.[26] Our roster has big overlaps with the town road and transfer station crews, and the volunteer fire and ambulance corps. No white-collar guys, except for Zach Galter, who joined because I did. (And I joined the VFW because of him.) We members do a lot of relaxing together, but we're supposed to be a service club. That's the purpose of this lobster sale. Every few weeks during the warm weather months, we sell boiled lobsters, clams, and grilled corn to benefit our daycare program, the lowest-priced one in town. The customer gets a good meal for less than restaurant prices,

---

26 Compiler's Note: The Turners started in Liverpool in 1734 as the 'woodturners,' another name for carpenters who used lathes. The first Turners Lodge in America was established in Worcester, MA, in1811. RMB.

and we net several thousand dollars for a day's concentrated effort. We Lodge brothers take turns boiling, grilling, cracking, and packing the food, and dealing with the customers, all while wearing silly lobster hats, aprons with salty sayings, and while lubricated by plenty of beer. God is in these details, I feel, as surely as He is in the intricate design of the pinecones.

Today, while things at the Lodge are going hot and heavy at the grilling and boiling stations, and while I'm toiling and chortling and swigging—I look around me and decide to just nurse this one bottle for the next hour or two and not reach for any more. Several lodge and town problems are becoming clear to me. One for the lodge, and also for the fire and ambulance crews, is that there aren't enough younger people joining. Can't keep institutions going without new blood. Beyond that, I'm bothered by the taking over of too much in this town by grabby guys like general contractor Jemmy Tillotson who're looking to gobble up chunks of weekender owners' wealth, rather than, as we craftsmen have done for generations, just making decent livings from our craftsmanship and the services we provide, and not engaged in rip-off tactics. We need a more moral sense of what we're doing here.

Zach comes over on one of our breaks and we get to talking. I tell him about Tracy's new focus on helping the town more, and that I'm wondering, what can we guys do. Turns out, he's been thinking along the same lines. Since local elections are also coming up this year, he's going to run for the planning board, and thinks I should run for selectman.

I don't feel qualified for that yet, I say, but I could maybe stand for the head of the Lodge, with a platform of recruiting younger guys for members, and some white-collar types, even a few weekenders. And we should do scholarships to trade schools like the Guardians are doing for colleges. Make the organization more viable and relevant. I mean, it's not revolutionizing the world, but why not try to make our little corner a bit better?

Zach likes it, and calls over his brother Harv, now well-settled in at The Chancellery. Harv listens to my spiel and says he's on board. He's going to push The Chancellery to do more with the town, like open up their hockey rink for locals, one night a week.

"The three of us could get some good stuff accomplished, couldn't we?"

The Happiest Funeral

(thoughts of Rose Serkin)

For Sadie Durmaz's send-off, the Congo church is mobbed to the rafters. Literally. I've never seen so many people in the balcony, which is usually only used by the choir. So many Cobblers and Gobblers in one place! Only Sadie could bring them all out, from big homes and small, from remote farms and from apartments over garages, plus three vans' worth of geriatrics from Moorehead.

Crotchety, foul-mouthed, squirrely, generous, a great gossip yet an incredibly moral person—no one could be neutral about her; you loved Sadie or you merely tolerated her, but she would not be ignored. Nor could any of us avoid, not even her closest pals, avoid now and then being zinged by her acerbic tongue.

What is a life well lived? On the evidence of this funeral, it is not a matter of having had significant achievements like winning prizes or elections or becoming famous. Rather, it is existing in a manner that touches others in positive ways and imparts to them an indelible sense of having had direct interaction with a unique and very interesting specimen of humanity who has enriched their lives.

That sort of a life seems to have more of a chance of occurring in a small, interior New England town than it does in a big city. In celebrating Sadie, then, we are also celebrating Jericho's Cobble. Reverend Trainor understands that; it is partly why he keeps the ceremonial parts of the service brief, to allow Sadie's eulogists lots of time to step up to the pulpit, adjust the microphone, and regale us with stories.

Feels more like a Friars Club roast than a funeral.

Many people have a Sadie story to tell, and the tales all provoke gales of laughter from a crowd that's mostly not inclined to dissolve in muffled sobs—Fred Ritter being an exception, quietly dabbing at his tears, and Beetle another, just sitting very still. Sadie's small kindnesses. Her vanity license plate. Her legendary drunks, before she swore off the sauce. Her unexpected love of basketball, so intense that a great moment of her life was when a visiting Harlem Globetrotter lifted her up on the court so she could dunk. Her claim that to save money she and her dog GoFetch used the same hairdresser. Her insistence on singing the 'Marching Mountaineers' anthem every time she passed Stillwater Mountain High. Her love of soft-serve ice cream—easier on her dentures than the hard stuff, she said.

New to me, among the stories, were those of Sadie's last two months at Moorehead. In one story, she imagined that being dead would be like sleeping in on a Saturday morning, feeling no pain and having absolutely nothing to do and nothing to fret about.

I learned that on her deathbed, knowing that she would die soon, she asked for a double Scotch on ice and a cigarette. No cigarettes, she was told, because she was on oxygen, but she slurped down the Scotch and then asked the nurse to re-do her lipstick so she wouldn't scare the undertaker. Two hours later, she was gone.

Aimee, who's sitting with me, doesn't want to go to the pulpit and tell her Sadie story – which tickles me, since Aimee is so often voluble on every subject—although she does claim that Sadie and she got along quite well for two such seemingly disparate people, the quintessential New England small-towner and the quintessential transplanted urban California hippie. Aimee's story is that when lawyer Ade dumped her for his drab second wife, and all of Aimee's friends were consoling her on this great loss, Sadie alone was adamant that Aimee should say 'good riddance' and take it as opportunity to start doing greater, wilder, more Aimee-ish things in life, without reference to a man—any man.

"Best advice I ever got," Aimee says.

A Brief Encounter

(diary entry, Laurie Milch, May 7, 2004)

Bumped into Vinny Djere at The Buttery, both of us on the same errand, ice cream cakes for our mothers for Mother's Day. Haven't seen each other since there was snow on the ground. While we're waiting for the cakes to be packed up, he asks how I'm doing with my college-prep stuff, and I tell him that the history teacher Mr. Miller—yes, old bowtie is still there!—and Mrs. Morely—Alice—are helping me, and I'm loving it. Reading and writing up a storm. What about the bucks for tuition? Not getting there as fast as I'd like, Vinny, but working on it. Maybe, he says, maybe I should hit up my faraway Dad for tuition? Worth a try, I agree, and I ask, what about you, what're you doing on college prep? He's saving up, too, from living at home while working at The Chancellery. Maybe, I say, maybe for post-9/11 vets there's a tuition-payment program that you could tap into? A good idea, he admits, and says he'll give that a spin.

We swear we're both going to keep at this college stuff, because that's the way the future happens for people like us, and we make a pact: we'll keep pushing each other to get it done.

And then he asks, how's Alice doing?

Oh, pretty good. Has a boyfriend—at her age! They went on a cruise together, but now, according to Alice, they're cooling it a bit.

Smart thing to do, we agree.

Then it hits me. So I ask him, would he escort me to the Stillwater senior prom in a month?

He says yes.

The Clabbered Butter Transaction

(thoughts of Kelly Murtaugh Lydner)

Behind the scenes is where the real changes in the Berkshire Buttery Co-op are taking place—a transformation that the public won't see; in fact, the new owner's plan is to deliberately leave untouched those operations that directly interface with customers, such as the signage, the restaurant's old booths, the ice-cream counter, the gift shop, and the retailing of certain farm crops. But the Co-op is no longer a co-op.

For the previous 115 years, since begun in 1889 by my great-grandfather Diarmuid Murtaugh and his neighbors, it was a non-profit for the benefit of its farmer-members. Now it is owned by a Delaware-based, for-profit chain of rural-area food marts that purchased the Buttery's name, buildings, and all else in exchange for paying off the considerable mortgage, plus a $2,000 apiece payout to the 150 remaining members—I'm one. That small amount per family doesn't come close to equaling what we each put into the co-op in the last fifteen years or so since it began to slip into the red, but something's better than nothing.

The new owner is able to use the "co-op" identity but to close those parts of the operation that were actually cooperative—the wholesale buying of equipment and supplies for farmers, and the wholesale acquisition of members' dairy products. The new owners do plan to continue to vend specialty farm products, which they can mark up significantly for resale. That's why I'm at the Buttery today.

After establishing our condo in Florida, Corey and I have come back for a few months, renting one of the Cobble townhouse-complex's units, since our farmhouse is no longer ours. Ina Mornay, who now owns the farm, has moved into the big house until she can finalize plans for a new one. Anyway, I'm also at the Buttery today at Ina's request, as well as that of the Paredeses, to broker an arrangement to sell the farms' strawberries, blueberries, heirloom tomatoes, designer lettuces, and vats of clabbered butter, the latter, I point out to the new Buttery manager, made from my great-grandmother's ratios and techniques.

This fresh-faced hotel-school grad sitting opposite Jorge and me in what used to be our Gang of Six's favorite meeting booth is working his way up the corporate ladder but knows little of the needs of farmers. I intrigue him by saying that I'll personally loan The Buttery my great-grandmother Liona's framed "receipt" for the butter, so they can use the lovely story of the tie between the clabbered butter and the origin of The Buttery, which will help them retail this special product at $50 for two pounds.

In this negotiation, I'm tickled to see, I'm pushing harder on behalf of our successor farm-owners than I ever did for myself! Well, I do want the old farm to keep going as a farm. Jericho's Cobble needs it.

Smiles all around. Contracts will be sent to Ina and Jorge in an email. And they will soon commence deliveries to the Buttery of their fruits, butter, lettuces, and tomatoes. And in the fall, they'll sell the Buttery artisanal decorative gourds—Ina's idea.

We'll make a farmer of her yet.

That's Old News

(thoughts of Grace Newington)

In the display celebrating the 100th anniversary of the newspaper were items that shocked Sam and me: the 1981 front-page photo of Hoke Klecko in handcuffs, and the headline identifying him and his brother as the prime suspects in the arson of town hall. We had not known that our mild-mannered lawn-care specialist had been involved in that arson and in the murder of an accomplice about to turn state's evidence—matters that occurred twenty-plus years ago and that remain central to the village's collective memory, but that are not part of what weekenders or recent full-timers know.

In this instance, for us, ignorance is not only bliss, as the old adage insists; ignorance also allows the space and time in which to form a counter-narrative—such as our positive impression of Hoke, which developed as he did our yard work during the decade we've been in the Cobble as weekenders. Sam and I are not the sort of New Yorkers that keep our distance from workers who toil on our property—plumbers, painters, yardmen, whomever. We try to interact with them as the fellow Cobblers they are. That's how we became a bit friendly with Hoke, as he made us aware through conversation of his devotion to his vegetable garden—we've also been its beneficiaries—and of his esteem for his wife, Frankie, and of his doting on his grandson, Morrie.

To the current moment: Hoke has to have assumed that the newspaper's centennial display would contain such a photo of him in connection with the arson, and that we would see it, being aware that I, as a columnist for the paper, would be likely to attend the anniversary event. So Hoke cannot help but figure that we Newingtons now know something about the dark part of his past, and wonder whether it will alter our relationship to him.

Sam maintains that were we still living in Manhattan and had turned up a similar piece of disturbing information about one of our regular repairmen, we'd simply drop the guy so as not to expose ourselves to someone known to have previously committed violence, and we would easily find a replacement from among the city's myriad of similar service providers. But out here in the country, the conditions are not the same. This particular ex-con is a neighbor and a friend—someone who, if we dropped him as our yard guy, we would still bump into regularly at the grocery store, the church, the coffee-shop, the recycling center, in encounters that could be awkward. Dropping Hoke, actually, would be downright un-neighborly of us—and also unjustified, since nothing in his work for us over the past decade, or in our interactions with him, has given us reason to part ways.

Even so, we've been mulling for a fortnight how best to deal with this. Now the moment to do so has arrived. Hoke and his grandson Morrie, a graduating senior at Stillwater, plus another helper, have shown up in our yard with their rakes, blowers and trucks, to do the spring cleanup of what has accumulated over the winter, the rotted leaves, fallen branches, etc., so that the yard can be mowed for the first time since October and primed for planting of annuals.

With an unsmiling nod at me, Sam and his cane go out to meet Hoke and his crew. I deliberately remain inside, out of sight and of earshot.

What I see through the curtained window, after Hoke and Morrie have removed their noise-cancelling headphones to speak with Sam, seems to be friendly banter, with Sam giving Morrie an extra-enthusiastic handshake, presumably to congratulate him on his forthcoming graduation from high school. Then Hoke and Morrie put their headphones back on and return to their noisy work on the yard.

The action: Sam's knowing inaction, his refusal to alter the status quo.

Sam comes in the door and sees me. "Didn't mention the TCC exhibit to Hoke, Grace. Didn't need to. That photo of him … is old news. And after all, this is the country of the second chances."

"Indeed it is! Now: How about really giving yourself that second chance?"

“New Birdsong Exhibit:

‘An Abiding Friendship’”

by Felicity Ringell,
***The Country Caller*, issue of May 27, 2004**

On Saturday, May 22nd, the Birdsong House’s new exhibit opened, bringing dozens of visitors to the venerable historic house museum, many for the first time.

Entitled “An Abiding Friendship,” the exhibit charts the amity and clandestine “forbidden love” bonding Eleanor Birdsong, the town’s celebrated poetess, and Mrs. Selwyn Markham Whitbred, wife of the legendary J. C. “Bucko” Whitbred of Whitbred Manor, from 1863 to 1877, a year before Birdsong’s death.

The storied Birdsong House, seized by the town for unpaid taxes in 1949 and deeded in 1957 to the Jericho’s Cobble Civic Association, has been a museum since 1960 and is now on the National Register of Historic Buildings.

Its current exhibit, mounted in the parlor that served as the law office for Eleanor’s brother Lucas Birdsong, features framed personal notes to “E” from “S,” photographs of the two women together, some of these from private archives and from the files of the Institute for the Wayward (1864-1884), for which both Eleanor and Selwyn served on the board, and Birdsong’s tartan skirt, which several of the photos show her wearing.

Another featured item is a framed copy of Birdsong’s 1862 poetic gloss on Hamlet’s famous "to be or not to be" speech, which the exhibit interprets as expressing E's then-unfulfilled yearning for S.

Upstairs in Eleanor's bedroom suite, the desk in which she kept Selwyn's notes has been moved away from the wall, and a mirror has been hung at an angle to reveal the hidden compartment in the desk's undersides where the notes had lain, undisturbed, for 125 years.

The exhibit stresses, in addition to the women's intimacy, their "progressive" views on abolitionism, feminism, and the proper treatment of mental illness. As an example, there is a letter from Birdsong to the Reverend Horace Butternut, then-pastor of the Congregational Church, pressing him to a more prominent abolitionist stance.

Birdsong House Executive Director and UMass doctoral candidate Mary-Beth Flaherty attributes the large uptick in attendance to recent articles in "feminist" and "radical" magazines that she had alerted to the forthcoming exhibit. Because of the new interest in the Birdsong House from such out-of-towners, the House, for the first time, is requiring visitors to reserve tickets in advance, by phone or through the new website. Only a dozen people at a time are being admitted. The suggested donation entrance fee is also higher, $10, twice what it had been.

Ms. Beresford said that the JCCA was pleased with the new income from the Birdsong House and opined that while the exhibit documents behavior that was "considered shocking at the time, and that some people do not want to feature even today, it is as much a part of the Cobble's heritage as any other."

It's Not the Money

(dialogue, Doug Flipkens and Pat Tolland)

"You wanted to see me, Doug?"

"Yessir, boss. I've been offered a job on the *Springfield Republican*, and I'm inclined to take it."

"A much bigger city and a daily paper—I can see why you'd want that. Straight-out reporting?"

"Actually, I'll be deputy arts and entertainment editor to a guy who swears he's going to retire within a few years."

"Nice."

"He particularly liked the clip of my review of *The Glass Menagerie* production."

"Ha! Sometimes old man Tolland guesses right, hmm? Are they paying you a lot more? Can we match the offer?"

"Actually, I figure that with the somewhat higher expenses of Springfield, I'll about break even on my new salary, at least until I get a raise or two."

"So it's not the money that's taking you away from us?"

"Haven't been meeting a lot of interesting, well-educated young women around here, Mr. Tolland, and I'm also afraid that the *Caller's* change to a nonprofit will not help me to become a better reporter and drama critic."

'How so?"

"If *TCC* is more dependent than ever on contributions, there'll be even less incentive to really critique a local arts production and maybe irk donors."

Katy Melchior Sketches Out an Idea

(her thoughts)

So I'm sitting and charcoal-penciling on my pad in a corner of Jim's bakery café, looking out to the courtyard, about 11:30 on a Wednesday. Quite a warm day for May, with some people seated outside. I'm not really paying attention to the hour, since I don't need to be home until 2:30 to get my kids off the bus from school.

I'm the only Black in the café, but in the Cobble I'm used to that. I'm sketching out an idea for a full-sized piece, ideally to be sited in this very courtyard, a piece based on old Hallie Prince, who's always around the café and is so much at home in it, reading her papers and nursing a pot of tea, looking up from the page to chat with a passer-by, which happens often because she knows everybody and everybody's glad to see her and to say hello. I'm thinking of a Hallie sculpture as the welcoming spirit of this village, sitting on half a bench, but only on half, so that a live person (or two) could plop down alongside. Plastic spectacles and ears, a rope mop for hair, arms of one-inch pipes, gloves for hands, long pants of wood, the newspaper a pasteboard able to gently move in the breeze, a head that nods every so often, both of these motions powered by a little battery-motor I'll conceal in the torso...and who comes over to peek at my sketch but Grace Newington and Aimee Bishop.

Earlier I noticed them at a far table and waved but didn't go over to say hello since they were deep into a conversation and I don't really know them well enough to interrupt. So I only overheard snatches of their chatter. It's about divvying up the gardening-column subjects for the summer, now that Grace has "cut the cultural umbilical cord"—not sure exactly what that means other than that she and Sam have moved up here from

Manhattan full-time—and Aimee confiding that her "thing" with her wild-and-crazy guy is "developing," as they are "both changing." Don't know exactly what guy Aimee's referring to, but there aren't too many around here who fit her "wild and crazy" description, so it's probably that son of the painter Oregon Wilberson. Haven't met him yet. Would like to.

Most times when I'm drawing in public, strangers come over and ask what I'm making. Usually I don't want to talk about it so I politely discourage them. But up here, such a refusal to chat with people that I actually know, even if only slightly, would be unnecessarily rude. So I show Grace and Aimee the sketch for the reading-and-sipping figure, explain that it is Hallie as the welcoming spirit of the village, and that she'll sit on half of the bench, and how the newspaper in her hand will move, etc.

"That's perfect for this spot," Aimee says, as Grace nods agreement, and asks whether it has been commissioned. No, I say; it's just my idea.

Then Aimee surprises me by asking whether I've ever done anything "site-specific," say, for a garden. I reply that I haven't, but that it's an intriguing notion.

She is revamping a client's garden, and it could use a sculpture as a centerpiece. "Would you be up for that?"

"Certainly," I say, trying to suppress my excitement; and add that "of course I'll have to visit the site with you, get to understand your design and also to know the client a bit and determine what sort of piece might fit the site and the owner's persona."

Aimee's smiling, as though she presumed that such conditions would be necessary – and on impulse I invite both her and Grace to visit my studio and see what I'm working on, a dozen sculptures in various stages of completion.

I bring my coffee and stuff over to their table and we get out our calendars to set a mutually convenient date for the studio visit. Then Grace asks how my husband Ernie is doing as the new VP of the Guardians outpost, and we go on talking from there.

After a while of our conversation, I begin to feel that I could actually become friends with these women.

EPILOGUE:
Memorial Day, 2004

Preparing for the Annual Invasion

The trees have greened, the ground has warmed,
and as the sun nears its yearly high point
the attendants are sprucing up
our monuments and markers,
adorning us with new patriotic flags.

We are the dead of all of America's wars,
from before there was a United States
through to the most recent overseas 'mission.'
We are the ultimate sacrifices, the direct and the corollary damage,
the givers of the last full measures of devotion.
We have served for you, killed for you, and died for you,
so that you can enjoy
freedom, safety, and democracy.

Many of us war dead, mostly the more ancient of us,
have had our energies absorbed into the universe,
re-settled in voles, mallards, deer,
sparrow, skunk, even a bear,
animals that on starry nights wander this cemetery
without knowing just why,
although we who remain here sense their kindred presence.

Once or twice each cycle some of you living humans invade,
out of a vague notion of obligation
coupled with the fear of joining us too soon;
some of you read the names of our battles
and scratch your heads over how many of them
you do not recognize;
but at least for a moment we are impinging on you.

When first we war-dead come here we are bitter,
more so than compatriots who never served under arms,
and we are angry at all who do not deign to care

about our sacrifices, our dashed potential,
our wasted chances to love and be loved.

Eventually, in our interment, we come to understand more
and forgive more;
the unfulfilled promise of one life assuring the enduring promise
of freedom for all American lives.
So come and visit us today, please!
We are glad to see you—now and then.

The Marchers and the Marched-Upon

(thoughts of Sam Newington)

Preparations for the parade begin several days before Memorial Day. The three-block Main Street business corridor is dotted with American flags and 'no parking on parade day' signs. Cars are banned from the route, even though it's a state highway.

This Memorial Day morning, family cars bearing marchers and onlookers arrive at the western end of the village, disgorging clusters of prospective marchers who meander into formation, and multiple watchers of the parade, who position themselves on the sidelines, unfolding beach chairs and otherwise claiming prime positions at the curb. Shortly, there are more people on Main Street in Jericho's Cobble than on any other day of the year. Red-white-and-blue outfits predominate among the watchers, who know that they too will be seen along with the marchers.

I left my cane home so as not to be inadvertently mistaken for a vet, which I am not, since I never served, and I walk slowly past the vets as they are assembling. Uniforms from closets and bureaus have been brushed off and tried on; some did not fit this year although they did in the past, others have long since been mothballed in favor of service caps or blazers with medals pinned on the breast. No more World War I vets, but there are a dozen World War IIs, all still able to walk, some with canes, plus contingents from the Korean War and the war in Vietnam, and smaller clusters from more recent conflicts. Those no longer able to walk are being chauffeured in antique convertibles. On the sidewalks and near the Eastlund Library, gaggles of variously uniformed marchers chat casually with one another. Lots of grins and handshakes and admiring of each other's spiffiness. Today all our men and women vets are honored, regardless of rank. Yet the officers still tend to hang together, as do the enlisted men. I nod to those in both groups that I know, among them Duke Duhamel, Charlie Mulroney, Lionel Parkford, Ernie Melchior, Jim Skupski, Andy Borska, and Zach Galter, but I do not attempt to chat with them, as I refuse to intrude on their military chumminess. Here and there among the vets are men whose patriotic service I was unaware of. In the crowd of on-lookers I also spot several whom I know to have served in the military but who choose not to march. In 2004, with a war going on in Iraq, their bitterness at what I presume were bad armed forces' experiences seems less warranted.

On the library's lawn two bands form up, one of schoolchildren, the other of more senior musicians, stalwarts of the town band who like to tootle and thump at public occasions. Where would this parade be without their blaring and beat-keeping, which spurs us on-lookers to clap in time with the music, although their melodies are more enthusiastic than enchanting? Nor would the parade be the same without its flag-holding leader, historian Richard Bond Miller, in his Civil War uniform. Rumor is that he has put in his retirement papers to Stillwater Mountain, so this may be his last parade. Well, he's going out with a smile. Maybe that smile means he's planning on remaining in the area, after all.

Shaping up to follow behind Miller and the veterans are all the non-military who can lay claim to membership in any quasi-official town group, with or without a uniform—the firehouse crew, accompanying their gleaming machines, the ambulance crew with theirs, the elected town officials, the clergy, the school principals, the Boy Scouts, Girl Scouts, Cub Scouts, and Brownies, and then other groups who might not seem to be parade-worthy units such as the school ball teams, and, bringing up the rear, the child-care center denizens, replete with moms pushing strollers with tots in them and accompanied by family dogs and slightly older siblings riding patriotically-decorated bicycles.

The line-up of the parade is several blocks long—longer, in fact, than the Main Street business district.

And there's the step-off!

Each fresh group of marchers in passing by provokes new bursts of applause from the watchers, plus hand-waves, bright yells, flag-flappings, and cheers worthy of an unexpected football touchdown.

Even in the first block or two of marchers, the distinction between the armed-service paraders and the other marchers is fairly slim, and what separates the marchers from the marched-upon spectators becomes even more tenuous and porous as the parade goes on, and it completely dissolves prior to the marching-by of the last group, the childcare center, at the eastern edge of the Main Street business district.

After that bunch has passed in scattered formation, the parade swells to three and four times its original size as everyone on the sidelines joins in. Thereafter it proceeds leisurely toward the parade's end point in the town cemetery.

I don't know if in every other small town a cemetery is the standard concluding point of patriotic parades, but it seems very fitting in ours, and readily done, since the cemetery is only a few hundred yards beyond the business district. In Cobblers' minds, a parade is not complete unless and until we are all among the gravestones, honoring our forebears.

There's no rush to get to the middle of the cemetery, where the benediction will be held, and there's no continued cadence to march us there, the drummers having ceased their pounding. As Grace and I walk along, I am reminded of the parallel path to this paved one, the nature trail that follows the route past the older, larger estates—Whitbred, Eastlund, Dawson, and the part of the Renwick state forest where the Pequabogue massacre marker stands. Today I'd rather be walking on the paved road, along with our neighbors, while keeping in mind all of the nature path's history.

I am also content to be among these neighbors, because to me they are as much part of the attractiveness of this corner of the world as its natural surround and storied past.

We Cobblers and Gobblers take our time arriving at the

cemetery's center, an area deliberately left open for such ceremonies; en route, I take note of dozens of pleasant conversations and greetings occurring, with lots of handshakes, pats on backs, hugs, and chaste kisses on cheeks. I wave at the Moorehead night-nurses, Maria and Jack, who were so helpful to me when I was in their care—I'm glad to see them in daylight, and out of the rehab setting. I hail fellow slow-pitch softball players and express the hope of rejoining them soon on the diamond. I take note of other Cobblers that we know, people for whom important transitions are in process, such as Pat Tolland, who is exiting the weekly newspaper as it becomes a nonprofit, and choir director Vic Leighton, who Grace tells me will retire soon from the Congo church.

Grace's and my quick toting up shows that we know as many Cobblers as we do weekend Gobblers. I yearn to tell them all that Grace and I have decided, now that we've moved here permanently, to become more involved in the civic and cultural affairs of the town, and that I may start a one-man stock-analyst and advisory firm. Just now I don't say a word about it; there will be more appropriate moments and venues to do so.

We pass recently-filled graves, among them those of Sadie Durmaz, William Beecher, Pamela Markle, and Chad Stucnowicz, each with fresh flowers brought by a few mourners come to pay respects. I look around for Chad's father Starker, the usually-ubiquitous traffic-director and proud veteran, and am informed that he is in serious medical decline but nonetheless here, sitting in the fire truck with his medals on but not descending from that chariot, too proud to let us see him diminished yet still desirous of attending one last ceremony before his own burial here.

We pass by the graves of the eighteen-century slave pair, the Archers; the solitary markers of the nineteenth-century farmer-friends Liona Murtaugh and Lisette Niedermeyer; the substitute soldier Lester Throckenberry; and those of many others who had no headline accomplishment during their lifetimes but whom we understand from our research readings in the Eastlund library to be worthy of attention.

At the center of the cemetery we come to a stop and stand around in bunches. Ceremony aplenty is in the offing, including rifle-shot salutes, benedictions by the clergy – Vern is particularly sensitive and clear in his remarks—and reciting the names of the dead of many wars, from the Revolution onward. Tiny 'veteran' flags adorn those whose graves are nearby. On the older headstones, the faded inscriptions can barely be read.

Each year, a Whitbred Elementary student recites aloud Lincoln's Gettysburg Address, that paean to the fallen and to the pillars of the country they died to preserve. This always-stirring recital, and the sounding of 'taps' by the best trumpet-player in town, are for me the highlights of the ceremony, as they are for most of the crowd.

Nine months ago I lay on an operating table in the hospital and it was not a far reach to imagine being dead and in this cemetery. The place is more beautiful than I realized then, and it is now fuller with friends, neighbors, and adopted forebears, and it is also more patient and eternal than I had even imagined.

I'll be content to lie in here when it's my turn to do so.

But not yet.

And, God willing, not too soon.

Grace and I are realizing now that as Cobblers pledged to this town and these hills and streams and forest and these neighbors and these adopted forebears, we've got all the time in the world to work on becoming our best selves.

Appendix

Residents of Jericho's Cobble Present and Past *(selected list)*

NATHAN ARCHER, slave (1743?-1779).

RUFUS BARTUMS, Whitbred estate stable manager (1842-1914).

WILLIAM BEECHER, restaurateur.

GERTRUDE "GERTIE" MERKIN BERESFORD, trustee, JCCA; oral history interviewer.

ELEANOR RUMMET BIRDSONG, poetess (1803-1878).

LUCAS BIRDSONG, brother of Eleanor; attorney (1802-1869).

AIMEE BISHOP, broadcaster; entertainment editor, TCC; garden designer.

ANDREJ "ANDY" BORSKA, third-generation plumbing service owner.

HUGO BORSKA, his son; pharmacy clerk; guitarist.

STACY BORSKA, Andy's wife; plumbing-office manager; board member, MFA; Class of '73 group.

REV. HORACE BUTTERNUT, minister, First Congregational Church of Jericho's Cobble (1811-1869).

ADEMANTE "ADE" CASTELMARA, attorney-at-law.

GEOFFREY COLLIER, ret'd. banking executive; treasurer, JCCA.

CHELSEA COLVER, ex-wife of Wm. Beecher; horsewoman; dance instructor; dance critic, TCC.

CELIA DAWSON, sampler-maker (1835-1854).

EMENTHA HELGELUND DAWSON, her mother (1814-1854).

OSCAR DAWSON, Ementha's husband; knackery and tannery founder (1802-1863).

MARIA DELACROIX, night-nurse, Moorehead Rehabilitation Center.

VINCENZO "VINNY" DJERE, Gulf War veteran; Chancellery groundskeeper.

MALCOLM "DUKE" DUHAMEL, ret'd. editor-publisher, TCC; chorister; past president, Guardians #267.

EZEKIEL DUNSMORE, banker; Bucko Whitbred associate, (1840-1905).

SADIE DURMAZ, widow; ret'd. party-line telephone operator.

HÉLOÏSE MARCEL EASTLUND, tennist (1890-1947).

NILS EASTLUND, her husband, (1868-1929); stock trader; founder, Valodia.

MARY-BETH FLAHERTY, exec. director, The Birdsong House; clogger.

DOUGLAS "DOUG" FLIPKENS, reporter, TCC

MERLIN "MERL" FORSTMANN, ret'd. television network news anchor; board member, TCC.

CHRISTINA "TINA" M. GABIANCO, housewife, garden-supply store assistant.

MAISIE BIRDSONG GAITSKILL (1899-1943), singer and chorine.

BETH GALTER, ass't. op. mgr., Valley Hardware Fuels; treasurer, Valodia; Class of '73.

HARVEY "HARV" GALTER, her husband; Viet vet, former building contractor; purchasing mgr., Valley Hardware.

ZACHARY "ZACH" GALTER, his brother; Vietnam vet; pharmacist; member, Guardians #267.

CASIMIR "CHIP" GARUZELSKI, ret'd. women's sports director, The Chancellery.

STUART "STEWIE" GLOBUS, senior, Stillwater Mountain High.

EDWARD "EDDIE" GRISWOLD, Mass. State septic systems inspector.

LILIANE GRISWOLD, his wife; ass't. mgr., Whitbred Branch of the Southern Berkshire Banking Corporation; volunteer EMT; Class of '73 group.

LOUISE GUTWIND, exec. sec'y, The Chancellery; volunteer, FIND; Stillwater Class of '73 group.

REV. PETER HICKLE, minister, First Congregational Church, (1930-2002).

JEANNIE JOHNSON, proprietor, Get'nGo sandwich shop.

HOLCOMB "HOKE" KLECKO, lawn care specialist.

LAMARR "LEM" KLECKO, Hoke's older brother; housepainter (1934-1985).

MORRIE K. LARNO, Hoke's grandson, senior, Stillwater Mtn. High.

APRIL LASKO, editor-in-chief, *The Country Caller.*

VICTOR "VIC" LEIGHTON, music director, Congregational Church.

REV. AARON LODEN, minister, Congregational Church (1904-1993).

GEORGE T. LODEN, his brother; WW I veteran, Chancellery tennis coach (1892-1938).

COREY LYDNER, farmer.

KELLY MURTAUGH LYDNER, his wife; farmer; Board of Estimate member; Class of '73.

POLLY MALDONE, stay-at-home mother of two.

PAMELA RENWICK MARKLE, ret'd. First Selectman.

ERNEST "ERNIE" MELCHIOR, regional manager, Harwin House Hardwares; member, Guardians #267.

KATHERINE "KATY" MELCHIOR, his wife; sculptor.

HENRY OLIPHANT MERKIN, farmer; private, U. S. Army, War of 1812 (1795-1816).

DELIA MIDDLETON, single mother; FIND bookkeeper (1955-1999).

JANE MILCH, scheduler, Moorehead Retirement Complex; board member, Valodia; chorister; Class of '73 .

LAURIE MILCH, her daughter; babysitter; senior at Stillwater Mtn.

RICHARD BOND MILLER, Stillwater Mtn. history department chair; town historian.

ALICE HADLEY MORLEY, ret'd. third-grade teacher; jogger; board member, Valodia.

INA MORNAY, managing director, Estabank; real estate investor; owner, Prince's Pharmacy.

CHARLES "CHARLIE" MULRONEY, SR., CEO, Mulroney's Marmalades; member, Guardians #267; former, Mulroney's Supermarket.

CHARLES "CHUCK" MULRONEY, JR., his son; vice-president, Small Luxuries, Inc.

DARLENE "LENE" MULRONEY, wife of Charles; CEO, Small Luxuries; former owner, Mulroney's Supermarket.

HERMAN MURFREES, ret'd. farmer; WW II veteran; former selectman; chorister.

DIARMUID "MUDDY" MURTAUGH, dairy farmer, Buttery Co-op founder (1853-1914).

LIONA MURTAUGH (1855-1919), his wife; farmer; mother.

JONATHAN MENAKER "DOC" NASH, veterinarian; skier; WW II veteran; (1923-2003).

GRACE NEWINGTON, freelance book editor; gardening columnist; chorister.

SAMUEL "SAM" NEWINGTON, her husband; stock analyst.

HEINZ NIEDERMEYER, Civil War deserter, farmer (1841-1893).

LISETTE GORDON NIEDERMEYER, his wife (1851-1893).

JOOST "BEETLE" OOSTENDYCK, entrepreneur, investor.

ANGEL PAREDES, farmhand; Ecuadorean immigrant.

LIONEL PARKFORD, ret'd. CEO, Balthazar Transports; horseman; foxhunter.

VERONICA "RONNIE" PARKFORD, his wife; ret'd. fashion model.

MARC POSNER, corporate lawyer; photographer.

MARTHA ERDMANNS POSNER, his wife; board member JCCA, Eastlund Library, MFA.

CLETUS "CLETE" PRINCE, owner pharmacist, Prince's Pharmacy, (1878-1948)

HENRIETTA "HALLIE" PRINCE, his daughter, retired, former pharmacy owner

LETITIA PAWLIS RENWICK, (1888-1983); founding trustee, JCCA, MFA.

FELICITY RINGELL, reporter, TCC.

DANTE "DANNY" ROMANO, owner, Valley Hardware; member, Guardians #267.

REV. JEDEDIAH SAMPSON, founding minister, Congregational Church; slave-owner (1718-1799).

MARY MERCY SAMPSON, his wife (1725-1804).

ROSE SERKIN, VNA nurse; townhouse "mayor."

DR. SANDOR "RUSTY" SERKIN, her ex-husband; physician; syndicated columnist, (1933-1998).

JERRI SCHUSSLER, Massachusetts State representative; former schoolteacher.

SKANASKA, sachem, Pequabogue band (16??-1736).

JAMES "JIM" SKUPSKI, Vietnam War veteran; baker; café-owner.

ELSTON "SUNNY" SUNFORTH, Broadway investor; proprietor of Sunny's Barn, (1910-1958).

BENJAMIN "BENNY" STELTENHAM, hockey coach, Sprouls Preparatory Academy.

JACK STOLTZFUS, night nurse, Moorehead Rehabilitation; husband of Maria Delacroix.

CHADWICK "CHAD" STUCNOWICZ, Valley Hardware DIY-section supervisor.

JOSEPH "STARKER" STUCNOWICZ, Chad's father; recycling center foreman; volunteer fireman; ret'd. minor league baseball pitcher.

ALONZO THORNTON (1923-1993) senior jurist, Merriam County; board member, FIND; poker game host.

LESTER THROCKENBERRY, farmhand; substitute soldier, corporal (1845-1864).

PATRICK REESE TOLLAND, publisher, The Country Caller.

DR. GLENDA TRAINOR, emergency-room surgeon; chorister.

REV. VERNON TRAINOR, her husband; minister, Congregational Church.

ANELISE CHELMSFORD WHITBRED, early settler (1717-1763).

JOSHUA COMMODUS WHITBRED, her husband; first settler (1700-1755).

JOSHUA C. "BUCKO" WHITBRED V, their great-great-grandson; entrepreneur; banker, (1818-1894).

SELWYN MARKHAM WHITBRED, Bucko's wife, (1825-1890).

ROBERT OBREGON "OREGON" WILBERSON, painter; WW II veteran (1918-1993).

CULLEN WILBERSON, his son; fisherman; hunter; kayak instructor.

JUSTIN YOUNGBLOOD, owner, Dawson's Inn, (1870-1925).

VANCE YOUNGBLOOD, Justin's son; owner, Dawson's Inn, (1898-1993).

CLAUDE ZOLDANO, retired Massachusetts State Police sergeant.

About the Author

Tom Shachtman has published forty books, most recently *Echoes, or The Insistence of Memory*, and *The Memoir of the Minotaur.* His histories include *The Day America Crashed*, *Skyscraper Dreams*, *Absolute Zero and the Conquest of Cold*, and *The Founding Fortunes*; his social analyses, *Rumspringa* and *The Inarticulate Society*; the classic coffee table book, *The Most Beautiful Villages of New England*; and an eclectic trilogy of short novels about sea lions, *Beachmaster*, *Wavebender*, and *Driftwhistler.* His award-winning documentaries have aired on ABC, CBS, NBC, PBS, and BBC. He holds degrees in experimental psychology and in drama and has taught writing at NYU and lectured at Harvard, Georgia Tech, the Library of Congress, Stanford, and other institutions.

www.ingramcontent.com/pod-product-compliance
Lightning Source LLC
LaVergne TN
LVHW030915080826
845145LV00013B/2910

* 9 7 8 1 9 6 3 6 9 5 5 7 1 *